*Can Sophie uncover th*

*family's past before it's too late?*

# STORYBOOK HOUSE

*Can Sophie uncover the secrets of her family's past before it's too late?*

# STORYBOOK HOUSE

Katie Jones

*For my Sophie and William.*

# CHAPTER 1

As we whipped past the trees I caught sight of the sign marking 5 miles to East Hampton and sank lower into my seat. My chest had started to tighten since we left New York; Mom, Dad and me squeezed into our old family wagon, which was crammed with all of our belongings that the removalist hadn't already taken the week before.

I had sat on the top step outside our house, watching sadly as two overweight strangers jammed the last sixteen years of my life into the back of the U-Haul, with absolutely no regard to the emotional value of the items. They were being damaged just by being removed from the place where they belonged. Sixteen years and it took only four and a half hours to remove all traces of us from the house.

I had spent the first sixteen years of my life happily ensconced in city life in New York. My parents couldn't understand my passionate pleading for us to stay; I went to a run-of-the-mill public school where I had never made any particularly close friends, and we lived in a small but comfortable house in Brooklyn. Surely a sea change to an historic mansion would be a lot more exciting, they argued.

But it wasn't school, our house or my neighborhood that I would miss in particular. It was the city. I saw my future in the city. On the weekends I would walk for miles to find inspiration for my latest drawings and the city never failed to disappoint. Whether it was the homeless couple that walked hand in hand through the park every morning, the people pushing against each other at Louis' deli on the corner of our street to get their first caffeine fix on their way to work, or just the bridge over the East River leading in to our little borough, there were an endless supply of subjects for my pencils. It was also a city that embraced artists, which I loved, because I couldn't imagine doing anything else. I had never been particularly sporty or scholarly.

The passing of my great aunt this spring had set in motion a series of events that had brought me to this miserable predicament. Poppy Farrell was a small and stocky woman who, at ninety-eight years of age, sported more wrinkles than a Shar Pei. But she had kind eyes and she would sneak me butterscotch candies when my parents weren't looking, and I loved her. It was her house that we were now speeding towards to take up residence. When I was a child I adored Poppy's house in East Hampton. She would create the most elaborate treasure hunts for me to follow around the gardens and through the secret passageways of the mansion, so I knew my way around there better than I knew my way around my school.

Her name was actually Gladys and no one could ever tell me why we all called her Poppy. To add to the confusion, she wasn't actually an aunt at all. My grandfather was a distant cousin and my dad grew up calling her auntie. She was the only daughter of a wealthy oil tycoon, had married young and in love, and her husband had gone to war and never come back. She never remarried so my father was the closest person she had to family but it had still been a surprise when she had left everything she had to him including her house.

When I was younger we would make the two-hour-long drive out to her imposing mansion that sat in the middle of millionaire row, backing onto the sound. Although there were thirty-four rooms in the main house she only lived in a handful of them and I would spend hours wandering through the abandoned rooms that lay heavy with dust. Back in the heyday the house had been full of staff, life and parties, but by the time we would go and visit the champagne had stopped flowing and the staff had been reduced to three: the grumpy housekeeper, Clara, a chef called Marcel who only knew how to cook a handful of tasteless dishes, and the gardener, Thomas, who never spoke to me. He didn't seem grumpy like Clara, just gruff and deep in thought.

We would pack up Dad's twenty-five-year-old Volvo station wagon on a Friday and brave the traffic to make it there by dinner to eat one of the six meals that made up Marcel's repertoire. In fairness to Marcel I always suspected that Poppy only liked eating those six meals so he had no opportunity to exhibit any creative flair.

Mom and I called her crazy Aunt Poppy because she would tell the most peculiar stories about the rooms in the house coming to life with mysterious strangers. She would tell us of parties in the grand hall, high tea in the formal sitting room, which had ornately carved ceiling roses, and visiting soldiers sneaking in through the greenhouse for stolen kisses with the maids. When I would excitedly pop my head into the sitting room to witness the tea party for myself it would be as I saw it last – empty and coated in a layer of dust that had not been disturbed for decades. I stopped looking after a couple of years and would simply roll my eyes at Mom and yawn when Poppy began yet another tale of intrigue.

Then when I was fourteen the trips suddenly stopped and my parents would look at each other with strained expressions whenever I brought up a possible trip to see Poppy. They would instead quickly make arrangements for us to do something else that weekend; trips to the beautiful galleries in the city were a regular excuse, and to my parents' obvious relief my love of art blossomed so much that I stopped asking about going to see Poppy.

Six weeks ago that all changed when Poppy had a heart attack. Thomas, the gardener, found her in the hot house where she had been tending her favorite rose bush, and although he called the ambulance, she never regained consciousness. The lawyers contacted Dad two days later with the news that the mansion and its staff were now his responsibility. They told him that she had been suffering from dementia, and her death was probably for the best.

Dad suggested to Mom that we could fix up the house and run it as a bed and breakfast. I could hear them discussing the idea in hushed voices at night when they thought I was asleep. Our house was small enough that I could hear parts of the conversation but not all and the grabs that I did hear made me realize my life was about to irreversibly change, and for some reason they were particularly anxious about my reaction.

I closed my eyes and began planning my future escape back to the city I loved.

> *I opened my eyes with the sun shining down on me and sat up in surprise. I was in a garden, enclosed on four sides by walls covered in jasmine. I closed my eyes again and breathed in the beautiful smells of the flowers, the freshly cut grass and salt and felt the sun warming my arms and legs. I felt very calm although I wasn't quite sure where I was and how I got here. I opened my eyes again and sat up taking in more of my surroundings. I was sitting in the middle of a patch of grass on a picnic blanket the size of my double bed.*
>
> *The garden was in two grass sections with a stone path running through the middle and a beautiful fountain in the center that made soft tinkling noises as the water ran over the edge of each of the three tiers into*

*the bottom which was alive with fish. My eyes were drawn to movement at one end of the pathway where a boy was running towards the gated archway leading out of the garden. He turned when he reached the wooden gate and looked back with a cheeky smile. He couldn't have been more than ten years old.*

*I pushed myself up into a standing position to run after him and it wasn't until that moment that I realized I was the same size as the boy. I was wearing a dainty floral dress with a white lapel that I vaguely remembered my mother making for me. 'Hurry up silly, girls are so slow!' yelled the boy, and turning, ran through the archway.*

*I ran toward the gate and, pushing on the solid wood, went through the arch.*

# CHAPTER 2

My eyes snapped open when I heard the sound of the tyres crunching on rock. I realized that I had drifted off and had vague recollections of chasing a young boy down a long path and the sweet smell of jasmine. The images faded from my mind as I stared down the long driveway to the imposing house. It looked darker than I remembered it; the large pine trees on either side of the driveway blocking out the light made the white stones of the driveway look gray, and the house loomed large in the front windscreen. As the car circled around the sculpture that sat in front of the house I closed my eyes and realized that I was holding my breath. I exhaled loudly and opened my eyes to see if my parents had heard but they were too busy analyzing the house.

Dad stopped the car and glanced at Mom. 'Here we go!' she said, sounding as excited as he looked, and opened the car door.

'Smell that fresh sea air!' Dad exclaimed as he climbed out of the driver's seat and stretched his arms above his head.

I climbed out of the car slowly in silent protest. 'In New York City the air smelt of excitement and anticipation. The promise that whatever you thought you were going to do was likely to change and become better!' I shot back.

'Sure kiddo, if excitement and anticipation smell like the body odor of the train commuters and the garbage truck that sat out the front of our house because the driver had a thing with the lady in number seven!' Dad said, smiling broadly and then continued stretching. I shot him a withering glare but he had turned his attention to the imposing pile of bricks that stood before us.

My negativity didn't seem to be rubbing off; they looked like they had just won the lottery. Which I guess they effectively had. My parents had both been teachers, my mother, a primary school teacher and my father a university lecturer. Mom had stopped teaching when I was born so they had been on one income for quite a while and this house had to be worth millions, despite the fact that it was completely dilapidated. Poppy had left some money in her estate and Dad had received a leave of absence and a grant from his university to prepare research papers while doing up the house.

I turned and glanced back at the long white stone driveway that we had just come down, the huge pine trees lining it, and the ginormous oak tree sitting next to the massive wrought iron gates that marked the entrance, and then slowly turned my head around to look at the house.

It looked the same as it had all of those years ago, the only difference being that now it appeared to be even more dilapidated. Three stories of imposing brick with a glassed-in conservatory off to the right-hand side. The stone pillars at the front of the house were still impressive in stature but had turned a muted gray, the white frames of the windows had paint peeling off them, the shutters were hanging off some of the windows, and the once beautiful green vines were dead in some parts, the leaves brittle and flaky.

I sensed movement in the small dormer windows above and glanced up, squinting against the sun's glare. The windows were framed by heavy drapes and I could just make out a shadow in the window at the end.

'Welcome back Master Edward,' came a stern voice from the front entrance. I looked over and saw Clara's steely gaze looking anything but welcoming. Her eyes looked haunted, she was very thin, and her hair had gone from pitch black to a charcoal gray. I had thought she was scary when I was younger but it was possible she was even more intimidating than I remembered. Her dark clothing did nothing to soften her harsh appearance. She glanced to the top of the building where I had been looking and then appraised me with an icy glare.

'Hello Clara! I told you on the phone to please call me Ted,' said my dad with a big teddy bear smile, as he started pulling luggage out of the trunk of the car. Fortunately he wasn't looking at her as his smile was not returned.

'I have made arrangements for you to sleep in the south wing. I hope that is to your liking. Please follow me.' She turned on her heel without checking to see if we were in fact, following her.

I turned my head back to the window on the third floor but the shadow had disappeared. Throwing a couple of my bags over my shoulder, I stumbled over the pebbles as I followed my family, wondering what we were about to walk into.

We followed Clara's black figure into the house and up the huge staircase. It was even worse inside than out. The wallpaper was coming off in strips exposing spidery cracks all over the walls and the floorboards groaned in protest with any movement. The patterned carpet was faded and coming up in parts and there were struts missing in the banister. Despite the solid brick exterior the inside felt like the whole building could collapse at any moment.

What a dump, I thought to myself. I turned around to look at my parents, expecting them to be looking equally dubious, but they were both looking at each other with the excitement of small children who have just been handed a puppy.

'We can start on the banisters,' said Mom, running her hands along the solid wood as the white paint flaked off.

'And I'll work on replastering the walls and give it a fresh coat of paint – it will look as good as new!' replied Dad, with a huge grin on his face.

I sighed and shook my head as I continued following cranky Clara up the stairs. At the landing on the second floor we turned right and passed a couple of rooms with closed doors. At the next door along the hall Clara paused.

'This will be your room Master Edward,' Clara said to my parents, who had momentarily left their critique of the banisters and were halfway up the staircase. She then continued down past a few more doors to the very end of the hall. 'And this is your room Miss Sophie.'

I paused at the door that Clara had indicated was my parents' room and peered into the space. It was as if I was looking into the past. The large four-poster bed had a floral printed bed cover and the matching floral curtains cascaded in large waves to the floor. Looking out of the window at the expanse of water was a small dark wooden desk and matching chair and at the end of the bed sat a gigantic soft green couch covered in cushions. Although the decor left a lot to be desired it wasn't nearly as old and moldy as I had expected and the view out the windows over the water was incredible.

'Well this looks very welcoming,' Dad muttered, giving me an encouraging pat on the shoulder as he walked past me into the room.

'Oh yes, how lovely,' Mom agreed, 'just like a Laura Ashley catalogue!'

I stepped back out of the doorway and glanced with trepidation along the passage in the direction Clara had indicated my room was. Clara's dark figure had disappeared. Probably off to stick some pins in voodoo dolls of our family I thought with a frown and started moping off towards my room. God knows what else she did in the house given she would have to be in her early eighties. I wondered unkindly whether she just had nowhere else to go and Poppy had kept her on for company even though she didn't seem to be doing a great job of keeping house, or whatever her role was supposed to be.

I stopped at the door to my room, took a deep breath and pushed it open. Light flooded in through two large windows onto the big bed, which had soft blue bedding and white pillows. Running along the windows were big window seats, which had cushions, propped at either end. I dropped my bags at the end of the bed, walked tentatively over to the window seat and nestled into the soft cushions as I looked around the room. The carpet had definitely seen better days but the room was sunny and clean and the scent of flowers and salt air drifted in through the open window. Not nearly as bad as I had been expecting. In fact, it was much more a haven than a jail, I thought, and breathed a sigh of relief as I hugged one of the pillows to my chest.

Leaning back on my window seat I closed my eyes and felt the warm sun on my body. After relaxing there for a few minutes I opened my eyes and glanced outside toward the house next door. If our house was the ugly duckling of the street the house next door was a shining star – light gray shingles offset against white shuttered windows. I sat up on my window seat and craned my neck to see a glistening blue swimming pool sitting in front of the house, a pool house matching the main house sitting next to it and a tennis court sitting beyond the house. Glancing down to the water again I could see they had a matching shed at their private dock, where two expensive-looking boats sat bobbing up and down with the currents.

I looked over to our dock, which sat alongside theirs. Every fourth board was missing and the pylons looked like they could fall over with the next strong wave.

Looking back at the house next door I could see the interior resembled a home decor magazine. As I squinted to see what looked like a gray-colored cashmere blanket draped casually over a pristine white couch I noticed some movement in one of the windows looking straight into mine. A boy was standing in the window watching me. His face was unbelievably handsome and he looked around the same age as me. Completely mortified, I ducked behind my curtain. Idiot! He had clearly been standing there watching me inspect their house like a half-witted burglar. I took a breath and slowly peered around the curtain trying my best to stay hidden. I needn't have bothered; the window where he had been standing was empty. I scanned all of the windows on the second story in case I had looked back at the wrong one, but no one was there. Strange, I thought his expression was so odd, like he had seen a ghost.

# CHAPTER 3

With my cheeks blazing red I half-heartedly pulled some clothes out of my bags and tossed them into the wardrobe, put my fluffy teddy bear on my pillow, and pulled my sketchbooks out of their squashed position in my backpack. In between pulling items out of my bag I glanced out the window at the house next door, but the boy did not appear again. After a while I gave up and walked back down the hallway to try to find my parents. They were not in their room so I decided to have a look around before starting the process of unpacking.

The house was unquestionably in desperate need of some TLC but I had to concede it did have a lot of character. As I wandered through each of the rooms I struggled to recall memories from the last time we had visited. We hadn't been here in more than two years and although I had known my way around the house so well when I was younger, I was struggling now to remember all of the nooks and crannies.

Also frustrating me was the fact that some of the closed doors I tried to push open appeared to be glued shut and no amount of pushing and pulling the handles succeeded in moving them. Absentmindedly I wondered why you would want to seal the contents of a room shut in such a permanent way. To mark it as a room not necessary to take care of? That didn't make sense given the state of disrepair of the unsealed sections of the house. Possibly to dissuade burglars I thought to myself, but then reconsidered; if anything, it made me more determined to get into the rooms for a look.

I vaguely recalled secret passageways leading from a number of the rooms but as I walked around the house and through the doorways that were not stuck shut, I couldn't remember the way to unlock them and which of the rooms actually had them.

One of the rooms, I noticed, was slightly less dusty than the others and had a well-worn leather armchair sitting in front of a beautiful fireplace that looked as though it had been used recently. I could see crystal glasses and a decanter on an old-fashioned copper-colored drinks trolley. This must have been where Poppy retired with her evening brandy. I sank down into the luxurious leather seat, understanding why it was so well worn, and looked at the two large bookshelves that towered on either side of the fireplace. There were books that looked to be hundreds of years old and I stood up to get a closer look at the spines for a clue on the contents. There were books on animals of the South Pacific and centuries old sea guides advising of the turning of the tides and storing of meats for extended sea travel. There was a beautiful encyclopedia and an atlas that looked as though it was half my height and fifty times my age.

'Wow,' I breathed out loud, taking in the impressive collection, and thought about the kind-hearted but completely batty librarian from my school in Brooklyn who was so passionate about books. What she would do to have access to this room! I wondered how long it had been sitting in this house unfound and unappreciated.

As I backed towards the door to leave I noticed several of the books on the lower shelf that did not look as aged as the others. I walked back to the shelf and, noticing that there was no title on the spine, I pulled out the one closest to me and opened it. It was a photo album, and even though I could tell from the smell of the books that they were old, the photos were in fantastic condition. The black-and-white images still looked as fresh as the day that they were taken.

I carefully turned the pages on the first album, not recognizing any of the faces. One after the other I looked through the treasure trove of memories, wondering who all of the people were in the photos and whether any of their ancestors would appreciate seeing some of these moments in time captured in these beautiful albums.

Finally I found an album where I recognized someone – Poppy. One of the albums was entirely dedicated to her wedding. I had only known Poppy when she had been old and wrinkled but she was a particularly beautiful woman when she was younger. Her hair had been tied loosely at the back and a wreath of flowers hung over her hair. Her dress was all elegance and lace with a chaste high neckline. I wondered how she had stayed single all those years after her husband passed away when there surely would have been a number of suitors lined up around the block.

As I pulled out the next album a photo dropped out of the pages and onto the hardwood floor. I picked it up carefully and looked at the image. It looked like a photo taken of the whole household, all of the servants in their finest black suits and crisp white shirts and ladies' maids in their black dresses, white bonnets and starched white smocks. I was amazed at the number of people in the photo. There would have to have been more than two-dozen servants. At the front of the group sitting down on a collection of chairs were what looked like a very young Poppy and her husband. The house sat as an impressive backdrop to the photo and every one of the faces in the image looked very stern, as was the fashion of photos from that day. Everyone except, I noted, one housemaid. The maid who stood over Poppy's left shoulder did not look sternly at the camera but smiled broadly. I gasped and looked closer at the photo. Her face was certainly a great deal younger but she was undoubtedly a maid who still worked for the household now. It was Clara!

What had happened to this woman that she had gone from being such a happy looking person to a dark and menacing figure who seemed to do nothing but skulk around the house. I searched through the rest of the albums but couldn't find any more photos of Clara. Putting the last of the albums carefully back onto the shelf I checked that the room appeared as it was when I had arrived and quietly walked out, closing the door gently behind me.

I wandered in and out of several of the other rooms that I could gain access to, noting the ones that I decided I would need to return to for a closer inspection. Some of the rooms really did seem to be stuck in the nineteenth century and it was amazing that even though the rooms and their contents were so dusty, everything, apart from the wallpaper and some of the plastering, had been preserved so well.

The sun was setting slowly over the water. I glanced at my watch and realized I had been walking aimlessly around the house for more than two hours. I quickly closed the lid of the beautiful antique music box I had been examining and headed off to check in with my parents, lest they think that I had headed for the nearest bus station, which I had threatened them with more than once.

As I wandered in the general direction of the kitchen I realized I was not paying attention to where I was going when I stumbled through open glass double-doors into the greenhouse. Every hair on my body prickled, and despite the summer sun and the warmth of the greenhouse I felt a chill run up my body. Turning on my heel I ran back into the house and followed the sound of voices to the kitchen.

Like my bedroom, I was pleasantly surprised by the kitchen. It was extremely comfortable and functional. I noted the irony that it was now fashionable to build a new kitchen resembling this one that was so old. The large marble table and white iron sinks were complemented by the newer stainless steel of the fridge and dishwasher. A large country-style wooden table big enough to sit twelve sat next to the double French doors leading down to the garden, and beyond that to the water. All around the kitchen were windows which gave it an airy, light feel.

My parents were deeply ensconced in what looked like the plans of the house. Marcel looked up from what he was doing and smiled at me. 'I am making omelets Miss Sophie. Would you like one?'

Good for you Marcel, I thought. That wasn't in the six-meal list that Poppy demanded – he must have branched out!

'No thanks Marcel, I'm beat. I'm going to head to bed.'

Both parents looked up, concerned.

'You need to eat honey, are you okay?' asked Mom.

'Yes, I just want to finish unpacking and go to sleep.'

'Alright then.' They both exchanged a nervous glance. Honestly, they had never been so overprotective and concerned about me having an early night before! I looked like a walking zombie; surely they didn't consider me a flight risk after only a few hours. Still, I thought, I had better set their mind at ease. 'Really I'm fine. I'm just exhausted. I'll see you in the morning. Goodnight.'

Walking back into my bedroom I glanced at the half-unpacked suitcase and felt heavy with fatigue. I'll finish it tomorrow I thought, moving sluggishly towards the bed. Too tired to even pull the covers over me, I flopped into the fluffy cloud and as soon as my head hit the pillows I was asleep.

# CHAPTER 4

*My eyes still felt heavy but I opened them to see the boy from the garden at the end of my bed. He looked older than in my dream.*

*I sat bolt upright.*

*'Who are you and what are you doing in my bedroom?'*

*The boy continued to stare at me as though I had said nothing.*

*'Who are you? What do you want?' I demanded again, pulling the covers up tighter around my chest.*

*He tilted his face to the side and appraised me. 'You really don't remember?' He sounded sad.*

*I closed my eyes trying to push down the headache that was starting to develop.*

# CHAPTER 5

When I opened my eyes there was daylight coming through the curtains. The large pool of drool on my pillow made me realize that I had been heavily asleep, but the memory of the boy standing at the end of my bed was still there. It felt as though his sadness vibrated through the room. I looked up quickly but there was no one there.

I rolled myself out of bed and quickly threw on jeans and a sweater, wanting to push the memory of the boy out of my mind. I had slept in, so my parents were already in town picking up supplies to begin the restoration. There was an amazing smell drifting up from the direction of the kitchen and my stomach rumbled. I realized that because I hadn't eaten the night before I was now famished. I wandered down into the kitchen where the obviously new and improved Marcel was making waffles.

'That smells incredible Marcel!'

'Yes, I have been taking some cooking courses since Madame Poppy passed away. I think maybe I wasn't so good the last time that you came, eh?' He smiled at me, handing me a full plate of waffles smothered in strawberries.

'Not at all,' I laughed nervously, focusing my attention on pouring the maple syrup onto the fluffy goodness that was sitting in front of me, knowing that he could probably see right through my lie.

'Actually, my mother wanted me to be a nurse like her,' he smiled, pulling down a framed photo from the shelf and passing it to me. In the photo a younger looking Marcel was hugging a round woman wearing hospital whites, a nurse's cap and badge, with a big smile on her face.

'You look like her,' I said passing the picture back.

After gulping down my plate of waffles made by the new-and-improved Marcel I spent the rest of the morning finishing unpacking my things. I carefully cleared a space on the bookshelves that were already laden with what looked like first editions of Enid Blyton books and fairytales from Hans Christian Andersen and put some of the antique-looking objects into a bag to move into one of the other rooms. China dolls were not really my thing. Every so often I would glance out the side window that looked into the neighbor's house, but the boy's blind had been pulled down so I couldn't even see into his room now. Once I had finished unpacking the majority of my stuff I went to the window again, but this time I looked out the front of the house. The sun was glinting off the water, which was as still as a lake, and there were people out and about walking their dogs and playing with their children in the soft sand near our little jetty. I decided to take advantage of the beautiful weather and spend the afternoon exploring the outside of the property to see whether my memories of playing outside would come back. I also took my sketchbook and a couple of pencils with me in case I found any inspiration during my explorations.

Making sure that I avoided the greenhouse, I walked out the front door and around to the left side of the house, where Poppy had designed a garden amphitheater. The tiered grass steps that you could sit on flowed down to a sunken stage that was surrounded on all sides by hedging. According to Clara, many years ago the mansion had played host to local productions of Shakespeare where all of the neighbors would come to watch with picnic baskets. I could imagine that the hedging that surrounded the theater would have been great acoustically.

Back in the day, when there had been a full-time gardening staff, I am sure it would have been beautiful, but with only Thomas left and the Shakespeare plays no longer a common occurrence the trees had grown out of control. The big trees blocked out any sunlight so the rock steps that curved around in a semicircle were covered in moss and the atmosphere was dark and damp.

I walked down the steps and onto the stage. Placing my sketchpad and pencils down I pretended to dance gracefully around the stage and finish with a bow. Even though it was a warm day I shivered. I could feel the goosebumps rising on my neck and down my arms. Strange that even though the theater was enclosed on every side by the ginormous hedge I felt like I was being watched.

I quickly left the mossy green stage, grabbing my pencils and sketchpad, and walked out through the entrance to the side of the stage. I walked further down the side of the property where there was a large oak tree and found a beautiful ornate chair to sit on, overlooking the water. On the chair was a small plaque dedicated to Poppy's deceased husband.

*And if I am not there for you to see*
*Do not be sad – where you are is where I will be.*

I sat down and gazed up at the beautiful big tree. Closing my eyes I breathed in the clean fresh air and pictured the couple sitting there, side by side. All around me I could hear sounds but it was so peaceful: the birds, the water lapping onto the shore and the wind softly tugging at my hair. The air was warm and even though the seat was shaded by the big tree I could feel the warmth of the sun on my arms and face.

The memory of the sad boy in my dreams came to my mind and I opened my eyes again expecting him to be standing in front of me. Of course he wasn't, but his face had been so clear and after a minute of feeling foolish I opened my sketchbook on my lap and started drawing him.

I stayed there for over an hour trying to get his face just right but the dream was fading quickly from my mind and by the time I gave up I was questioning whether that was what he had looked like at all. I closed my book, giving up and jumped up to continue my tour of the grounds. I did a large loop back around the house and up to the right was a small wooden gate surrounded with jasmine flowers. Funny, while we didn't have any of these flowers in Brooklyn the smell was so familiar.

I walked around the hedging to the heavy wooden gate and pushed against it but like some of the rooms in the house it wouldn't budge. Running my hand over the beautiful markings on the wood I followed the grain down to the middle. There looked to be a slot for a big old metal key, but the key was missing.

I looked around for an obvious place for someone to hide a key. I felt along the top of the posts that sat on each side of the gate but there was nothing. I followed the hedge around in a circle but it looked like the wooden gate was the only point of entry. I did another lap around to see whether the hedge had any gaps that I could squeeze through but it was far too dense.

'Sophie!' I heard Mom calling from the back of the house.

Looking back at the wooden gate my curiosity was peaked. 'Coming!' I yelled back and decided to concede defeat for today; I would have a look around the house and see if I could find the key later. Not tomorrow though. Tomorrow I had an entirely different challenge to conquer.

As I walked back up towards the house I saw movement in one of the rooms. Glancing up I spotted Clara standing in the window of the room next door to mine. I raised my hand to wave and she turned and walked away from the window. Shaking my head I continued walking back to the house. I couldn't know for sure but it felt like she had been watching me. I involuntarily shuddered as I wondered how long she had been standing there.

After dinner I again dragged myself up to my room,

my body heavy with fatigue. But unlike the previous night, as soon as I walked into my room I felt my mood shift. Something was strange. It was not immediately obvious what, but I was certain that some of my things had been moved around. The pillows on the window seat were fluffed up and some things on my desk weren't where I thought I'd left them. I wondered whether Clara had been cleaning in my room, but she hadn't said anything. They were only the sort of small things that someone who had been searching through my room might not have noticed. Someone who was looking for something quickly and hadn't put everything back quite the way it had been before. I felt a chill go down my spine and pulled my warm cardigan tighter around my body. Suddenly my little haven didn't seem quite as safe as it had minutes before. I realized with a sinking feeling in my stomach that maybe it wasn't my room that I was worried about but the fact that the following day was Monday.

# CHAPTER 6

New school. Generally the change that is most feared by teenagers moving around the country. Not me; I was going to get through the next two years and get out. I didn't need to make any friends because after I had completed my two-year sentence I was quite certain I would never lay eyes on any of those kids again.

When I walked through the front gates I got a few curious glances but it wasn't until I walked into homeroom that I drew any real interest. A couple of the girls who looked like their clothes were worth more than my family's car looked me over then went back to their conversation, and some intelligent-looking kids at the front glanced up at the door as I entered and then back at me like I had stepped off a spaceship.

After everyone rediscovered their manners and averted their eyes I slunk over to a free seat by the window and pulled out my timetable and a map of the school buildings that the surly looking woman at the front desk had shoved at me.

'Let me know if you need any help with that,' said a boy to my right. I looked over to where he was sitting. He was scruffy looking but with a really kind face covered in freckles.

'Thanks,' I muttered.

'I'm Percy.'

'Seriously? As in the steam train from *Thomas the Tank Engine*.'

'Yes, my parents are that cruel. Actually, I think I'm named after a great-grandfather or something,' Percy said laughing. He put on an official-sounding gruff voice and with a serious look on his face said, 'One of the founding fathers of our community. Our family has been living here for generations.' He smiled and winked.

His smile was infectious and I found myself smiling back. 'I'm Sophie.'

'Great to meet you Sophie. I hear that your family have just moved into the haunted mansion,' he said.

I snorted, 'I guess you could call it that. I'm not sure it's haunted by anything scarier than bad wallpaper and bathroom mold though.'

'Well, regardless, I feel it is my civic duty to advise you that you are likely to get a request from the social committee to hold the Halloween ball there later this year.' Looking around, he motioned toward the back of the room where a group of beautiful people sat, all looking the same. 'They've been itching to get their hands on a decent venue for years and I overheard them talking about the Storybook House before you arrived. I dare say they might even give you an honorary membership of the attractive people table if you loan them the house, and you could sit there and do nothing,' Percy added with a laugh.

'Thanks for the heads up. I'm not much of a social

committee kind of person,' I said rolling my eyes.

Just then the teacher walked into the room and everyone went silent. Well, I thought to myself, I know I said I wouldn't go out of my way to make friends, but Percy seems like a very easygoing kind of person …

For the next couple of classes there was at least one person who made a special effort to be nice and make me feel welcome and for that I was grateful. After each class I was led to the next one before my savior left me with a wave and a promise to find me at lunch.

When I reached the cafeteria I discovered that all of them were sitting on the same table. That figures, I thought to myself. Percy waved me over and I carefully made my way past the inquiring eyes and over to their table.

Percy introduced me to the group, which included Alex (who had cheerfully volunteered to be my lab partner in Chemistry), James, Emma, Megan and Alice, who I had spoken to in Art class.

'How are you finding our little school of overachievers Sophie?' Alex asked smiling.

'Everyone seems really nice,' I said politely.

'Everyone on this table anyway,' said Alice, a tall blonde girl with big dimples. 'You might not say the same thing about all the tables in the cafeteria.'

She started to point out the different groups around the room but based on the appearance of the groups I think I could have worked them out myself. 'The tables at the front are full of the math and science groups. They usually eat quickly and disappear back to their important work. The jocks and socialites sit towards the back because the girls don't eat the food and the meatheads need lots of space to throw balls at each other. And then you have all the mixed groups like us in between.'

As she pointed out the group at the back I spotted him. My neighbor who had caught me gawking at his house. He was looking directly at me with the same look on his face. His eyes were narrowed and he looked surprised. I quickly looked away, feeling my face burn with embarrassment. After picking at my food and staring at my plate for a couple of minutes I quietly murmured to Alice, 'I think one of the boys over there lives next door to me.'

'Really? Which one?' she asked, looking in the direction of his table.

I looked back up at the table he had been sitting on and he was gone. 'Oh, my mistake,' I said, unsure, searching the rest of the cafeteria in vain.

The bell rang for the next period and everyone picked up their trays and started heading off. 'What class have you got next Sophie?' asked Alex, in an overly keen kind of way.

'Umm, history in building B,' I said, glancing at my timetable.

'Oh,' he said, looking disappointed. 'I have gym class but it's right near building B if you would like me to take you?'

'Sure,' I said with a polite smile. 'That would be good, thanks.' Might have to keep my distance from this one, I thought. He was a little overeager and I wasn't looking for any kind of romantic relationship.

As soon as I walked into the classroom I saw him. He was sitting up the back pulling out his pens and textbooks. I had a minute to check him out before he looked up and saw me staring at him. He looked straight back down at his book and pretended not to see me but the muscles in his hand and arm were tense. The class had filled up and the only seat left was directly in front of him. I took a deep breath and nervously made my way over to the desk and sat down.

For the next fifty minutes I sat there wondering what he was thinking about behind me. I wasn't sure why but he seemed to be somewhat frightened or angry when he looked at me. It couldn't just be because I was spying on their house from my bedroom. I felt like there was an electrical current running straight into my back. I summoned all of my courage and when the bell rang I was prepared to turn around and confront him, but he was one step ahead of me and was already at the door before I opened my mouth.

I found Percy waiting for me at the door. 'Ready for some softball?' he said, pretending to hit a home run with an imaginary bat. He looked totally ridiculous and I laughed, despite my rising concern that I had created an enemy of someone I had never even spoken to.

My lack of sporting prowess had not changed with the move and despite one mildly impressive shot, which was an accident more than anything, I spent most of the class trying to avoid having to take the bat.

By the end of the day I was exhausted. I walked over

to the bike racks next to the car park and looked around the parking lot. There were expensive European cars in all different shapes and sizes. My jaw dropped when I saw the boy-next-door walk over to one of the shiny new cars and drive off in the direction of our houses. Of course he has a beautiful car, I thought to myself. He is a beautiful guy driving his beautiful car to his beautiful house, probably with his beautiful girlfriend. I, on the other hand, was riding my second-hand bike back to my falling-down house that everyone seemed to think was haunted. Pulling my bike off the rack I rode past the shiny cars and out to the road. This was going to be a long year, I thought, sighing.

When I got home there was no sign of the shiny black car next door. I walked in through the front door and Mom was finishing up on the staircase banister. The lacquer had been stripped back and the color underneath was a beautiful warm brown oak. 'Looking good Mom,' I said giving her a quick hug.

'How was your first day honey?' she asked anxiously, stopping her work and studying my face.

'It was OK,' I told her honestly. It really hadn't been as bad as I'd feared it might be. I picked up a piece of sandpaper and began running it gently along the grain of the wood on the staircase. 'There was a group of really friendly kids that welcomed me onto their table. They all seem really nice.'

'That's great Sophie!' I could hear the relief and encouragement in my mom's voice.

'And I have been told the social committee want to

use our house for the annual Halloween ball,' I added, chuckling.

'Well that would be lots of fun. Let us know when it is and we'll start planning.'

'You're kidding, right?' I said, incredulous. 'This house could fall down on top of them!'

'Don't be silly, the house is made of brick. We'll make sure the ballroom is in good condition and we could decorate the room with black crepe and we could go to Hank's and buy the pumpkins …' I started walking up the stairs already tuning her out.

'Sure Mom. I'm going to get started on some homework. Let me know if you want me to help with dinner.'

I ran my hand over the smooth wood, tracing the lines all the way up to the top of the landing, and walked down the hall to my room. Glancing out the front window that looked out over the water I caught myself thinking about the boy next door. There was something so familiar about him. Maybe I should just go over and introduce myself, I thought, but the look on his face each time that I had seen him stopped me in my tracks. I couldn't shake the feeling that he didn't really want to talk to me or that he was angry with me for some reason.

Dad had made me a makeshift desk and I sat down to start working through my homework. Out of the corner of my eye I caught sight of something propped up on my desk lamp. It was a thick, cream-colored envelope with my name written in beautiful cursive text. My hand froze as I reached for it. The treasure hunts that Poppy would create for me all started with the same cream-colored envelope, which would hold the first clue. But the card had not been here this morning.

# CHAPTER 7

With shaking hands I picked up the card and turned it over. It even smelt like her perfume. I opened it slowly and pulled out the card that was inside. It was definitely made of the same paper and there was no question about it – the writing inside was Poppy's.

*The treasure hunts were always fun*
*It's time to do another one.*
*It is in the place where we used to play*
*How I loved it when you came to stay*
*I would place the flowers in your hair*
*And all of our secrets we would share*
*Can you hear the water falling down?*
*And smell the grass? It's all around*
*Oscar and Lucinda are no longer there*
*Find some new friends that come in a pair*
*But please do not let anyone see*
*It must be you that finds the key.*

I read the card over several times before putting it down on the desk. She had obviously hidden something, but what? A key? And where was it hidden? I was completely confused and I had no idea where to start looking. I had played all over the house and there were so many rooms. And who had put the card there? Obviously not Poppy or I would have seen it when I came in on the first day we got here.

Just then I heard the creaking of someone coming up the stairs. Remembering her comment not to trust anyone, I hid the card under the cushions on my window seat and sat back down quickly at my desk.

There was a knock on the door and Clara's voice on the other side. 'Miss Sophie, dinner is ready.'

'OK thanks, I'll come down now.'

I opened the door, looking back into the room to make sure that the card was not visible, and once I was confident it was not I turned around to leave the room. I let out a cross between a squeal and a squeak and shrank back when I saw that Clara was still standing in the door waiting for me. She peered over my shoulder into my bedroom as if looking for someone or something and then, realizing that she was lurking, she pursed her lips, turned on her heel and marched back down the hallway.

# CHAPTER 8

The rest of the week seemed to drag on. I spent most of my time in class trying to figure out the riddle. It had to be from Poppy, but at the same time there was no way it could have been from her. She was dead, I reminded myself. But it was absolutely her writing and her stationery so someone must have put it there at her request. Why did she want me to find it? Why not my mom and dad?

I mentioned the card to my parents over breakfast one morning but didn't tell them what was written on the card. I was at a complete loss and figured that if I didn't mention any of the clues and just told them that I had found one of her treasure hunt cards then I wasn't revealing anything that I shouldn't.

Mom and Dad had no idea who had put it in my bedroom. Marcel asked what the clue said and Clara snuck a sideways glance at me from where she had been cleaning the back windows. Even Thomas had stopped in his tracks as he was walking out the door when he heard me mention the card. I filled the silence with a laugh and said I thought it was one of the cards that she had given me years ago because it looked old and I half remembered doing it with her. My parents looked dubious but everyone else had resumed what they had been doing with no further mention of it.

I did another full lap around the house and the gardens trying to put the pieces of the clue in context. It was 'in the place where we used to play.' I remembered being all over the house with her, but not at all clearly. Why was my memory so hazy? It wasn't that long ago that we had visited Poppy and yet I couldn't quite remember the last time. And who were Oscar and Lucinda? Was she pointing me towards a book? That didn't make sense – the library was at the front of the house and you couldn't hear the water in there. Although, it didn't sound like she was talking about the ocean because the waves either lapped or crashed, so maybe she was talking about rain. Where could you hear the rain? I guess you could hear it at the top of the house, but we didn't really go up there because that was where Marcel and Clara's rooms were. You could probably hear the rain in the kitchen and the greenhouse but I didn't really want to go back there; it gave me the creeps so I hadn't been back since the day we arrived.

I decided my best bet was to have a quick look around upstairs. I waited until dinnertime when Marcel was busy in the kitchen and I couldn't see Clara anywhere. It would only take a minute to have a quick look, I argued to myself. I would be in and out and Clara would never know I was up there. And really the house was ours, so technically I was allowed to go wherever I wanted. I went to the door at the end of the passageway that led to the upstairs rooms and quietly tiptoed up the stairs, listening for any sound of movement in the upstairs quarters.

There were eight rooms in all divided into two defined sections. This must have been to separate the male and female staff back in the days when it was not considered proper to see each other wandering around in nightclothes, I thought to myself as I passed a couple of open doors, noticing the scant furniture in the rooms. Back in the house's heyday there had been a lot more staff but it seemed that not all of them would have been live-in.

I walked past a wall of bells that had room names underneath them but stopped dead when I heard the sound of a voice. It sounded like it was coming from down the hallway. I couldn't tell if the voice was male or female but it sounded like the person was upset. I wondered which of the rooms was Marcel's and which room was Clara's. I tiptoed towards the sound of the voice. One more step and I would be at the door where the sound was coming from. The floorboard groaned under my step and I held my breath as the sound of the voice stopped. I heard a couple of quick footsteps and the door next to me was suddenly thrust open, Clara's severe face glared at me, self-consciously standing in the hallway.

'Are you lost?' she asked curtly.

'Um, no,' I responded, my voice sounding meek.

'Well then, is there something that you are looking for?'

'I was … I was … looking for the door to get out to the terrace on the roof.'

I tried to peer into Clara's room but she noticed and closed the door behind her, pushing me into the corridor.

Who had she been speaking to in her room and why wouldn't she let me see inside? She started to walk along the corridor and turned to make sure that I was following her.

'Were you on the phone?' I asked, curiosity getting the better of me.

'No,' she answered curtly. 'If you push in this panel a door will open,' she demonstrated, revealing a hidden staircase. 'Unfortunately the door at the top of the stairs which leads you into the clock tower and then out onto the rooftop terrace seems to be stuck for some reason.'

I walked up to the top of the stairs and tried as hard as I could to open the door but nothing I did would make it budge one inch. Curious, I thought to myself. Another door that seems to have been superglued shut. When I walked down the stairs Clara had an 'I told you so' look on her face. I thanked her for her help and she stood there blocking the hallway that led back to her room until I turned and walked back down to my room. Why had the room to the rooftop been sealed? Who had Clara been speaking to, and what was the answer to Poppy's riddle? I was more confused than ever.

It was in the final class of school the next day, while we were in Chemistry and discussing a famous scientist who went crazy and started naming the spiders around his house, that I remembered. Poppy had shown me how the earthworms in her flowerpots helped the soil turn, which she argued gave her a better rose. We had spent an afternoon digging in the soft soil at the bottom of the garden looking for worms. I had dug around in the dirt and pulled out two that were stuck together almost like they were holding hands and I had called them Oscar and Lucinda. Poppy had let me start my own little potted rose bush and I had put Oscar and Lucinda into the soil. It sat right at the door of the greenhouse where the grass crept up to the back door and you could hear the rain falling on the glass roof. It had to be in there – all of the pieces of the puzzle fit.

I raced out of my final class and headed straight for the bike racks. As soon as I was beyond the curious eyes of teachers I started to sprint and I ran around the corner of the sport center and straight into my next-door neighbor, sending books, pens and backpacks flying in the process.

'Oh my god! I'm so, so sorry!' I stammered as we both knelt down to collect our possessions.

'That's OK, are you alright?' he murmured, refusing to make eye contact. I realized he was wearing his protective football clothing so it was unlikely that he felt a thing in the collision, which made me feel even more stupid.

'Yep, still alive and kicking!' I said laughing lightly. His face twisted and he looked almost sad. As soon as he had all of his things he jammed them quickly into his bag and looked up at me like he was going to say something. But as he opened his mouth one of his teammates yelled out to him and he looked at me for what felt like a full minute before muttering, 'Well, see you,' and running down to the field.

'Weirdo,' I thought, but really I was disappointed. I wanted to speak to him and ask why he acted so strangely around me. It was not just in my imagination. I felt drawn to him and I could see from the natural way that he interacted with other people in our class that he was really kind and smart, not to mention good looking. I had discovered from Alex that his name was Charlie Crawford. He played for the football team and he had two older brothers who were both away at college. He had lived in the house next door to Poppy all of his life. Alex had provided me with this information in a begrudging way and then added for extra measure that he didn't date any of the girls at school, even though plenty of them had flung themselves at him.

I had to laugh; there was no way that I could see Alex as anything more than a friend so I wished he would stop trying. Aside from not being attracted to him in the slightest, Emma seemed very interested in Alex and I felt like I would be stepping on toes there. In the past couple of weeks she had made it perfectly clear that I was an unwelcome addition to their table too, which I think had stemmed from the unwanted attention that I was receiving from Alex.

Shrugging my shoulders, I threw my stuff in my bag, ran down the ramp to the bikes and sped home. I didn't have time to waste trying to uncover the reasons behind the strange behavior of my neighbor at the moment; I was certain that I had deciphered the code on the card and nothing else mattered as much as finding the hidden treasure.

As soon as I got home I checked that the house was quiet. I could see my parents down on the dock checking out the repair work that was needed but I couldn't see or hear Marcel, Clara or Thomas. I didn't want to wait to find out where they all were so I threw my bag on the kitchen bench and headed straight to the greenhouse. As I stepped through the door I had the same weird sensation that I experienced the last time. 'It's all just in your mind, all in your mind, there is no such thing as ghosts,' I reassured myself, and started looking around at all of the pots and bags of fertilizer and sprays. There were three long tables stretching 15 or 20 feet, two on each side and a big long one going down the middle of the room. There were hoses twisting across the floor and two long, rusty looking sprinklers that sat overhead. The smell was the same as it had been all those years ago, the sweet scent of the flowers and the earthy soil all mixed in together, and the sticky humidity that made me instantly clammy.

My mind turned to where Poppy had been sitting when she died. She had a bar stool that she would sit on to tend to her plants that was moved around the room depending on what she was working on, but I couldn't see it. Maybe Thomas got rid of it.

I took a deep breath, stepped into the room and made my way down the left side, smelling some of Poppy's roses that were still in bloom as I walked down the path. I marveled at the way the mind could recall memories with a single smell and I found myself remembering the names of the flowers that she would spend hours trying to teach me. For the first time since I had heard of her death and our subsequent move I felt sad that we hadn't come back when she had been alive. Even though I didn't pester my parents to venture back here I was surprised that we hadn't. I think my dad had occasionally come to visit her by himself but she must have been really lonely in this big house without any family and only having a few employees for company.

As I reached the end of the path I looked along the wall next to the double doors that led outside. The big rectangular pot that she had given me wasn't there. 'Crap,' I said to myself looking more closely around the door. I walked around the whole greenhouse, looking under the wooden benches and on the top of the table and was about to give up the search when I spotted, peeking out in the back corner, bright yellow paint. That had to be it, I thought excitedly, remembering that I had painted sunflowers on the sides of the earthy terracotta. I reached the spot in three quick strides and bent down to have a closer look.

It was stuck underneath one of the heavy wooden tables so I had to climb under, trying my best not to cover myself in soil. My curiosity at the contents of the pot got the better of me and I gave up and knelt down pushing other pots aside as I reached for the one that I had painted with flowers along the side. Using a small trowel I had grabbed off the table I began digging through the soil. She was right about the worms; they were long gone and the soil was dry and flaky, like it hadn't had water in years. It seemed to take me forever just to loosen the soil. The trowel hit something at the bottom and I pushed it aside and, using my hands, unearthed something wrapped in a plastic bag.

I pulled out the bag and as I peered into the dirt-covered plastic I suddenly heard someone yelling my name. My heart pounded and I tried to stand up quickly, hitting my head on the table above in the process.

'Ouch, crap!' I muttered as quietly as I could.

'Sophie?' Rubbing my head I shook off the dirt from the plastic bag and pushed it into the back of my jeans, pulling my T-shirt over the top to hide it.

'Oh there you are,' said Mom, raising her eyebrows while looking at the knees of my jeans that were covered in dark brown soil from kneeling on the ground. 'What on earth are you doing?' she asked, unable to mask her surprise.

I brushed myself down, smiled and sweetly said, 'I was thinking about growing some herbs.'

'Really? I mean, OK, great. That would be great. I'm sure that Marcel would love to have some fresh herbs to use in his cooking,' Mom said looking a little doubtful, and no doubt wondering when her daughter, who had no interest whatsoever in gardening, had suddenly developed a green thumb. Idiot! I thought to myself. She would have been more likely to believe me if I told her I was thinking about setting up a drug lab in the greenhouse.

'Dinner will be ready soon.'

'OK. I'll just get changed and wash up,' I said, racing past her and up the stairs.

As soon as I got into my room I quickly pulled off my soil-stained jeans and threw on a pair of sweat pants. I opened up the bag, barely able to contain my excitement. Inside there was what looked like a diary. I flicked through quickly, looking at some of the pages, but it didn't seem to make much sense. There were random entries in each of the months of the year that seemed to include a description of a location in the house with names next to it and then a year written next to the name. The writing was clearly Poppy's.

The plastic bag slid off my lap and onto the floor and I heard something inside clink like metal. Lifting the bag I reached in and pulled out a key on a necklace. It was the most beautiful key I had ever seen – detailed, ornate markings circled around the top of the key that flowed down to a narrow part that went into a lock with three prongs. It looked like an antique. I wondered for a minute if it would fit inside the gate that I had found in the garden but quickly dismissed the idea: that gate had a much bigger keyhole.

Hearing Mom yelling up the stairs I put the book inside my school homework folder and the key back in the bag and stuffed it under the cushions on the window seat. Heading downstairs I wondered what Poppy was doing when she died that required such secrecy. For her to have hidden the book in the pot and not told anyone must have meant that she didn't trust the people in the house but what was I supposed to do with that information? I had anticipated that once I found the location of the treasure it would make sense, but I was more confused than ever.

# CHAPTER 9

At school the next day I found my mind wandering to where the key might fit and why it would be so important that I keep it a secret. After dinner I had gone straight back upstairs claiming that I had more homework to finish off but really I wanted to have a better look at the diary.

The entries had to be in some kind of code because they didn't make any sense. Each entry had the name of a room in the house and a name or multiple names of people next to them and what looked like a year in brackets. I spotted one entry that had *Library. Percy Cunningham (b.1896)*. The entry had stood out because of the name: Percy had mentioned that he had been named after a great-grandfather and the year would have fit with someone being that old.

'Earth to Sophie? Come in Sophie???'

'What?' I looked up to see that everyone at the cafeteria table was looking at me for the answer to a question that I hadn't heard.

'I was asking how your first few weeks have been sleeping in the haunted mansion,' James said.

'Do you think it's really haunted?' Alex asked with a nervous laugh.

Just days ago I would have laughed and rolled my eyes but receiving notes from people that I knew to be dead had weakened my conviction. Still, I didn't want to seem crazy to my new schoolmates so I simply shrugged my shoulders. 'I don't think so, but don't some people believe that spirits are everywhere?'

'I do,' Megan said. 'We should have a séance at your house Sophie!' she followed up excitedly.

'That's a great idea Megan!' enthused James.

'Please! You won't find me walking into that decrepit old pile of bricks! It will probably fall down on top of us,' Emma said sarcastically.

Ignoring Emma, I looked over at Alice but she had a faraway look on her face. 'Are you free Alice?' I asked her, quietly hoping she would laugh away the idea of ghosts too, but she didn't.

'No, I have to help my mom out tonight. Sorry.' She smiled apologetically but I had the feeling that she wasn't at all sorry not to be participating.

I wasn't thrilled at the idea of a séance either but Emma's rude comment made me determined to do it, if only to get back at her. As Emma was the only one that poo-pooed the idea we ended up agreeing to meet at my house at 8 pm that night. I wasn't at all surprised when Emma turned up. She seemed to be very much a follower and not a leader.

When they all arived I led James, Alex, Megan, Emma and Percy up the front steps and took them into the library. I had never done a séance before so I had looked around the house for somewhere suitable to hold it and decided that the library seemed like the most comfortable and least dusty room in the house. It also had loads of atmosphere with the old books and fireplace.

My parents were happy to hear that I had friends coming around but seemed less enthusiastic about the idea of a game to summon the spirits. Marcel had laughed and made a joke about summoning his mother to ask for her recipe for pumpkin scones. 'Best in three counties,' he said winking at me.

My friends wandered into the room looking around in awe at the paintings and old books.

'You should definitely let the social committee have the ball here Sophie. Even if it isn't haunted, this place is fantastic!' Percy said enthusiastically.

As I had never participated in a séance let alone led one, I happily relinquished that role to Megan, who seemed to be the most spiritual of the group. She went around lighting the candles that I had foraged from around the house and ordered us all to sit in a circle around the coffee table and the Ouija board she had brought. A couple of us giggled nervously and Megan silenced us all with a look.

'Close your eyes and put one finger on the planchette,' she commanded. She was so serious none of us dared make any jokes. Even Alex, who was inappropriate at the most awkward of moments, kept his mouth closed.

'We have come here tonight to summon the spirits!' she said in a confident voice. I opened one of my eyes and looked around the room at the others. Emma had a smirk on her face, Alex and Percy looked like they could erupt into laughter at any minute, but James had his eyes firmly closed and looked like he was taking it very seriously. I muffled my own giggle and closed my eye again.

'Is anyone there?' she waited several minutes and appealed again.

'Is anyone there???' She raised her voice.

My mind started to stray and I wondered how long people usually wait until they just give up the ghost, so to speak, and stop playing. Suddenly the planchette began to move. We all opened our eyes and looked down at the board, which had firmly swung across to YES.

I was so shocked I took my hand off the board and received a swift reprimand from Megan. 'Sophie, put your hand back on the board or you might break the connection!' I did as I was told and she appealed to the spirit again. 'Are you a man or a woman?' The planchette swung to the letter M. She then proceeded to ask a series of questions that became stranger and stranger the more she asked. 'Can you tell us your name?' The planchette started moving. P…E…R…C

'PERCY!!!' Megan groaned and smacked him on the back of the head. The rest of us fell about in fits of laughter while Percy protested his innocence.

'What?! I didn't do it. One of the others must have been spelling my name!!!' He put his hand on his heart and Megan looked around at the rest of us but no one was prepared to confess.

As much as Megan wanted to try again the rest of us were clearly not taking it at all seriously and the spell had been broken. We sat around in the library telling ghost stories until Mom popped her head in the door and suggested it might be time for bed. It was 11 pm on a school night after all, she argued.

Even though Megan was a little disappointed we couldn't find a legitimate spirit they all headed off, happily planning another ghostly encounter soon. Even Emma had a smile on her generally sour face when she left. It completely softened her eyes; she should try smiling more often I thought to myself as she left.

I too was dubious at the existence of ghostly spirits in the house but my mind went back to the entry in Poppy's diary that had said, *Library. Percy Cunningham (b. 1896)*. Was it the boys or Emma pushing the planchette around or had it really been Percy's great-grandfather in the room with them. I felt a shiver run down my spine as I reluctantly waved goodbye to my friends, returning to their normal houses.

At school the next day our hippie and Earth-loving art teacher declared the weather glorious and sent us all outside to sketch the autumn leaves. 'Probably just an excuse for a smoking break,' one of our classmates muttered as we were ushered out the door. Alice and I walked around the back of the round art workshop and found a patch of grass under one of the big trees.

'So, were you really busy last night?' I pressed her when we both had our sketchbooks open and had started to draw. She looked at me for a minute with an obstinate look on her face.

'What do you mean? I was helping my mom.'

'Don't get me wrong I don't mind,' I continued. 'In fact, if it wasn't at my house I think I would have probably given it a miss too! I just got the feeling yesterday that you weren't that interested in attending a séance.' She looked off into the distance at something I couldn't see and seemed to consider her answer carefully. Slowly her resolve seemed to crumble and she let out her breath with a big sigh.

'You didn't grow up here so you wouldn't have heard any of the rumors but you know in every small town there is a local crazy woman that everyone decides is really a witch and people throw eggs at their house on Halloween and dare each other to ring their bell. Well that was my grandma. She believed in the spirits and she thought that she could communicate with them. Actually, I think she may have been institutionalized more than once. My mother was so embarrassed or sick of her antics but either way I think she also decided that Grandma was nuts and moved out of home at the age of sixteen. After my grandpa died I was the only one that would visit her.' She looked sad and then confused. 'The funny thing is that to me what she said actually didn't sound that crazy. I believed her and I don't think that the spirits are a world that we should be tampering with, you know?'

I opened my mouth to tell her about my theories on Percy's great-grandfather but the teacher came out at that moment to call us all back to class.

# CHAPTER 10

On Friday my parents left early in the morning to stay overnight at some little village not far away that had kitschy antiques, and Marcel went into the city for the weekend.

Since it was only me at home, Clara and Thomas also made themselves scarce and I found myself enjoying having the place to myself. I spent a couple of hours after school looking around for where the key might fit. As expected, it didn't fit into the big wooden gate in the garden. It also didn't fit into any of the doors that seemed to be superglued shut. I looked for jewelry boxes and cabinets with locks, but after a while I started to get hungry and gave up. Hanging the key around my neck, I went to the kitchen to make myself some dinner.

Marcel had left a shepherd's pie in the fridge so I heated it up in the oven and watched out the windows at the rain starting to fall on the water. I still felt a longing in my heart to return to the city but I had to admit that it was pretty spectacular to watch a storm rolling in over the water towards you, minutes before you heard the raindrops falling on the roof.

After dinner the rain was bordering on torrential. I was tired so I had another half-hearted look around for a place to fit my key but finding nothing I dragged myself up the stairs and headed off to bed. I was too tired to even change into my pajamas so I just pulled the key from around my neck and put it down on my side table.

I woke to a loud rumble of thunder and, opening my eyes, I rolled over to look out the window. It was pitch black outside, the rain still belted down, and I realized that I had left my window slightly open. I groaned and rolled out of bed to pull the window secure. I snuck a look over at Charlie's room but his blinds were drawn, the lights were off and the house looked vacant.

Suddenly I heard a loud noise out in the hall. Glancing at the clock I couldn't believe it was so early; it was close to midnight but I felt like I had been sleeping for hours. I heard another noise in the hallway. Strange, I thought to myself, my mom and dad were the only ones who would be walking around out there since their room was on the same level. Thomas had a little cottage that was separate from the main house, around the side near the garden theater, and Marcel and Clara took the main stairs, which were on the other side of the house. I heard the noise again and remembered that Marcel wasn't even here and it seemed a bit late for Clara or Thomas to be up. I walked over to the door and peered out into the hallway just in time to see the back of a young boy disappearing down the stairs.

'Wait!' I called out, but he showed no sign that he heard me. I followed his figure down the hall and turned left at the top landing of the main staircase, but he was gone.

I looked either side of the staircase for signs of movement when suddenly there was a sound directly beneath me.

'Hello?' I squeaked out, my bravado having disappeared at my bedroom door.

I walked down the stairs slowly, each step creaking under my feet. When I walked through the door into the kitchen I was briefly blinded by the daylight, which flooded through the windows.

The boy from my dreams was there, talking to a man sitting at the table with his back to me.

'The weather is wonderful!' the boy said sounding obstinate.

'I don't care what it seems like now, there is a storm coming and I don't want you in the middle of the water with that girl when it does,' the man countered. I couldn't see his face but it looked like he pushed his fingers to his temples.

The man took a deep breath and tried again. 'You really shouldn't be spending so much time with her and that Crawford boy anyway. These people are not like us Gus.'

'You're wrong Dad.' I heard a noise behind me and looked around for a split second, turned back around and the kitchen was in darkness again. I heard the sound of the door leading outside open and rounded the corner in time to see his back disappear down the stairs to the beach and the dock. I ran through the rain down the grass toward the dock but just as I reached the gate I lost sight of him. He must have gone out on the dock. I had to warn him that our dock had holes in it or he could fall. 'Hey!' I called out. 'Be careful down there! HEY!' I didn't realize I had gone so far down the dock until it was too late. I felt my feet come out from underneath me and held my breath as the water came over my head.

Following the boy around the house I had felt dazed, as if in a dream, and my legs had felt as though they were made of cotton wool. As soon as I hit the cold water I was awake and alert, and I realized that I was in deep trouble.

I had done a little bit of swimming at school but I was no athlete and the storm had churned up the water. There also seemed to be an undercurrent that was pulling me away from the jetty quicker than I could swim into it. It didn't help that I was being weighed down by the heavy tracksuit pants and sweater that I had worn to bed so I used some of the strength that I had left to pull off the sweater.

I continued to struggle against the waves that kept slapping me again and again. As I came up for air I called out for help but doubted anyone would be able to hear me in the howling wind, and I kept getting hit by the waves as I opened my mouth, which made it impossible not to inhale mouthfuls of seawater. I felt myself getting heavier and heavier. I closed my eyes and waited for the water to overcome me but instead felt strong muscular arms wrap around me and pull me through the water on my back and then out of the churning water and onto the dock.

# CHAPTER 11

As I lay there gasping for breath and coughing up water I glanced at my savior, who was also gasping for breath on the wooden boards. Expecting to see the boy I had followed I was shocked to see Charlie looking at me with a mixture of relief and shock. As soon as he had his voice back he opened his mouth and yelled at me, 'ARE YOU INSANE?!!'

Stung by the anger in his voice I used the remaining strength that I had to push myself up to stand and yell back at him, 'What is your problem? You spend all your time at school avoiding me and then if we happen to run into each other you look at me like I'm the strangest thing you have ever seen. You don't even know me. I have no idea what I ever did to make you hate me so much! You should have just let me drown!' As soon as the words had left my mouth I felt the hairs on the back of my neck stand up and my head felt heavy, my stomach churned and I felt like I could be sick. I collapsed back onto the dock and looked up at the stars as I closed my eyes.

*When I opened my eyes again I was standing at the start of the dock looking back at the end where I had just passed out. I felt disorientated. The sky was still a light-gray color and the rain had eased to a heavy mist. In the spot where I had just passed out was a man leaning over another form lying on the aged wooden platform. I walked out onto the boards, moving slowly like I was wading through quicksand. As I got closer I realized the man was crying. I felt like I was intruding on a private moment. 'Gus,' he said but it came out as a sob. The form beneath him was the boy that I had followed to the pier and he wasn't moving. The man looked up and I gasped – it was Thomas.*

I opened my eyes and felt the wooden boards in my back. One by one the pieces began to fall into place, the cogs in my brain turning to reveal a past that had lain buried in my brain. Buried to protect myself from the pain of loss. The boy was Thomas's son and, what felt like a lifetime ago, he had been my friend. His name was Gus.

The memories crashed into me one by one and I couldn't believe I had blocked them for so long. It all made so much sense now: why my parents didn't bring me back here, why they were so anxious of my reaction to moving here. I remembered Charlie too; he had been more than a friend.

The only memories I couldn't bring to my mind were the day that Gus had died. A tear rolled down the side of my face and I struggled to sit up. Charlie was sitting next to me watching me carefully. The anger had disappeared from his face. 'You remember now,' he said, and it was more of a statement than a question.

I could feel more tears welling up in my eyes but I didn't want to start blubbering in front of him so I pushed myself up and started to stagger off down the dock.

'Wait!' he called out.

'What! What do you want?' I choked out using up the last of my energy to fight back the tears.

The initial shock had worn off and he almost looked like he was going to laugh as he stood there and looked me over – I must have looked completely ridiculous. 'You're soaking wet. Come with me.'

I quickly assessed my options: my parents and Marcel weren't there and the only people in the haunted mansion were Clara, who was likely to yell at me for coming inside soaking wet and making a mess, and Thomas, who I realized had held me at arm's length this whole time as he more than likely blamed me for the death of his only child.

'Come on Sophie,' he said. His voice was gentle now, like a person soothing a lost animal.

I felt all of my resistance crumble. 'OK,' I conceded.

I could feel him watching me even as we walked up the wet grass leading up to his house. He led me through the double French doors leading into the living area. The house looked exactly as I had expected – a Ralph Lauren catalogue come to life – and I felt myself feeling self-conscious, standing on the doormat, dripping wet, while Charlie stripped down to his boxer shorts and ran to fetch us towels. I watched his back muscles as he jogged across the living room and into a room behind the kitchen, which I assume was the laundry. He came out a minute later clutching two of the softest fluffiest towels I had ever seen and as he wrapped it around me I realized that I had started shivering. I wasn't entirely sure whether it was from the cold or the shock starting to sink in. Charlie led me up to his room and passed me some of his clothes, taking me to a guest room down the hall to change.

After I had changed into his dry sweats and towel-dried my damp hair I wandered back towards his room to find him pulling a shirt over his head. I stood in the crack in the doorway watching his muscles stretch as he pulled each arm into the shirt. Not wanting to get caught staring at him I quietly cleared my throat and he turned around to the sound. His face looked sad and his eyes probed mine.

'What happened to you?' he asked, his voice hoarse. 'Where did you go?'

'I remember now,' I said slowly, 'but I don't remember everything.' I tried to order my thoughts into an explanation. 'That summer when Gus died we went back to New York and my parents took me to see a psychologist. She said that my mind was blocking the memories because they were too painful.'

'So you didn't even remember me?' he asked sounding wounded.

'I'm sorry,' I said sadly, shaking my head. 'I don't know why.'

'I missed you,' he said so softly I wasn't sure if I had heard him. He cleared his throat, 'You left right after he died, I had no idea where you lived and you didn't write me. I hadn't seen you in years and I didn't know if you were alive or dead so when I saw you standing there and everyone had always spoken of the house being haunted I wasn't sure. I know it sounds completely ridiculous …'

'You thought I was dead?' I laughed softly but his face was so serious I quickly stopped.

'And then when you came back I wasn't sure whether you were pretending that you didn't know me or if you hated me or blamed me so I tried to keep my distance but I have watched you. Sorry, what I mean is that I was watching you before, walking out on the dock in the middle of the rain and I couldn't believe it. When he had died in the same way. He drowned that day that you went out in the boat. Do you remember being on the boat?' he asked gently, his eyes searching mine for some recollection.

Again, I searched my mind for some shadow of recollection, some vague memory that could shed some light on that day, but nothing came. I shook my head slowly. 'No, I don't even remember planning to go on a boat. Look at me – do I look like the outdoorsy type?' He laughed and I resisted the urge to reach out and touch the dimple on the left side of his face.

The memories were coming back thick and fast now and I could see how I had developed feelings for Charlie since I had arrived – it was because they were already there. The summers we spent at Poppy's had involved happily looking around the house for the treasure hunts that she had left for me but they had also been spent playing endlessly with Charlie and Gus.

Charlie was smart and kind and sensitive but also really athletic. I remembered that his mom had called him her toasted marshmallow because he was strong on the outside but soft in the middle. Gus would make fun of that nickname. Charlie was always the last one into whatever crazy idea that Gus had thought up because he never liked to get into trouble. That last summer when Gus died I had my first kiss.

The three of us had been jumping off Charlie's dock into the water and I had pretended to drown. I realized now how stupid I had been, but I thought it was funny then. Both boys had jumped off the dock to my rescue but Charlie was the stronger swimmer and had reached me first. He had held my nose and started to try to perform mouth to mouth. Just having his mouth on mine had sent tingles over my body. His hair was dripping on my face and his breath had tasted like saltwater and the caramels that we had been eating earlier. I had pulled the back of his head closer and after he got over the shock that I had tricked him he had kissed me back. It had felt like we had been there for hours but it must have only been a minute because we broke away when Gus reached us. 'That was not funny Sophie!' Gus had said, out of breath, with an angry look on his face, and he had stormed off down the beach.

'I think he's just angry he didn't get to you first,' Charlie had said with a smile, water still running down his face and into his dimple. I reached out and followed the pathways the water had taken down his face and he had lent back into me and started kissing me again. When I had returned to the house Gus was still mad at me. That must have been only a week before his death.

Gus had been the rebel of our motley gang. His mother had died a few years earlier and I think he had used that as an excuse to play up. He was always looking for things that we could do that were likely to get us into trouble if we were caught, and we were regularly caught by my parents and Thomas. It was with Gus that I had spent hours around the mansion trying to find all of the secret passageways, even after his dad had told him to cut it out. When Gus came up with each new harebrained plan I knew it was not a matter of if but rather when we would be caught and how much trouble we would be in when we were. But I adored him. His mother dying so young had caused a deep-seated gratitude for his friends and the family he still had and he was as loyal as a basset hound. I trusted him with every secret and he was the person that I would turn to if I was ever upset. He taught me everything I knew about trust and loyalty as well as useful tricks from Gus's handbook of mischief.

He had broken his arm trying to climb to the top of the oak tree that stood at the entrance to the property. Another local boy had dared him to do it. Charlie and I had tried to convince him not to but Gus couldn't resist a dare and had leapt straight onto the lower branches, falling before he reached halfway. I could vividly remember Thomas shooting Charlie and I a withering stare, more than likely thinking that we had put Gus up to it, and screaming at him that he could have died if he had fallen from the top.

I searched my mind for memories of Thomas in the days after Gus had died but I couldn't find them. If I had been on the boat with him why had I survived? Did Thomas blame me, as he seemed to when Gus had fallen out of the tree?

I looked back up at Charlie now, his eyes were staring into mine, his face deep in thought.

'I understand why you were so upset, now that I remember what happened that summer,' I said. The memory of his lips on mine that day at the beach were overpowering and it took all of my control not to reach over and touch his lips. I wondered if he had the same memories or if he had completely forgotten our kiss. His smile interrupted my thoughts and he said quietly, 'You and Gus were my best friends. I'm happy you came back.'

We sat there in silence for a minute and he slowly leaned towards me. My heart stopped as I thought he might be leaning in to kiss me. I closed my eyes but felt him reach around me to grab his wet shorts off the bed and then hang them over his heater. My face flushed red again and I avoided looking at his face. I felt so foolish; time had passed and he obviously didn't have the same feelings for me that I still had for him. Surely he would have moved on, found someone else. He must have a new girlfriend and he would call her later and recount the tale of the lovesick ridiculous next-door neighbor who seemed to have a death wish and some kind of amnesia. My face went from red to pale as I felt all of my energy draining out of me again and I pondered how I was going to walk from Charlie's back to my house.

'You look a little sick Sophie,' Charlie said quietly, and I realized he had been watching my face again. 'Are you feeling alright? Are you hungry? Do you want me to get you something? Food, hot chocolate?'

I looked across at his soft pillows and warm-looking quilt as I felt my eyelids getting heavier. Stuff the new girlfriend I thought to myself, if he even has one. We used to be best friends and I physically don't think I can make it back to my bed. 'Actually, I am feeling a bit tired, do you mind if I have a rest?'

'Of course,' he said, pulling back the covers on his bed. I eased down into them and snuggled into his soft pillows. He pulled the covers over me and lay down on top of the quilt next to me with his head on the pillow looking right into my eyes.

'Tell me about what you've been doing the past couple of years,' I said looking at his muscular arms and thinking that at least physically he seemed to have changed a little. He was bigger and stronger than he had been when we were fourteen-year-olds. He rolled onto his back with an arm behind his head.

'Not all that much,' he said evasively. I wondered what he wasn't telling me. Was he keeping it from me to spare my feelings or had he really not been up to much?

We ended up talking for hours without him directly answering my question. When the light of dawn started to peek in through the windows and I couldn't hold my eyes open any longer I fell asleep with Charlie watching over me, like he was concerned I might head back down to the dock if he took his eyes off me.

# CHAPTER 12

When I opened my eyes again a couple of hours later he was no longer next to me. I rolled over to look around the room, getting tangled up in his covers, but he wasn't sitting at his desk or anywhere else in the room. Out of the corner of my eye I noticed a piece of paper on his side table next to me. I picked it up and written in scratchy handwriting was a note from Charlie: *I had to go to training. I didn't want to wake you because you looked so peaceful. C*

I smiled and buried my face in his pillow – it smelt just like him, a mixture of aftershave, sweat and saltwater. A horrible thought came into my head: god, I hoped that I hadn't been snoring! I sat up in the bed and looked around the room again.

It looked a lot different in the light of day, post near-death experience. The walls were painted a very pale shade of gray and his queen size bed had been pushed against the wall next to the door so when I sat up I could look out of the window and straight at our house, over to my bedroom. I imagined him sitting on his bed the day that we arrived and seeing me standing in the window, gaping at their beautiful house with its perfectly landscaped garden. No wonder he had a look of shock on his face that I had mistaken for anger; he must have thought I was very peculiar with my strange form of amnesia. I got up and walked around his room, looking through his book collection, his trophies and his photos, wondering if there would be one of his girlfriend that I had concocted in my mind, but the photo frames on his shelf looked mostly like they were his immediate family – his beautifully manicured mother, handsome father, and two brothers who looked like older versions of Charlie.

His desk was covered mostly with homework that I recognized – history paper, math take-home test, various textbooks, a lamp and stationery.

One of his desk drawers was slightly ajar and I could see the glass from another picture frame glinting up through the crack. I glanced guiltily at the door, not wanting to be caught snooping around his room but curious about whether it was a photo of his girlfriend. I wondered if she would match this house; would she be one of the tall, blonde cheerleaders who giggled politely and flipped their hair when they talked to him at his table in the cafeteria, or maybe one of the social committee that wanted to use my house as a terrifying sideshow for the Halloween ball. What did it matter to me if he had a girlfriend? I was being completely ridiculous.

Just because we had been close years ago didn't mean that he would have any feelings for me now and I was acting like a crazy stalker going through his bedroom and looking in his drawers. Shaking myself for being nosy, I quietly pulled his clothes off and slipped back into my jeans and sweatshirt that had been hanging on the back of Charlie's desk chair. They still felt a little damp and I was disappointed to leave the warmth and comfort of Charlie's sweats but I felt like I had better not steal them – that might push me back into the crazy stalker category.

I peeked my head out of the bedroom door to see if the coast was clear. Not hearing any noises coming from the rest of the house I decided I must be alone. I glanced behind me at the desk drawer again and decided a little peek wouldn't hurt. It wasn't like I was being completely crazy. If someone caught me I could explain that I was going to write him a little note back to thank him for saving my life. I pulled the drawers open slowly and soundlessly and gasped at my face looking back at me from the photo frame. It was Gus, Charlie and me sitting together on the beach. I was smiling joyfully at the camera with my arms around Charlie and Gus, who were both looking inwards at each other or me with broad smiles on their faces. I touched our faces and instead of the happiness making me smile it made me feel sad. We had been so happy, the three of us.

I also felt the occurrences of the night before come crashing down on me like a ton of bricks. It had seemed like a dream. Gus appearing at the top of the stairs, leading me into the vision of the past where he was having an argument with his dad, and finishing with him lying dead on the dock, Thomas's sobbing body clutching his son to him. It had seemed like a dream but I was more positive now that I had not been dreaming.

Somehow I was able to see the visions in the house. I walked over to the window looking back over to my room and shivered. Poppy would tell stories of ghosts in the house, and even though I still thought she was a little crazy and I couldn't quite bring myself to admit it, my conviction that there was absolutely no such thing as ghosts had been rocked. Was Gus in the house? There was only one way to find out.

Taking a deep breath, I slid the photo back into the drawer and closed it. I grabbed a piece of paper and quickly wrote Charlie a brief note with my grateful thanks, picked his clothes off the ground where I had dropped them, folded them carefully and put them on top of the desk. I tiptoed quietly out of the house – even though I could see no sign of his parents – and made a beeline for the beach that joined the two properties.

I paused at the gate and looked out at the water and the dock where Charlie had pulled me to safety, and then looked back up to the house. Trying to swallow my nerves I walked through the back door, into the kitchen, looking for a distraction, but no one was there. I made myself breakfast and pottered around downstairs for as long as I could but realized after my second helping of toast that I was only prolonging the inevitable. I would have to go up to my room eventually. I thought back to all of my dreams of Gus. He had never hurt me in any way; in fact, I think he was trying to help me to remember. But he did lead me out onto that pier last night and if it wasn't for

Charlie I would have drowned. I felt nervous as I headed up to my bedroom. Would Gus be there? Was he some sort of angry ghost out for vengeance?

The sound of a creak on the floorboards behind me almost gave me a heart attack and I whirled around to find Clara walking out of my parents' room holding the dirty linen that she must have taken off their bed.

'Clara! You scared me.'

'Sorry Miss Sophie.' She glanced down the hallway in the direction of my bedroom and I wondered whether she knew that I hadn't slept in my bed last night.

'It's fine. I just didn't know you were up,' I said, trying to make it sound like I had been in the house the whole time. I backed down the hallway towards my room, thinking about how Clara always seemed to pop up without warning.

As I walked into my room the hairs on the back of my neck stood up. I spun around and immediately saw Gus sitting at my desk.

'Morning.' Not an angry, vengeful ghost then, but the same Gus I had known all those years ago.

Stifling the urge to scream I took a deep breath, walked over and sat on the edge of my bed and forced myself to really look at him. He looked exactly the same as I had remembered, the same as he had in the photo – tousled short, sandy blonde hair, big brown eyes, and even though he looked almost transparent, I could still see the olive tone of his skin and the freckles that speckled the top of his nose. I resisted the urge to reach out and try to touch him, wondering what it might feel like or if it would feel like nothing was there.

'I thought you may have run away and got yourself certified for seeing ghosts,' he said, winking at me. The initial fear that I felt quickly subsided and I felt myself smile.

'I have to say, now that I remember, you always did have a strange sense of humor,' I said. It felt strangely natural to fall into conversation with Gus like I had never left. Like he had never died.

'You died,' I said, sadly now, looking up at him.

'Just my body, not my witty banter!'

I shook my head, willing him to stop joking for a minute. 'But was it my fault that you died? I can't remember what happened that day but when I saw you talking to your dad in my visions last night he was begging you not to come on the boat with me; there was a storm coming. What happened? Was it me? Did I make you go?' I said lowering my head, feeling the tears start to well in my eyes. I felt so powerless and frustrated: why couldn't I just remember that day?!

'No,' he said, kneeling in front of me so that our eyes met. 'It was never your fault.' He tried to touch my arm but his hand went right through me. It felt strange and cold.

My mind was all over the place and I recalled a memory from the day that we moved into the house. When we had got out of our car and I had seen a movement at the top of the house.

'Was that you standing in the window the first day that we arrived? I saw someone standing in the window.'

He shook his head, looking confused about where the question had come from. 'No Sophie, I was in the tree we used to climb in the driveway, planting dreams in your head, but you wouldn't have seen me. I finally made it to the top of that stupid tree!'

'How can I see you now then?' I asked confused.

'I needed you to remember me, to be able to believe that what you were seeing was not just in your dreams. Otherwise you would not have been able to see us.'

'So I can see you now because of … wait what? Did you just say *us*?'

He smiled and nodded towards the closed bedroom door. 'You can come in now,' he called out. I looked with alarm from his face to the door and back again, quite certain that I was Alice in Wonderland and I had toppled headfirst into the looking glass.

Just then I saw movement out of the corner of my eye and Poppy walked through the door and into the room. 'Hello my darling Sophie,' she said lovingly. 'I am so glad you are here, we are going to need your help to save the house.'

'Save the house?' I repeated nodding to myself and wondering how hard I had hit my head when I landed on the dock last night. 'This is crazy. I've gone mad, right?

How am I even having this discussion?' I debated in my head about whether I should try to go to sleep and when I woke up it would all have been a ridiculous dream. I lay back on my bed and closed my eyes for twenty seconds. Forcing them open I looked down the end of my bed but they were still there and both of them looked concerned.

'Are you feeling quite well?' Poppy asked.

'No, I feel ridiculous!' I pushed myself into a seated position. Resigning myself to the fact that they weren't leaving I asked the obvious question. 'And how exactly am I supposed to save the house?'

'Do you remember when Poppy would tell us about the rooms coming to life?' Gus asked.

'Yes, we thought she was crazy,' I mumbled, looking at Poppy apologetically.

'Well there is a key, and in every room of the house there is a clock. The key goes into the back of the clocks and when you wind them you can see the spirits from the other side. You can see them and speak to them the same way that we are doing with you now.' He looked at me, making sure that I was keeping up. 'The key will only work on the full moon. If you wind the key twelve times at midnight you can do this without them being able to touch you or hurt you. But if the key is wound thirteen times then the spirits that are present in the house will be able to interact more with the living. They will be able to touch you, to hurt you. They could potentially bring down this house and cut off the barrier between the living and the dead.'

'But it is not a full moon and I can see you both.'

'Yes, because we live in the house. You have to either have died here, or while living here, or have a connection that ties you to the house, like we do, so we are here all the time. We inhabit the house, the other spirits that come in or out just do so on a full moon. The spirits can roam freely on the full moon.'

'And you need a key,' I said slowly and somewhat incredulously. I suddenly remembered the key that was on the necklace I had found on Poppy's treasure hunt. 'You need a *key*.'

A key that goes in the back of the clocks? It must be a small key. Maybe like the key that I had dug out of a flowerpot. Poppy watched my face putting it all together and looked at me beseechingly, 'Did you follow my clue and find the key?'

'Yes, I hid it under my cushions,' I said, crossing the room in three steps I flung the cushions aside. The key was gone. 'No, no that's not right. I was tired so I left it on my side table last night.' I rushed over to the other side of the room, but my side table was empty save for a book. I pulled the room apart trying to find it, but it was definitely missing.

'Crap! I swear it was here last night.'

Poppy looked dismayed. Gus looked thoughtful and then put his hand on Poppy's shoulder. 'It's OK, we still have time,' Gus said reassuring her. 'Sophie will just need to solve the murder before the next full moon and then we will know who has the key.'

I looked at the two of them, barely comprehending what they were saying. 'I'm sorry, whose murder am I supposed to be solving?'

'Mine dear,' said Poppy. 'I didn't die of natural causes in the greenhouse.'

'Whoever has stolen the key is the same person who murdered Poppy. If you find the key then you will find the killer,' said Gus.

# CHAPTER 13

I started feeling tired and dizzy. The previous night was taking its toll on me: I had almost drowned and then spent the rest of the night with Charlie. My eyes felt heavy and I lay down on my bed. I went to sleep with Poppy and Gus debating who would have been most likely to commit murder and steal the key. My dreams were full of Thomas whacking Poppy on the back of the head with a shovel, Marcel stabbing her with a kitchen knife and Clara slipping poison into her brandy. After a fitful couple of hours I woke up feeling worse than I had going to sleep. I was relieved that Poppy and Gus appeared to have vanished and wondered again whether I had just dreamed the whole night. But my mouth tasted of saltwater from my near drowning and my head was pulsating so I accepted that it probably wasn't a dream. I walked across the hallway into my bathroom and downed a whole glass of water with a couple of aspirin.

My stomach was rumbling so I walked down to the kitchen to get myself something to eat. Pulling the fridge open I was balancing eggs and bacon in one hand and a container of juice in the other when I heard a noise coming from the pantry. I closed the door of the fridge and quietly put the food on the kitchen bench. I slowly walked around to the open pantry door, pulling out a weapon from the utensil jar on my way, without looking what it was.

'Hey!' I yelled, jumping around the corner of the door and brandishing my chosen weapon. The culprit yelled and dropped the packet of flour that he had been holding. A white cloud puffed up from the bag. It was Marcel.

'Oh, it's just you! Sorry, I didn't mean to scare you,' I said, relaxing my shoulders. 'I thought you were a robber or something.' Or something alright! I thought, maybe a pair of crazy ghosts that were haunting me or a killer on the loose.

I saw Marcel's eyes go to my right hand, which was clutching my weapon of choice. 'Just out of curiosity, if I had been a robber, were you planning on tenderizing me?'

I looked at my hand and realized that I had grabbed a mallet. Laughing, I put the mallet down on the table. 'I thought you were in the city for the whole weekend.'

'I was going to stay all weekend but I decided to come back early,' he said, looking back into the pantry for whatever he had been looking for and scooping up flour at the same time. Some of the flour looked like it had gone through a crack at the base of the wall and I racked my brain trying to remember if there had been a secret passageway out of the pantry. I realized that I had been staring at Marcel so I quickly backed out of the pantry and busied myself with cooking eggs and bacon.

'Oh, OK.'

I wasn't sure whether he was telling the truth or not. Listening to Poppy and Gus talk about who was likely to be the killer, it was decided that it had to have been one of the people in the house. This narrowed down the candidates to a very small pool of three people, who I was stuck with alone until my parents got back. I wondered exactly when Marcel had returned to the house and whether he could have had the chance to take the key from my table. I thought back to the times I had felt that some of the items in my room had been rearranged; perhaps the person who stole the key was searching for it? I winced realizing how easy I had made it for them to find, leaving it on my table and not taking better care to hide it like I had hidden the diary. I needed to be careful with what I said but I also needed to figure out who had taken the key before the next full moon. It had to be the same person who had killed Poppy.

Marcel walked out of the pantry with all of the ingredients to make a cake and started pulling out tins and mixing bowls.

'What are you cooking?' I asked trying to sound conversational and friendly.

'A chocolate cake. I make one every year for Poppy's birthday. Today she would have been ninety-nine.'

Well, that's nice, I thought to myself; surely he hadn't murdered her. Idiot! My subconscious fired back. What an amateur investigator I was. The person who had murdered Poppy had been smart enough not to leave any trace of what they had done so they weren't likely to be stupid. Making a cake every year would be an easy thing to do to alleviate suspicion. *What suspicion?* There was no open murder investigation, I thought to myself as I pushed the bacon around in the skillet. As far as the killer was concerned, he or she had gotten off scot-free.

'Were you here? The day that she died, I mean?' I asked trying to sound casual, as I scooped my bacon and eggs onto a plate with my back to him. I turned and snuck a glance at his face – he had his nose scrunched up like he could smell something off.

'Oh yes. It was terrible. She seemed so alive. She had just finished off eating her usual jam toast and took her cup of tea into the greenhouse and I was washing up the dishes when I heard Thomas yell out. We called the ambulance but there was nothing they could do unfortunately.'

I struggled to think of a way to ask whether he believed the place was haunted without sounding obvious but I could think of nothing, so I gobbled up my lunch, washed and dried my plates, and waved goodbye.

I walked out through the greenhouse and had a look around for anything that might be a clue but nothing seemed to stick out and I figured the killer would have had months to clean up any evidence, so I walked out the back door and into the sunshine. As I walked down towards the beach I thought about how she had died. The coroner had ruled natural causes but I wondered how likely it was that they investigated. She was ninety-eight and showing signs of dementia. They may have done some looking around, but the main beneficiary of her death was my dad, who was miles away in a lecture at the time she died.

Looking out across the water it seemed strange to think of what had happened only several hours before. The storm had passed and the sun was peeking out through the fluffy white clouds. Apart from the wet grass you wouldn't know that it had been raining for half the night. My eyes drifted across to Charlie's house and I felt butterflies in my stomach. Last night had been horrible and scary but it had also been amazing. All of the memories that had come flooding back had brought up all of the feelings that I had for not only Charlie but also Gus.

My eyes wandered past the gate of the closed-in garden and I instantly remembered where Gus and I would hide the key. I wondered whether it was in the same spot. Walking over to the wooden gate I felt along the side of the two sandstone pillars on either side until my finger caught on a nail that stuck out. Jackpot! I could feel the key hanging from the nail. I pulled the key off, careful not to drop it into the beckoning branches of the hedge. If I dropped it in there I'm not sure I would ever be able to find it without poking my eyes out. The key went into the slot and turned easily like it had been used very recently, and I wondered who had been coming in here and locking the gate when they left, almost like they were closing the rest of the world out.

As soon as I walked through the gate I had my answer. Where the sunken theater had been overgrown and forgotten this garden had been lovingly maintained and nurtured. It had to have been the work of a gardener. It had to have been Thomas. The water trickled down from a fountain that sat in the middle of four intersecting white stone pathways. Perfectly trimmed topiary framed the bottom of the fountain and each of the three stone pathways that didn't lead up to the gate led to a bronze archway that was dripping in jasmine flowers. On each of the four corners sat lush green lawn, which looked to be freshly mowed.

'Wow!' I breathed out in a sigh.

'Thank you,' a voice said from behind me and I spun around, startled, because I hadn't heard anyone walking up behind me. Thomas was standing there with a mixture of sadness and pride on his face. He closed the gate behind him, which made me feel a little nervous, but only for an instant. 'This was his favorite place and I couldn't bear to see it die along with him. I still come here, sit on one of the seats and pretend he is here with me,' he said in explanation, gesturing at the wondrous garden that stood before us.

'I am so sorry for what happened,' I said quietly. 'I know that is not going to change anything. I can't even remember that day. In fact, until very recently I didn't even remember Gus.' My voice faded towards the end of the sentence, feeling like maybe those words were hurtful. 'I'm sorry, that must make me sound like a terrible person, the truth is that he was my best friend and I don't know why I would have blocked him out,' I said as the tears started running down my face.

He passed me a tissue from his pocket. 'Come and sit down Sophie,' he said, gently leading me down the pathway to one of the seats. I knew that he was one of my possible murder suspects but I felt nothing but safety in his company, so I followed and sat down next to him on the seat.

'Your parents did explain the situation to me before you arrived. Actually they offered to pay me for a full year if I wanted to move on and not have to see you. I guess in case seeing you brought back too many painful memories.' He paused and took a deep breath, his face clearing a little. 'I can't say I wasn't tempted. But I realized that you, and this garden are all that I have left of him.' He paused and collected his thoughts again.

'I don't blame you Sophie, you have to know that. Gus made his own decisions and he was, well, a bit of a troublemaker to be honest. That is probably the wrong choice of words. I know he didn't do drugs and he wasn't violent, but he was very mischievous. I know that he had strong feelings for you too. Maybe he used the naughty behavior to cover up his sensitive side,' he said, chuckling to himself.

'Yes, we could be a little cheeky,' I said as a weak attempt to alleviate some of the pain he must be feeling.

We sat in silence listening to the fountain and the wind blowing through the jasmine for some time before he looked up at me and in a hoarse voice said, 'You know, after his mother died I caught him taking some of her jewelry. I was so sad and the thought that he might be stealing her things made me furious and I lashed out and smacked him. I can still vividly remember his tear-streaked face when he led me to his room and pulled back his sheets: he had been sleeping with all of her clothes and her things in his bed because they smelt of her.' He cleared his throat. 'I never hit him again.'

We sat there in silence again, the only noise coming from the trickle of the fountain. It felt like it could be an opportune moment to find out how much Thomas knew of the existence of Poppy's key. I glanced guiltily at him out of the corner of my eye. 'I remember when I would come here in the summer Poppy spoke of spirits in the house – do you think there was anything to that?' I swallowed hoping my bad acting wasn't too obvious.

'As in do I believe in ghosts?' he asked looking at me with a raised eyebrow. He laughed, 'No I don't. I hope that there is something in the afterlife because I find comfort in the thought that my beautiful wife and son will be together again but …' he paused and shook his head sadly, 'no, I don't think they are walking among us.'

I debated telling him then and there that I had only seen Gus this morning and then decided against it; he already thought that I was a little crazy. Changing tack, I looked up at him again. 'What happened on the day that Poppy died?'

His eyes misted over as he remembered, 'Well, I had been working in the shed at the bottom of the garden and I was walking back up towards the house when I heard a smash in the greenhouse. When I walked in the first thing that I saw was her favorite rose bush. It was on the ground, the terracotta pot she had just potted it into was knocked over, and her teacup was smashed. That is when I saw her in the chair. Her eyes were open wide and she looked like she had fallen backwards into the chair. As soon as I saw her I called an ambulance and I tried to resuscitate her, but she was gone.'

'Was there anything strange that you noticed at the time?'

He looked at me, 'Strange? Like what? And why the sudden curiosity?'

'Oh, I'm thinking of writing my English piece on the house and I thought it might be interesting to have some information in there about Poppy. It just got me thinking about when she died, and my parents didn't really tell me anything about it.' Must get better at lying I thought to myself, but Thomas just nodded. 'Now that you mention, there was something that I found a little strange. I found a small red clip or broach in her hand, shaped like a cross, with bits of thread on it, like it had been attached to something and she had ripped it off.'

'Did you keep it?' I probed.

He shook his head. 'No. Her hand was wrapped around it tightly and I didn't want to pry it out of her fingers in case it was something that was important to her.'

We sat there in silence for a few more minutes, taking in the perfume from the jasmine trees and the sound of the water in the fountain, completely relaxed in each other's company. It was a pleasant surprise to feel this relaxed given that after last night's revelations I felt it was likely that Thomas held me at least partially responsible for Gus's death.

After leaving Thomas in the garden, with a promise to keep the garden our little secret, I climbed back up the stairs to start on my homework, which I had been woefully neglecting.

'Hi gorgeous,' Gus said as soon as I sat down, and I jumped up with a start.

'Crap Gus, you can't keep on letting yourself in here, you scared me.'

'Would you rather I said BOO!' he laughed. I rolled my eyes and turned back to my homework.

'Go away, I have to study or I will never get out of this godforsaken place!'

'Why would you want to leave here – it has everything that you could ever want. Nice beaches, fresh air … good-looking men …' He pretended to flex his muscles and wiggled his eyebrows at me. I threw my pencil at his head. It went straight through and bounced off the wall behind him.

'Have you done any sleuthing Nancy Drew?' he asked, ignoring my violence.

'Yes, I spoke to Marcel at lunch and I just spoke to your dad – he didn't do it.'

'How can you be so sure?' he asked, but I could see that he looked relieved.

'He doesn't know anything about Poppy's ghosts and I think if he did know he would have tried to find you already. He misses you so much Gus. He said that he hoped you were with your mother. Where is her spirit?'

'She has passed on,' he said quietly, not making eye contact with me.

'Why haven't you passed on?'

'I think some spirits can't let go but mostly those of us with unfinished business have to first resolve it – to find peace and move on.'

'What is your unfinished business?' I asked gently, trying to be careful not to upset him.

'If I tell you, you have to keep it a secret. It's really embarrassing.' He looked up at me with a timid look on his face.

'Promise.'

'OK.' He came over and held his hand up like he was going to whisper it in my ear. I lent the side of my head towards his transparent hands. Instead of whispering he half yelled in my ear. 'To get my first kiss from you,' he flopped back on my bed and started laughing and I turned back to my desk feeling foolish.

'You're an idiot,' I huffed. 'He also mentioned that he found a cross-shaped pendant of some sort in her hand, like it had been ripped off something or somcone.'

Gus stopped laughing and looked thoughtful but then shook his head. 'I don't know what that would have been, but it's a start.'

A sudden knock on the door sent my heart racing again. 'SOPHIE!' I opened the door and my mom peered around my shoulders, looking around the room.

'Mom! You're back!' I hadn't realized that they would be back so soon.

'Hi honey, yes we came back a little earlier than expected. Were you just talking to someone?' she asked, looking around again.

'What? No. Oh, but … yeah, on the radio. They had a guest and he was an idiot, just giving him a piece of my mind.'

'Right, well I found a friend of yours at the front door when we arrived. Alex someone from school.'

'What? Why is he here?' I asked too loudly, and Mom hushed me. 'OK, well if you're heading back downstairs can you ask him to come up?'

'He's a nice-looking young man, isn't he!'

'Ugh Mom, NO! Don't even think about it!' I stood up and pushed her out the door. The last thing I needed was my mother trying to match-make me with Alex!

She walked back down the hall and I used the opportunity to duck my head back in to look where Gus had been sitting on my window seat. He had disappeared. The next minute Alex came lolling up the hallway looking like a great big golden retriever puppy.

'Hey Soph!'

God I hated that he called me that. In my mind nicknames were reserved for people that you were really close to and he was not one of those people.

'Hey Alex, what's up? Come in.' I opened the bedroom door wide after he walked in to avoid him getting the wrong impression.

'You said in class the other day that you were getting behind so I thought you might like a study buddy for a couple of hours to finish the assignment on the chemistry experiment.'

I had no interest in chemistry or spending the next couple of hours with Alex but unfortunately I did need to pass this class and this was probably the only way that would happen. I groaned inwardly but gave him a polite smile. 'Yeah, sure, thanks. That's really thoughtful of you.'

I heard Gus snort from the corner of my bedroom and I swung around to see him lying on my bed, hands behind his head chuckling away.

'Is this guy for real?! He's trying to get into your pants by doing chemistry homework!'

I looked at Alex, then Gus, and back to Alex again. Alex showed absolutely no sign that he had heard Gus.

'Calm down princess he can't hear or see me.'

Alex turned around to look at me and saw the peculiar look I had on my face. 'What?' he asked. 'Is something wrong?'

'Sorry, no I just thought I might have left my Chem book at school but it's right there in my bag,' I recovered, as quickly as I could.

The next two hours were a test of my terrible acting. Alex was doing the best he could at helping me while trying to get as close as he could at every opportunity and Gus spent the whole time running commentary on Alex's futile attempts to come on to me. At one point Alex went to the bathroom and I tried my best to get Gus to leave but he was having too much fun at my expense and if anything his rude comments escalated. In the end I was able to tune him out and Alex and I got everything finished.

'Thank you so much for the help Alex.' Despite what I could see his intentions were I was really grateful for his help. It would have taken me twice the time to complete the work we had just done alone. Unfortunately, my enthusiasm seemed to help him summon the courage he needed, and turning around he puffed out his chest and cleared his throat and I could already see what was coming but it was too late to stop him, '… you to wanted maybe ah, um, want to go to the dance with me?' he stammered out in a jumble of words.

'Sorry, what?'

'I thought maybe we could go to the dance together.'

'Wow, that is really sweet Alex, but I'm already going with someone else.'

'Oh, OK, no problem. I better go then. I'll see you at school tomorrow.'

It was like I had popped his little balloon of courage. He piled the last of his books in his bag in record speed and then hightailed it out the door.

'Who are you going with?' Gus asked, looking

curious.

'Who am I going with to where?' I asked distractedly as I packed up my books. I felt guilty like maybe I had just used Alex.

'To the dance.'

'Oh that. I didn't even know there was a dance.'

Gus snorted, seeming satisfied.

# CHAPTER 14

After finishing off the rest of my homework I walked down to Poppy and George's seat under the oak tree to get some fresh air. I carried my sketchbook down with me but I put it to the side and left it unopened. I knew I wasn't really up to drawing today. There were so many things running through my head as I looked down towards the dock.

The wooden boards had dried and the water was at high tide, lapping up onto the posts and running back over the reeds at the top of the sand. I left my book and walked down to the start of the deck, looking out to the water. Glancing around me at the boats gently rocking in the water and then back up at the beach at the water lapping up the sand my mind wandered into the past. I wondered where Gus had drowned and where they had found his body. Had I been there? Did I find him there all cold on the sand with the water and seaweed lapping over him? A shiver ran up my spine and I walked back up to the seat to grab my cardigan.

'Hey there stranger!' I heard Charlie's voice coming from his end of the beach and I smiled, turning around to see him walking up wearing shorts and a T-shirt.

I walked back up the hill and met him near Poppy's seat.

'Hey yourself!'

'How are you feeling?'

'A little exhausted to be honest. After last night's activities, plus I just spent the past two hours going through a Chem assignment with Alex Whitfield.' I threw in the end of the sentence just in case he had seen Alex leaving and thought we had been on a date.

'What are you doing?' he asked gesturing towards my sketchbook, which lay unopened on the seat.

'It's nothing,' I said sitting back down on the seat and tucking it under my legs. I had never shown anyone my sketchbook, not even my mom. I felt like it was a little glimpse into my soul, I suppose how some people felt about their diary. He tilted his head and looked at me with a questioning expression and I looked away a little embarrassed.

'It's just, well my parents used to take me to all of these galleries in the city and it kind of inspired me to … uh … draw. They're my drawings.'

'You're an artist?' he asked smiling. 'Can I have a look?' he sat down next to me, so close that I could feel the warmth radiating off his body, and reached out his hand and looked at me with a pout and big sad puppy-dog eyes. After a minute I relented, and pulling the book from under my legs, I handed it to him with trepidation. I felt like some of my deepest secrets were in that book and I wasn't sure I wanted to share it with anyone, let alone someone that I had a huge crush on. I watched him nervously as he studied each of the pages, looking for signs that he might find them childish, amateur, knowing from the brief glance at the artwork in his house that he had obviously been surrounded by fine art.

'Wow these are really great Sophie,' he said sincerely as he got towards the end of the drawings. He turned to the last picture, the one that I had done a few days ago from my memory of the dream of the boy standing at the end of the bed; the boy who had been so sad because I couldn't remember him – Gus. I looked at the picture now, tracing the lines of his face with my eyes and remembering him standing at the end of the bed. It was actually a very close likeness of him and I was surprised that the simple act of drawing the image had not sparked any recollection in my mind.

Charlie stopped dead on the page and sat still for a minute with his head tilted and examined the picture carefully. I watched his face nervously until, after a couple of long minutes, he flicked over another page and, seeing that this was the last drawing in the book, looked up at me with curiosity, 'Did you do this one today?'

I shook my head, 'No, actually I did it a couple of weeks ago.' I looked at the confusion in his face and opened my mouth to tell him about what had happened after I had left him that morning but I couldn't find the words, and I really didn't want him to think I was mad, so I decided to tell him half of the truth.

'When we moved here I started having dreams about Gus. I think it must have been my subconscious trying to help me remember.' I shrugged my shoulders to make it seem less dramatic and he smiled.

'Oh yeah? Was I in your dreams?' he teased lightly.

'No way, they would have been nightmares,' I laughed, teasing him back. 'I thought you hated me, the way that you'd been looking at me since I arrived.'

'I admit, I was upset and a little hurt that you never contacted me and then when you moved in next door you appeared to be pretending not to know me,' he conceded, and closing the sketchbook he handed it back to me.

'Do you want to go for a walk along the beach?'

'The other day when you asked me about what I had been up to while you and your family were gone ...' he sounded nervous and he hesitated.

'Yes?' I encouraged him.

'Well the truth is that I was a little messed up when Gus died and with you gone I had no one to talk to. Apart from my parents of course and I didn't really want to talk to them so I acted up and I got into trouble.' He muttered out the last part of the sentence and I put my hand on his arm to make him stop walking.

'What kind of trouble?'

'I believe the lawyers referred to it as grand larceny.' I studied his face to determine whether or not he was kidding and I realized he was serious. 'It was a car and I was granted probation because it was a first offence and because there were extenuating circumstances and I ended up taking a year off school, working on my dad's building sites.'

'Wow, I'm so sorry, I wish I had been here for you.' I felt terrible but Charlie cut me off.

'This is completely not your fault Sophie. We were both going through a hard time'

We walked in silence for a while until Charlie asked what I was thinking of doing after school. We compared our plans for college and I confessed that I intended to go back to the city. Charlie spoke a little of his older brothers and how they rarely came home from college so he felt guilty applying for colleges too far away.

I mostly listened to him. Although he had just dropped a bit of a bombshell on me it was so easy to be with Charlie it felt like I had never left. I thought again about whether to tell Charlie about Gus and what was going on inside the house but I still didn't really know if I believed it myself and when he looked my way and smiled with his beautiful dimple it made me wish that it was all a dream.

# CHAPTER 15

At school the next week the dance that Alex had invited me to was the only topic of conversation and I found myself unlucky enough to be in the thick of it. I realized quickly enough that it was the annual Halloween ball that Percy had spoken to me about on my first day of school and just as he predicted, the social committee had my haunted house firmly in their sights. As soon as I walked into the lunchroom I found myself bailed up by Camilla and Priscilla Ascot, perky identical twins wearing identical pearl necklaces, with their beautifully styled red hair tied in matching blue ribbons and holding matching clipboards.

I noticed Percy sitting at our table laughing hysterically behind them and as soon as I could get away from the twins, by telling them I was sure my parents would be delighted, I walked over to the table and hit him on the arm.

'Why are you hitting me? I warned you, didn't I?'

'I don't want to even go to the ball but it will be hard to avoid if it is *at my house*!' I said glumly, picking at my sandwich.

'Well, you'll need to find yourself a date then,' he said, looking around the room at the potential candidates.

‘Who are you going with?’ I noted that he didn’t seem to be volunteering.

He blushed, ‘I was going to ask Alice.’

‘Really? I had no idea. Should I find out if she is going with anyone?’

‘Yeah? You would do that? And can you maybe feel out whether she would even want to go with me so I don’t make a total ass out of myself?’

‘Sure. I had better ask someone soon because Alex asked me to go with him and I told him I was already going with someone else.’

I continued to pick at my sandwich. My mind went back to the past and I started to run through all of the hidden passageways that Poppy had shown me. ‘Maybe I can avoid it even though it is at my house. There are more than a dozen secret passageways I could hide in!’ Percy laughed at me but the thought cheered me enough to eat my lunch.

# CHAPTER 16

After school I wandered over to do some sketching at the football stadium. It was quiet and I knew that no one would bother me. I opened up my sketchbook and started drawing the flags flying over the top of the bleachers. I paused for a moment and again considered who might have killed Poppy. I was positive it wasn't Thomas so that narrowed it down to Clara and Marcel.

Marcel seemed so jovial and friendly, I didn't really know much about him though. He had been working in Poppy's house for the past fifteen years and he looked like he was in his forties. Apart from the photo of his mom, who he mentioned had passed away, he didn't seem to have any family. I couldn't see any reason for him to have murdered her apart from the restrictions she put on his cooking, but that seemed an unlikely motive for murder.

Then there was Clara. She was as closed as a clam. She carried herself with a general disdain and her sour features didn't really endear her to you. She had always been intimidating but after hearing her talking to herself upstairs, and noticing her keeping an eye on me when I was exploring the property, she seemed even stranger than I remembered. Even though she had been in the house the whole time when we would visit when I was a child I knew even less about her than I did about Marcel. But she had been with Poppy for more than forty years and I could see no obvious signs of a motive. If I had to pick one of them as a suspect over the other it would be Clara but that was only due to her grumpy demeanor. You'd think it would be easy with a pool of only two suspects but as I thought more about it I realized I wasn't even sure that it was someone in the house – what if some random stranger had wandered in? Granted it seemed unlikely, but who was even to say she was actually murdered? Then again, someone had definitely taken the key from my room.

Sighing, I looked down to the field where the football team had come running out from the change rooms under the stands. The cheerleaders also came out from the other side of the stand to do their practice. There goes my peace and quiet I thought to myself as I looked down at my drawing, which I had barely started since I was so wrapped up in my thoughts.

I searched the players on the field until I saw familiar brown hair bobbing around the field and felt my cheeks flush. After speaking to him on the beach about his criminal offence I had tried and failed to picture him stealing a car. How did he even know how to do that, I wondered. Out of the corner of my eye I saw two of the cheer squad were hovering nearby, watching Charlie as he threw the ball to another one of the players. Uh oh, I thought to myself. It looked like they were closing in for the kill – maybe they would ask him to the dance, or at least ask him out. We had spent over an hour walking along the beach talking about everything about our lives and he definitely had not mentioned a girlfriend.

Without thinking I quickly jumped up out of my seat like I had been electrocuted and yelled out, '*Hi Charlie*!' He looked up at the stadium to where I was sitting, smiled and waved at me.

Oh my god, you idiot, I thought as I sat down just as quickly as I had jumped up. If I could have dug a hole and buried myself in it I would have. I have no idea what that might have achieved but I figured there was no way he would want to go to the dance with me now.

The two girls looked up at the stadium to see where the screaming fan was, frowned, and started speaking to him anyway. Eventually, one of the girls laughed and touched him affectionately on the arm and then they wandered off in the opposite direction so I couldn't see whether they were happy or annoyed.

I should have run then and there but my curiosity got the better of me and I waited around like a crazy stalker until Charlie finished, wanting to apologize for my outburst but also wanting to find out if one of the cheerleaders had asked him to the dance and whether, god forbid, he had accepted. By the time the team started wandering out of the change rooms the sky had turned a pink-orange color. I didn't see Charlie walk out of the rooms and packing up my books I chastised myself for being so desperate and creepy. But just as I was turning to leave, I heard someone sneak up behind me and the world went black as two strong hands covered my eyes. 'Guess who?'

'Ha, ha, very funny,' I said feeling a tingle run down my spine as I pulled his hands off my face.

'You waited for me.' He gave me the full force of his dimple and I looked down feeling embarrassed about asking him to a dance I didn't even want to go to.

'Yeah, there is nothing I won't do for a free ride home,' I laughed too hard at my own joke and then quickly sobered up at the memory of screaming his name out earlier. 'Hey listen, I just wanted to say I'm so sorry about the yelling before – I feel stupid.'

'Oh, was that you? I didn't know. Girls come down here and yell my name all the time,' he joked, and I smacked him on the arm. We walked towards the car park in silence while I mustered a semblance of courage.

'So, I saw you talking to the girls down there earlier,' I hesitated. Having never asked anyone out before, and certainly no one that I cared about, I felt strangely nervous.

'Yessss …' If he knew where I was going with this line of questioning he wasn't going to make it easy for me. I took a big breath and let it out in one long sentence.

'Well, it seems everyone is lining up dates for this Halloween dance thing and I wasn't going to go because it's not really my thing but I think I have to go now because the tall red-haired twins, I forget their names but you know who I'm talking about because they sit at your table and they seem to be organizing it, and they have decided they want it to be at my house, and I was thinking that maybe I could hide in the secret, god I'm rambling and I think I might just stop talking now if that is OK,' I quickly took another big breath and held it so that my voice came out as almost a squeak. 'Are you going to the dance with one of those girls?'

'No,' I was momentarily relieved until he continued. 'I'm like you – it's not really my thing … so I actually never go to the dance.'

'Really? Right, well OK, sure.'

We kept walking in silence until we reached the bike racks. He may have been hoping that I would not continue with my rambling and never bring the topic up again, or maybe he was waiting for me to invite him, but I was far too embarrassed to put myself out there again so soon, so I just said nothing.

He waited while I unlocked my bike and pulled it out of the rack. When I pulled on my helmet and went to throw my leg over he reached out and touched my leg to stop me.

'Didn't you say you were getting a lift with me?' without waiting for an answer he lifted up my bike and carried it down to his car.

As we drove towards our houses I snuck a glance at him out of the corner of my eye. I had already lost most of my dignity, I thought to myself, I may as well find out for sure whether or not he had a girlfriend.

'Won't your girlfriend be disappointed that you won't go to the dance with her? I mean, that is, do you even have a girlfriend?'

He chuckled and turned to look at my face, taking his eyes off the road for a moment.

'Why? Are you concerned that I never recovered after my first crush disappeared from the face of the earth?'

'I was your first crush?' I asked, briefly distracted from my question.

He looked embarrassed but quickly recovered. 'You didn't know?'

'No. You have girls lined up around here wanting to date you, I would have thought you would have picked a new one every week.' But as I said the words I didn't believe them; the Charlie that I had known growing up was not that guy. Who really knew anyone though; I would never have picked him to be the type to hot-wire someone else's car.

'What about you?' he threw back.

'What about me?' I snorted, considering my entire dating pool was sitting in the car with me.

'I always wondered what you were up to after you left. Where you were, whether you were back in New York, what your friends were like, if you had a boyfriend.' He brushed past the last part, as if it were incidental, but he looked over at me as he said it and it felt like more than that.

My cheeks flushed again and I felt my heart squeeze. He had thought about me. And then I felt guilty. He hadn't crossed my mind once. Not intentionally, of course, but you would have thought that I would have remembered something – a feeling, some semblance of a memory.

We spent the rest of the trip in silence but each time he changed gears his hand would come close to touching the side of my leg and I would hold my breath.

When we reached the top of my driveway Charlie insisted on driving me to the front door. He started to turn the steering wheel to pull into my driveway and I grabbed his hands.

'Absolutely not, you will have to drivc all the way back up again and then drive down your driveway. I will just get out here,' I protested, still holding one of his hands on the wheel and using the other to start to undo my belt. In all honesty I think I was more concerned by the prospect of an interrogation from my parents if they saw me being dropped off by a member of the opposite sex.

'No way,' he fired back, trying to pry my fingers off. 'That is a long driveway – you could be attacked by the local wildlife.'

'Argh, you are so annoying! I lived in New York. What could possibly happen to me in this boring little town!'

We ended up settling on a compromise: he would drive his car into his garage and then walk me around to the beach access. As we drove down Charlie's driveway I took in his house in all its splendor. Similar to our property, theirs also had beautiful big trees lining the driveway but theirs were light-gray-colored olive trees, seemingly placed

evenly every few yards the whole way down the drive, which gave the entry an almost Tuscan appearance. The house itself seemed to glow with the lights that lined the drive and lit up the side of the house. I bet the social committee didn't see this house as a potential Halloween ball venue, I thought with chagrin.

Charlie parked the car and walked me around to the side of the house. The security light didn't reach down the side and I felt myself trip a couple of times on the loose white stones around the pavers. Both times Charlie righted me before I fell, and I felt a tingle down my spine as his soft warm arms held on to mine until we reached the light around the back of the house, leading down to the beach.

'It's OK, I'll be alright from here,' I said, a little embarrassed that I had lost my footing and landed on him.

'OK.' He seemed uneasy and unwilling to let me go. Perhaps he thought I would fall over again and hurt myself properly and he would be found to be negligent in his care.

'Really,' I insisted, 'I'll be fine! There is enough light out here for me to see and I will wave once I get to the back door, OK? I'll see you tomorrow, thanks for the lift.' I walked off quickly so he wouldn't have a chance to change his mind, and when I reached the back door of the house I turned and gave him a quick wave. He was still standing where I had left him and he waved back, but I couldn't see his face.

I walked back into the house through the greenhouse and realized too late that there was a person standing at one of the working benches. I stopped in my tracks as soon as I spotted Clara's dark form leaning over one of the tables, her face in her hands. As soon as she heard me her body tensed up and she turned her back to me. She reached into her pocket and pulled out a tissue, which she brought to her face before she turned around to face me. I stood still as a statue until I could see her face. Her steely resolve was back in place but I could still tell that she had been crying. Why had she been crying, I wondered. Was it from guilt over what she had done to Poppy or was it sadness from Poppy's passing. Now that her mask was back in place I couldn't tell.

'Dinner is ready Miss Sophie,' she announced like we had been in the middle of a conversation, and then she turned on her heel and left the room without another word. I stood there for a couple of minutes trying to deduce why Clara had been crying and could not come to a resolution so I followed my nose and the smell of Marcel's latest concoction into the kitchen.

My parents were sitting at the table and as I sat down for dinner I realized I had left my bike in the back of Charlie's car and I didn't have his cell phone number. I didn't want to confess to my parents but I knew it would take me at least forty minutes to walk to school in the morning. As I wolfed down my salad I wondered how quickly I could eat my dinner and head upstairs to see if Charlie had his curtains opened or closed. Maybe I could try to get his attention and ask him to leave the bike near our gate. No one here was going to steal it. Most people around here had purses worth more than my old rusty bike.

But when I got upstairs Charlie's curtains were firmly pulled shut and I couldn't even see if there was a light on inside.

# CHAPTER 17

The next morning I woke up to light drizzle tapping softly on the windows. I groaned as I remembered my bike was being held captive in the boot of Charlie's car and I would have to walk to school. As I gobbled down a bowl of cereal I debated whether to tell my parents but decided it was not worth the interrogation that would inevitably follow.

I pulled on my rain jacket and some comfy shoes and headed off down the drive with a big black umbrella that I had dug out of the cupboard near the front door. Unfortunately, the umbrella seemed to be the same vintage as the house and it started leaking the moment I opened it. I kicked the stones and resigned myself to the fact that the bottom half of my jeans and my shoes would likely be soggy by the time I reached my homeroom class.

I had just walked out the imposing front gates when I heard the sound of a car engine behind me, followed quickly by the sound of a car horn. I spun around as Charlie drove up so that the passenger door was next to where I was standing. The car window went down and Charlie, who was wearing a black hooded jumper and a pair of jeans, and looking handsome and dry, called out, 'Now don't pretend that you didn't leave your bike in the back of my car deliberately Sophie Weston!'

I was already wet, probably looked like a drowned rat, and was irritated at the implication. Was he so arrogant to think that I had done it on purpose? Stupid expensive-car-driving jerk! I didn't need a lift, I just needed my bike.

'Thanks for dropping my bike off, now I can ride to school,' I said sarcastically and walked around the back of the car to take it out. As I reached for the handle of the boot to open it I heard the door lock. Urgh! What game was he playing? His door opened and he jumped out with a big blue golf umbrella, not a leak in sight.

'What are you doing?' he asked as he held the huge umbrella over both of us.

'I don't need a lift from you. I am perfectly able to ride my bike.' I said obstinately. But by now the rain was borderline torrential and he raised his eyebrows as I huddled closer to him to stay dry.

'Get in the car!'

I couldn't be bothered arguing with him and I knew from the night before that he had seat warmers that would help dry my wet pants.

'Fine,' I relented, 'but only because you have stolen my bike.' I immediately regretted my choice of words given he had been convicted of stealing a car, but when I looked at his face he was chuckling quietly to himself.

He walked me around to the passenger side door and I wondered again if he had a girlfriend and how she would feel about another girl being in his car. I thought back to the previous night, seeing him on the football field with the girls laughing and touching his arm.

'So, I didn't realize that part of the athletic training for football includes fending off the advances of the cheerleaders.' I realized my statement had come out sounding a little like an accusation. He looked at me with a bemused smile.

'My, my, Miss Sophie, are you jealous?'

'Absolutely not,' I said a little too hastily. 'I just wondered what your girlfriend might think about it, that's all.'

'Who said I had a girlfriend?' he said, clearly entertained. 'And I don't think you should throw stones at me when you are standing in a glass house,' he said, glancing across at me.

'And what do you mean by that?!' I challenged him, feeling my cheeks flaming red.

'You seem to have a little admirer yourself!'

'I have absolutely no idea who you are talking about,' I said, knowing full well he had to be talking about Alex, and annoyed that he had managed to dodge the question again. I hoped that Charlie would know that I was absolutely not interested in Alex, but I guess it didn't hurt for him to think that someone was interested in me, as there seemed to be a large number of girls interested in Charlie, girlfriend or no girlfriend.

'In fact, now that I think about it,' he continued, 'I would say that more than one of the boys at your table seems to follow you around school like a little lovesick puppy.'

Now I really didn't know who he was talking about.

'I am not sure how this became about me, but I am positive you are mistaken,' I said trying to sound aloof, but it came out sounding mildly hostile.

He chuckled under his breath and looked over at me with a curious expression. 'Did you know that your face squishes up when you're cranky? All those summers with Gus and I ribbing you, I think you developed a way of trying to mask when you were annoyed, but we could always tell in your face when we got you. It's all up here.' He touched his hand to my face just above my nose between my eyebrows and ran his finger lightly up towards my hairline. I closed my eyes as tingles ran down my spine and I couldn't speak. He took his hand off my face and when I opened my eyes again his eyes were back on the road. I could still feel the pathway his finger had made across my face.

As we pulled into school and he took the keys out of the ignition he turned to me and said with a serious face. 'The answer to your question is no.'

'What question?'

'Do I have a girlfriend? No, I don't have a girlfriend.'

'Oh,' I said, surprised, and followed him, climbing out of the car.

I went around to take my bike out of the boot but he had already locked it and as I turned to protest he was already loping off towards the school buildings.

'Hey! I have to get my bike out so I can ride home!'

He turned around with a wicked-looking dimpled grin. 'Already put my keys away – I guess you'll have to ride with me again! See you later!'

I couldn't stop thinking about him for the rest of the day. Picturing that day on the beach, years ago, when we had kissed. I was pulled up twice by teachers and hit by a basketball while daydreaming during sport. By the time school was over for the day I was a bundle of nerves and had built a friendly lift home into a romantic date. So when I turned up to the car and Charlie had two of his friends with him I was more than a little disappointed.

He introduced them as Pat and Ben and they chivalrously allowed me the front seat. The whole way home the three of them joked about one another's skill at football and I sat there feeling uncomfortable with my stomach twisted in knots. I glanced across at Charlie a couple of times during the drive and he looked relaxed and happy. I was confused. This morning Charlie had made a point of telling me he didn't have a girlfriend, he had deliberately kept my bike prisoner and had almost seemed flirty.

'Sophie?'

'Sorry, what?' the whole car had gone silent waiting for me to answer a question I hadn't heard.

'I was asking whether you are enjoying living here?' Pat said from the back seat.

'Oh yeah, it's great.' I wondered whether that sounded unconvincing and I felt Charlie look at me cautiously from the driver's seat. 'Have you lived here all your life?' I asked Pat, trying to deflect the question.

'Yep, born and bred. Or you might say born and

inbred around here,' he laughed, and it made me feel a little more relaxed.

'I hear your house is a potential venue for the ball Sophie,' Ben commented. 'What's it like? Is it spooky?'

'Well, we haven't had any reason to call the ghostbusters around just yet but I think with a bit of decoration the spirits might be coaxed out of the walls and floorboards.' I let out a fake giggle and the two boys in the back clapped and snorted with laughter.

When we reached Charlie's house he parked the car and turned the ignition off. The lights in the car went off and we were immediately thrust into darkness. I felt a jolt of electricity run up my body as he leaned over me, thinking for a moment that he was going to kiss me in the car, in front of his friends. He reached his hand to the glove compartment brushing the top of my legs and pulled out a torch. Turning it on, he held it up to his face.

'I thought after last night's stumbling maybe it would be easier if we had a torch!' he said teasingly. I was so deeply embarrassed that I had thought he was going to kiss me. I could feel my face was flushed a deep shade of red again and I could feel tears welling up. I was immensely grateful that the lights were off and none of the boys could see my face, particularly Charlie. I had to get out of there and quickly.

We all piled out of the car. I quickly grabbed my bike out of the boot and waved goodbye to Ben and Pat, the latter giving me a pat on the back like a puppy and enthusiastically saying he would see me at school. Charlie started to walk me over to the side of the house.

'You were a little quiet in the car. Is everything alright?' he asked me.

'I'm fine,' I said hastily, but realized I didn't sound fine. 'Really, go back to your friends.'

'Sorry about tonight. I forgot; Pat and Ben always come over on a Tuesday night. You can come and hang out if you want? You're my friend too.'

So that was it then. I was a friend. Nothing more. I felt stupid and emotional. I could feel the tears start prickling and knew I wouldn't be able to stop them when they came.

'You don't need to walk me, I'll be fine by myself,' I said defensively, trying to stay ahead of him so that I didn't have to make eye contact. I could hear his friends talking and throwing the football back and forth and I was relieved that we were likely out of earshot.

'Are you OK? Sophie?' I could hear the genuine concern in his voice but I really didn't want him to keep following me. I had almost reached the side of the house and the cover of darkness.

'I'm fine, really,' I said again. 'I'm quite capable of getting myself home.'

I pushed the bike around the corner and held onto the handlebars each time I almost tripped. I didn't look behind to see if he was there and I didn't look over at his house to see if he was watching me reach the back door. By now the tears were streaming down my face. Instead of going through the kitchen I pushed the bike under cover, went around to the greenhouse and ran up to my room.

I was sobbing into my pillow quietly when I felt the hairs on the back of my neck prick up. Turning around, I'm not sure why but I expected to see Poppy and was surprised instead to see Gus. He was sitting on the window seat looking over at Charlie's house. I buried my face back in my pillow and waited for him to make a joke or a rude comment but instead there was silence. There is nothing he could have said to make me feel better so I was grateful he didn't try. I wondered whether he'd been watching out the window when I arrived home.

After a few minutes my embarrassment eased, my sobs slowed to sniffles and my breathing returned to normal. I grabbed a couple of tissues and wiped my face. Gus was looking at me now, his head tilted to the side and a serious look on his face.

'Do you want to talk about it?'

'Not really, no.'

He moved over to the bed and lay down next to me. His face was just inches from mine and I could still see the freckles on his translucent skin. I wanted more than anything for him to wrap his arms around me and give me a hug. It wasn't just to have someone, anyone, give me some affection; I knew that I could just go downstairs to my parents. No, I wanted Gus to touch me. To be able to turn around and move my body back into his and lie there like that until morning. But I couldn't touch him, he couldn't hold me. The thought brought fresh tears to my eyes and I closed them so that he couldn't see. I felt exhausted, like I had run a marathon.

'I don't like seeing you sad Sophie. Is there anything I can do?'

'No. At the moment I just want to go to sleep.' And escape this dreadful day I thought to myself.

'OK, I'll go and let you sleep.' He moved to get up off the bed.

'Wait,' I called out and stretched my hand to him. 'Please stay. Please stay with me.'

He lay back down on the bed, closer this time, and the sensation made the hair on the back of my arms prick up.

'Close your eyes Sophie.' I closed them obediently. 'When I was a little boy and still scared there were monsters my mom would say to me, "good dreams, good dreams here to stay, bad dreams, bad dreams go away."' He repeated it several times and I felt myself drifting off to sleep with the sound of his voice.

Before I lost consciousness I mumbled, 'I wish we'd never come back here.'

'I'm so happy that you did,' he said quietly. I half opened my eyes and saw Gus's face next to mine and he was smiling. I closed them again and drifted off to a dreamless sleep.

# CHAPTER 18

Having decided that I'd been friend-zoned by Charlie, I effectively avoided him for the rest of the week. I rode my bike to school early in the morning, and then ran to the bike racks and took a longer route home in the afternoons so that he wouldn't see me if he happened to pass me in his car. I'd also avoided history class by volunteering to assist with moving around books in the library, as they were preparing to renovate part of it.

By the end of the week I hadn't gotten any closer to figuring out Poppy's likely murderer, I had no date to the dance, and I was being hounded by the social committee twins and all of their slaves. The only way I could get them off my back was by promising to take them back to my house on Friday night to have a look at the ballroom. Which is how I found myself getting a lift home in the back of the twins' shiny new Audi. I hoped they didn't notice that I smelt their leather seats the whole way home. Their car was probably worth the same as my old house in Brooklyn, I thought to myself as I inhaled the leathery scent.

As we drove up the driveway my reservations about them using our house as some Halloween freak show eased. They gushed about how beautiful the house was and were unable to conceal their excitement. They talked in animated voices about stringing up decorations on the trees down the driveway and setting up pumpkins with lights in them to guide the way. They kept doing that annoying twin thing where they finished each other's sentence. I sat back, relieved that no one seemed to need any input from me.

I had given my parents the heads up and they were waiting at the front door. They were overjoyed to have found in the twins the enthusiasm that had been lacking from me. As they clucked over the placement of electrical sockets for the DJ booth and locations for the drinks and snacks area, I tuned them out and walked into the ballroom for the first time since we had arrived. I had to admit it was a fantastic Halloween ball venue. The paint was peeling off the walls in lots of places but with the harsh light of day gone, fairy lights all around and the decorations, it would look perfect. Marcel had volunteered to make Halloween treats and even Clara, who was usually so sour, was standing next to Mom offering to help decorate the room.

I wandered over to the windows and was looking out at the garden, listening to the twins talk about their lighting scheme, when I heard one of them mention the moon. I spun around, 'Sorry, what did you just say?'

'Well I just think it's going to look amazing with the moon shining down over the water. You know, because it's going to be the same night as the full moon.'

'Oh shit!' I muttered under my breath, my face draining of all color.

'Are you OK Sophie?' Mom asked, studying my face.

I realized Marcel and Clara were also both looking at me with quizzical expressions.

'What?' I plastered a smile on my face and turned to look at them, feigning calm. 'Yes, all fine, A-OK. I um … I just have to … I just realized that I have some homework I need to finish. Do you mind?' I asked my parents, on my way out the door. Mom shook her head, but I saw her shoot a look at my dad.

I took the stairs two at a time and ran along the hallway to my room. Barreling through the door I half expected to see Gus sitting on my bed with his cheeky grin, ready to make a suggestive remark, but he wasn't there.

'Gus?' I called out to him, trying not to be too loud in case one of the people in the house heard me calling out the name of a dead person. Guaranteed they would think that I was off my tree. I started pacing the room and calling his name again, softly but urgently.

He appeared in the middle of the room and I walked right through him. I felt off balance and cold for a minute and all of the hairs on the back of my neck went up. He opened his mouth to make a sarcastic remark but must have changed his mind when he saw the look of horror on my face. 'What is it?'

'We have a big problem.' I explained to him about the dance being the same night as the full moon.

'Well, you have two options, the first is to tell the twitlets to find another venue.'

'Nope, no can do,' I said firmly, shaking my head.

'The whole social committee are down there right now frothing at the mouth because the ballroom is so perfect. Option two?'

'Easy,' he said shrugging his shoulders, 'figure out the murderer and get the key back before the full moon.'

'That option isn't really going to happen at the moment either. I have narrowed it down to Clara and Marcel but I still can't seem to think of a way to eliminate either of them.'

'You could always just kill both of them,' he joked. 'No? Ok let's go and talk to Poppy. She always seems to have good ideas in times of crisis.'

He led me down the hallway and into the main bedroom, next door to my parents. My parents hadn't wanted to take Poppy's room out of respect to her, and the door had been closed the whole time we had been at the house. I half expected the door to be stuck shut like so many of the others, but it opened with a gentle twist of the doorknob.

The room was arguably the best in the house. The view was similar to mine as it was on the opposite end of the house, so it had two long windows, one across the front and one along the western side of the house. Where my side window looked into Charlie's house, Poppy's side window looked over the garden, and you felt as though you could be in the English countryside. While it was three times the size of my bedroom, it was furnished in a way that made it feel warm and cozy.

Poppy was sitting at her dressing table that looked out over the water, and it seemed as though she hadn't heard us enter the room.

'Poppy,' I said gently, pulling her out of her thoughts.

'We've hit a bit of a snag.' Gus explained the issue and Poppy sat and considered it momentarily before clicking her fingers. 'There was another device, one that could protect you from spirits. It was similar to the key but it wasn't in the form of a key, it was an old fob watch. You pulled a lever out of the back and put it in the room that you wanted to protect and the spirits couldn't get in or out.'

'Great, so I could put it in the ballroom and just make sure that no one leaves the room and they will be safe?'

'Exactly,' she said nodding her head.

'OK, it's probably not a foolproof plan but it will have to do! Where is it?'

'It's in a safe which is hidden in one of the secret passageways.' Her face furrowed with concentration and she shook her head. 'I just can't remember which passageway it's in, I haven't been to that safe in years.'

Gus and I looked at each other glumly: another treasure hunt, only this time we had no clues to start with.

Poppy sat up as though she had remembered. 'I know, go to the painting over there of the ladies.' I walked over and stood next to the painting she was referring to – two women in robes reaching up towards what appeared to be the heavens. I turned around expectantly.

'OK, now feel down the right-hand side and there should be a latch. If you pull it down the painting will swing away from the wall.' I did as she had described and the painting swung out and revealed a safe behind it. It was a beautiful old and ornate dark-charcoal-colored safe with a large knob that had numbers from one to sixty arranged around the outside and a big, heavy-looking handle.

'I thought you said the safe was in one of the secret passageways,' I said excitedly.

'Yes, it is, that is just my private safe, but it has copies of the blueprints to this house, which show all of the secret passageways. You'll have to check each one.'

'OK, how do I do this?'

'You will need to turn the knob to the right numbers. The password is my wedding date 02-22-1942. So turn it right to twenty-two, then left back to the number two, around to nineteen and then back to forty-two.'

I wound the wheel to each of the dates and the safe clicked open. Pulling open the door I was shocked to see piles of money and jewelry, including a beautiful big, diamond and sapphire ring sitting on top of legal-looking documents. I whistled as I reached in and grabbed two long tubes from the back of the metal box and held them up. Poppy nodded her head, confirming they were the blueprints.

'Poppy I don't want to sound nosy, but there has to be hundreds of thousands of dollars in there!' I said looking at her face.

'Yes, I never opened that safe. It has my wedding

ring in there and I couldn't bear to look at it. Please give the money to your parents, they seem to be doing a wonderful job sprucing up the place.' I wondered how I could get them the money without having to explain how I had found it: I couldn't just walk into their room casually carrying half a million dollars in hard currency. That would have to wait for another day I thought, refocusing my attention to the issue at hand.

Spreading the blueprints across Poppy's bed I noticed they looked the same as the ones my parents had been pawing over at the kitchen bench when we first arrived. However, these ones had one key difference: I could see marked on the pages at least a dozen entrances to secret passageways coming off a number of rooms.

'What am I looking for?' I asked Poppy. 'What does the safe look like?'

'You won't find it marked on that map, but use it to find the right passageway. The safe is concealed in the wall of one of the passageways. There is no code to the safe because it's hard to find. You have to look for ripples in the stone on the wall. When you find the ripples – there should be five of them – you need to run your fingers down the ripples. I think it might be in the west wing of the house.'

'OK, that narrows it down to around five,' I said, studying the images of the house.

'I'll come with you,' Gus volunteered, and even though he was a ghost and couldn't protect me, the thought of him being with me did make me feel better.

'Thanks Gus.' I smiled nervously at him and he gave

me an encouraging thumbs up and smiled back.

I walked back over to the safe to secure the contents but before I closed it, I noticed a manila folder propped up on the right side that I had not seen before with the words 'LAST WILL & TESTAMENT' written on the cover. It occurred to me again that it had come out of the blue that the property had been left to my dad and I wondered if there had been any other family who had been in the old versions and might have had a reason to knock Poppy off.

'Poppy, is this a copy of your will?' I asked, turning around and holding up the folder.

'Yes, all of my wills are in there,' she answered distractedly from the window where she seemed to be waiting for a boat that would never come.

'Do you mind if I have a look?' I knew she was a ghost and if she had said no there was really nothing she could do about it but I felt like it was polite to ask.

'Certainly. You need never ask my dear.'

I opened the folder and started to sift through the pages. There couldn't have been more than three or four versions because it wasn't a very thick pile of paper and it looked like the most recent version was at the top of the pile. I scanned my eyes down the page over all of the legal jargon that I couldn't understand and turned to the important section. *To Edward Douglas Weston of 16 Mossman Street* … That was Dad, and it bequeathed him all of the estate save a couple of gifts for other individuals. I looked further down the page. The other people's names popped out, $100,000 to Clara Rosenbaum, $100,000 to Thomas

Cutter and that was it. I turned to the last two pages looking for a mention of Marcel, but his name wasn't there. He was the shortest serving member of the staff, but even so, he had been there long enough to warrant a small bequest, surely.

'Poppy, can I ask why you didn't leave any money to Marcel?' I looked up from the pages, but she had disappeared. My curiosity piqued, I turned to the older version of the will and it was identical in every way but one. In this version Marcel was left $50,000. I checked back to the dates – the will had been changed less than six months before she had died. What had happened in those six months that had rendered Marcel stricken from the will, I wondered to myself. It was unlikely that Marcel was going to tell me, and I wasn't sure that Poppy would even remember if I asked her. I also wondered whether Marcel was even aware that he had been in the original will and, if he had known, was he surprised that he had not received anything after she had passed away. He didn't seem like the sort of person who would kill someone for $50,000 but I didn't really know him that well; maybe he was a closet gambler and he had to pay back some loan sharks. My imagination was going wild but at least now I had one of my two suspects with a motive.

At the back of the manila folder, behind a couple of clear plastic files, what looked to be a newspaper cutout was poking out. I pulled the scrap out and unfolded it. It was a local newspaper clipping reporting the drowning death of a boy. A boy that I knew very well; a boy who was standing right behind me. 'Local boy drowns after sailing during freak storm,' I ran my hand over the picture of Gus's face smiling out at me like he was posing for a yearbook photo. There was no mention that I had been in the boat with him and I felt sadly relieved about that.

I turned to look at him but he was looking at the blueprints scattered across the bed. I quickly tucked the newspaper clipping into the pocket of my jeans, pushed the rest of the paperwork back into the safe and secured the door, ensuring that it looked like no one had touched it.

# CHAPTER 19

Gus and I started going through the passageways first thing on Saturday morning. It had been years since I had gone into them but with the help of the blueprints my memories came back relatively easily and it was really nice being able to spend the day with Gus. We joked about all of the trouble we had gotten into when we had slept the night in one of the passageways without telling our parents. Thomas and Dad had gone berserk but Mom had been too relieved that I was OK to be mad at me.

Most of the passageways were made out of stone apart from the ones at the very bottom of the house that had dirt pathways. All of the entries had a lever or a button to get the hidden door to open. Some of the doors sprung open like they had been open recently and others needed to be pulled and pushed to get them to open. It made me wonder if Clara or Marcel had been going through the passageways looking for the key before I had arrived and unearthed it from its hiding place in my garden pot.

One difference I noticed from when we were children was that some of the exits from the passageway into rooms were boarded up. How strange, I thought to myself, they seemed to correlate to the rooms that had been sealed shut from the inside of the house too. I must remember to ask Poppy why the rooms had been sealed. What was inside these rooms to warrant them being closed up from all possible points of entry, even the entry that was hidden in the passageway?

I had just finished checking the wall of the last of the five passageways that we had flagged as being a possibility when I climbed out of the exit under the stairs and was met by Alice standing at the front door talking to my mom. I must have looked ridiculous because both of them turned and looked at me like I had grown an additional head. I quickly closed the passage entry behind me. Wondering what Gus was thinking behind the door, I looked down at my T-shirt and jeans and realized that I was covered head to toe in dust, dirt and cobwebs.

'Speak of the devil,' stammered my mom.

'Hey Alice,' I replied, trying to sound casual.

'Hi Sophie,' Alice said in a surprised voice.

Just then Marcel came through the door laden with fruit boxes from the market. He bustled past Alice, took one look at me and whistled. 'Miss Sophie you look like you have been rolling around in the dirt with spiders!' he chuckled and kept moving into the kitchen to offload his parcels.

Alice, god bless her, continued on with her invitation as though nothing had happened. 'I was just telling your mom that a group of us are having a bonfire on the beach this afternoon if you are free. Just in front of Percy's house – it's about half a mile down the beach towards the lighthouse.'

'That sounds great. I'll have a shower and get changed and meet you down there.'

We waved goodbye and before my mom could ask what I had been up to I muttered about needing to shower and headed upstairs. It was then I noticed that Clara had been standing in the sitting room near the bottom of the staircase. So now both she and Marcel knew that I had been sniffing around in the hidden passageways. I wondered whether either of them would be concerned as to why I was poking around in there.

I popped my head into my room to check if Gus had come back upstairs but there was no one in there so I grabbed my towel off the hook on the back of my door and walked across the hall to the bathroom. I turned on the shower, pulling off my clothes as the water warmed up and steam filled the room.

'Wow you just slammed the exit to the passageway in my face – that was so cold Sophie!'

I spun around to the sound of Gus's voice in the bathroom and hit my elbow on the shower rail in the process. Whimpering, I quickly grabbed up the towel and pulled it across my naked body.

When I finally turned around rubbing my elbow, Gus was facing away from me but I couldn't tell whether he had been standing that way the whole time and I eyed his back suspiciously.

'Get out of my bathroom you pervert!'

'Calm down! I didn't see anything princess!'

I kept my eyes on him as I pulled the shower curtain

back and let my towel drop at the same time as pulling the curtain across between the two of us.

'Is this what you do with your power of invisibility in the afterlife? Creep into girls' bathrooms?' I said squeezing a big blob of shampoo into my hands and rubbing it through my hair.

'Not all girls' bathrooms.' His voice sounded clearer and I looked around the shower curtain. He had turned around with his hands over his eyes and was peeking between the gaps in his fingers. I pulled the curtain across further.

'Who was the guy at the door that you didn't want me to see?'

'There was no guy. It was a girl, called Alice. She invited me to a party on the beach if you must know.' I scrubbed my hair harder, unsure whether I was trying to get all of the dirt out or trying to get Gus out of my head.

'Ahhh a party! And will there be boys at the party?'

I finished rinsing the suds off and turned off the faucet. 'Yes *Dad*, there will be boys at the party. Now turn around again – I'm coming out and if I so much as see you sneak a peek, when I find that key I will turn it too far in the clock just so I can kick your butt!'

'Whatever, I'm not looking.'

I snuck a look around the corner and saw him standing next to the toilet with his back to the shower. I quickly wrapped the towel around me and used another towel to dry my hair.

'So, who are the guys that will be at the party? Any of them as ridiculously good looking as me?'

'Several,' I said with a giggle as he turned around with a look of mock horror on his face.

'I think that's doubtful. Is the scientist going to be there?'

'Who?'

'You know the guy that likes to come over and study.' Alex, I thought with a cringe.

'Yes, probably.' This news didn't seem to concern him too much.

'And what about Don Juan next door? Does he still remember who you are?'

Ah, so this is what he had been fishing for, I realized. I thought it was unlikely that he would feel threatened by Alex but Charlie was an entirely different story. I frowned and turned around as I pulled on my bra and T-shirt and then my pants, with my towel still wrapped around me. When I turned around again he was facing me.

'What?' I murmured pretending not to have heard him, but he wasn't fooled.

'You know what – will he be there?'

'No he won't be there and of course he remembers me. We're friends.' The last statement came out sounding far too sour and he picked up on it straight away.

'Friends? Didn't want to pick up again where you left off?'

'See you later Gus.' I threw the towel is his direction. It went through him and landed in the hamper.

'Oh that is cold Sophie! Sophie?'

But I had already walked out of the room and made

my way quickly down the stairs and out of the house. The last thing I wanted to think about was Gus gloating about my situation with Charlie.

# CHAPTER 20

Spending the afternoon and evening with Alice was just what I needed. She was so happy and friendly that I forgot all about what was happening at the house – and with Charlie – and was able to relax. She told me about growing up in the Hamptons with a single mom who didn't have any money and three siblings and I felt an instant connection with her given that my family were not flush with cash like most of our schoolmates. Her mom now had her own providore and cheese room just out of the center of town and Alice was really proud of her. I promised that I would have dinner there one night during the week and was genuinely looking forward to it after hearing all the stories of the chaotic house.

As we walked along the beach I heard all about the trouble that her brother and younger twin sisters had gotten into, and how her brother had always been the instigator of the mischief, and it made me think of Gus. We had been walking slowly for about twenty minutes and I realized we were back on the beach out the front of Poppy's.

'I wonder if your grandma ever spent time with Poppy – she would have given your grandma a run in the crazy lady stakes!' I said to Alice.

'Actually, when I visited my gran in the nursing home towards the end of her life she did tell me she spent a bit of time at that house.' Her face clouded over, as though she was recalling something particularly disturbing that she had witnessed, and again I felt tempted to confide in someone about the crazy goings-on over the past few weeks, but I hesitated.

'Really?' I pressed her wanting to hear more but also suspecting I knew at least part of what she had heard. 'What did she say?' I asked, studying her face.

Her face cleared a little and she tried to laugh it off, 'Mostly she talked about the good old days. I think Poppy liked to have the occasional casino night back in the day and I think my grandpa might have been a little bit of a closet gambler.'

I could tell she wasn't being entirely honest with me so I pressed her further. 'So nothing spooky then? It seems that most people I've spoken to are surprised I can sleep there every night.'

She laughed again but then her eyes narrowed and she seemed to be looking at the rooms up the top of the house. I tried to follow her gaze to see what she was looking at and, out of the corner of my eye, saw her involuntarily shudder.

'What? What is it? What are you looking at?' I asked.

'Nothing. Do you want to go back?' she whispered.

'No really, your body was just shaking,' I said, feeling genuinely concerned. I reached out and touched her arm and noticed it was covered in goosebumps.

'I'm sure it's nothing, it's just that,' she hesitated, 'I thought I saw someone watching us. It looked like … like … an old woman.'

'Really? Where?' I squinted against the sunlight but I couldn't see anything. Was it possible that she saw Poppy, or maybe it had been Clara? I looked up towards the house again but I couldn't see anyone in the windows.

'Never mind, I'm probably just delirious from hunger! Let's go back.' She pleaded with me and, pulling my arm, started to walk off down the beach.

We walked in silence for a few moments as I wondered again whether to tell her about the ghosts in the house. I had the feeling that it was unlikely that she would laugh at me, especially after what she had told me about her grandmother and the spirits, but again I hesitated.

'I guess the social committee would be wrapped with having your house for their dance?' Alice asked, and immediately thoughts of ghosts and haunted mansions were replaced with the mundane teenage horror of inviting someone to a dance.

I chuckled, 'Yes the twins were frothing at the mouth! Speaking of the dance, I forgot to ask you, do you have a date?'

'No, not yet. There is someone I was going to ask but I haven't summoned up the courage and I, um, actually also wanted to make sure you were OK with it.'

'Who is that? And why on earth would you need my permission?' I asked as I watched her head turn around to the group setting up the wood for the bonfire.

'Well, I know you are both quite close, so I hope you haven't already asked him, but if you have that's OK, I'll just ask someone else but …' she hesitated again and then looked at her feet, seeming to reconsider whether she should say anything at all.

I was completely baffled. 'The anticipation is killing me! Who are you talking about?'

'Percy,' she blurted out, looking down at her feet.

'*Percy?* Well that's perfect,' I said, smiling at her when she tentatively looked up, 'because he was trying to muster up the courage to ask you,' I said, setting her mind at ease.

'Really?' she squealed. 'That's great! So when do you think I should ask him? Or do you think that I should wait for him to ask me?'

She sounded unsure of herself again and I laughed. 'Why don't you go and ask him now!'

Alice started to walk back to the bonfire and then paused and looked back at me pensively. 'Who are you going to ask?'

I glanced back in the direction of the house, 'I'm thinking about taking a ghost.' She followed my gaze, her face looking a little pinched, and then gave a half-hearted laugh. I wondered again what she had seen in the window.

Percy, Emma, Alex and a few of the other kids that would sit at our table unloaded all of the supplies from James's truck and soon enough we had built a roaring fire with logs around for us to sit on. Percy came and sat next to me and handed me a stick and some marshmallows. He looked ecstatic, and after he sat down he turned to look at Alice with a big smile on his face and she smiled back, so I assumed they had locked in their date for the dance. Alex, who had been just behind Percy, looked disappointed that the seat next to me had been taken, but he moved around to the other side on the log next to mine and sat next to Emma, who beamed at him like he was her favorite person in the world. Unfortunately for Emma, Alex didn't seem to notice and turned his back to her to listen in to the conversation between me and Percy.

The topic of the dance came up and from the sound of it half of the group had not yet locked in dates and some had decided to go in a group. I was relieved to hear that this was a possibility given I had yet to ask Charlie and was now convinced that he might have been trying to let me down gently when he said he didn't go to the dance. Maybe he just didn't want to go with me. I had successfully avoided him for a week and had almost convinced myself that he had not seen my minor meltdown.

'Who are you going to take Sophie? Now that the most eligible bachelor is otherwise occupied,' Percy asked, pulling up his collar and running his hands through his hair.

'I think the group idea sounds pretty appealing actually.'

He put on a pretend shocked expression, 'Really? I would have thought you'd muster up the courage to invite the football stud that you always look at on the other side of the canteen, whom I am well aware lives on the other side of your fence.'

My face went crimson and I punched him in the arm. 'Is it that obvious? I actually had my first kiss with Charlie years ago. But I'm fairly certain he does not still think about me that way unfortunately.'

'I don't know about that. I've seen him staring at you too, although sometimes his face looks like he's being tortured.'

I laughed off Percy's astute observation, but if he'd told me that a couple of weeks ago I would have been confused. Now that I knew where Charlie's feelings had been coming from it just made me feel a little sad that I hadn't been able to remember our past, and relieved that the majority of my memories had been restored. Not all though, I reminded myself. I was determined to rediscover that terrible day that was still buried in my memory. I just wasn't sure how to unlock that part of my brain.

I realized too late that our conversation was being picked up on by an eavesdropper.

'Charlie? As in Charlie Crawford? You can't be serious! Oh Sophie, I'm sorry to be the one to tell you this but he doesn't date girls at this school so good luck with that!' Emma said unkindly, sounding like she wasn't sorry at all to be the one to inform me how terribly misguided I was.

I quickly looked around and saw that, thankfully, Alex had gone back to the truck to pick up some more firewood so he didn't overhear that I was, in actual fact, dateless. I had heard Alex mention earlier to Percy that he was going to invite Emma. Given she had been so rude to me I wondered unkindly whether she knew that she was his second pick. I thought about mentioning that in a similar snide fashion to the way that she was treating me, but I just wasn't like that and decided to pretend she hadn't said anything. If Emma told Alex later that I was dateless I could always say that I had arranged to go with Percy but relieved him of his responsibilities once I learnt of his interest in Alice. That way no one could be offended and I could easily go alone … or just find somewhere to hide in the house!

Later, when we were leaving, Percy and Alice volunteered to walk me back down the beach, which I was grateful for. The sky had darkened and I knew that I would have felt uneasy walking alone along the dark beach. It soon became clear why Emma had made the mean comment in the first place.

'Don't worry about Emma,' Alice said. 'She's tried to invite Charlie to the dance for the past three years and has always been knocked back.'

'Well that explains a bit,' I said, putting the pieces of the puzzle together. 'She really doesn't seem to like me much.'

'Yes, I think she might also have a crush on Alex and he most definitely appears to have a crush on you,' Percy continued.

'For someone who was intent on not making friends

here I'm disappointed that I have managed to make myself an enemy.'

'Well, you know you have also made some good friends,' Alice said as she hugged me goodbye.

I watched Percy and Alice heading back down the beach, waving back when they turned around to wave goodbye. I was delaying going back inside. It was too dark to go back into the secret passageways, but I didn't even want to talk about the search, and I suspected Gus would be waiting for me in my room to do just that. There was also one murder suspect that I hadn't interrogated yet and I was avoiding that as much as I could. Clara didn't seem like a mean person, but her generally prickly demeanor made her unapproachable and a little bit frightening. I just wanted to sit outside and look at the stars.

After a while the air cooled down and I started walking slowly up to the house. I was looking up in the direction of Charlie's room, trying hard not to look like a stalker, when I saw a movement in my house out of the corner of my eye. My head snapped around to the direction of the movement but I didn't see where it had come from. Could it have been in my bedroom? I stood still and was squinting up at the house when suddenly the security light went on and temporarily blinded me. I rubbed my eyes and peered toward my bedroom again. My eyes were still adjusting but I could have sworn that I saw the outline of a person standing in one of the windows, looking out from the house. Watching me from my bedroom.

I blinked and rubbed my eyes again, looking

desperately into my windows, but the shadow had disappeared, leaving me to wonder if the outline was just my imagination. The goosebumps on my arms were not just from the cold but I pulled my jacket tighter around me and headed back up to the house. I wondered whether the figure I had seen was Gus. He had taken up residence in my bedroom at night since I had my mini meltdown and most nights I would go to sleep with him lying next to me or sitting on the seat beside the window, quietly watching me. But the shadow that I had seen had seemed like more than just a shadow, more solid than Gus's translucent body. I shivered again when I thought of someone going through my room. It was unlikely that Gus would be able to do anything in the event that someone did come into my room but it made me feel safer knowing that he was there next to me.

# CHAPTER 21

The next morning Gus and I were back in the same tunnels that we had been in the day before and we were no closer to finding the safe. I hadn't slept well at all, dreaming about ghostly shadows, and Emma pointing and laughing at me standing on the stage at the dance with no date.

'Are we sure that it even exists?' I asked Gus, flopping down on the floor to rest for a minute with my back up against the cold stone. 'I mean, what if Poppy is imagining this other safe.'

He shook his head, his eyes scanning the wall for any sign of uneven markings.

'I remember being down in these passageways with you almost every day we were together and I can't for the life of me remember noticing any ripples on the wall,' I muttered, starting to get frustrated. We had been down all of the same passages in the west wing yesterday and hadn't been able to find so much as a chip out of the walls let alone a ripple. I closed my eyes and pushed my fingers against my temples trying to force the memory.

'In fact,' I said, looking up at him moving along the passage, 'while we're on the topic of memory, I remember every day of my childhood spent here apart from one. No matter what I try I cannot remember that one day.' He turned around from his careful studying of the wall and, noticing my serious face, came and sat down on the seat and looked at me expectantly. I looked into his eyes and softened my voice, 'What happened the day that you died?'

'I don't remember,' he said so fast I could tell that he was lying. I raised my eyebrows to show him I didn't buy it. 'OK,' he relented, 'I remember parts of it. In fact there was one question that I asked you and you didn't give me an answer.'

'Oh yes, what was that?' I pulled my foot out of my shoe and started to rub the sole.

'I asked you what would have happened if I had been a faster swimmer? What if it had been me that pulled you from the water?'

That was unexpected. I started to shake my head but I couldn't say it. In my heart I did know that I had feelings for Gus but what was the point of telling him.

'I'm sorry Gus, I can't spend my life in love with a ghost. I don't know what you want from me.'

'I want you to tell me that you had – I mean that you have – feelings for me too.'

'What is the point of saying it, it doesn't make a difference,' I argued.

'It makes a difference to me. I'm not imagining things. I know that you have feelings for me too Sophie. I mean what does Charlie have that I don't have, besides a heartbeat and an inheritance?'

'Money? You think it was about money?'

'No. Well, I mean ... I ...' I could tell that he regretted his comment but it was too late to take it back.

'Thanks a lot Gus! You know what? I've had enough of this ridiculous search, we're just wasting our time. I give up!' I jumped up, pulled on my shoe, and stomped off with Gus protesting behind me to come back. I am sure he could have probably just vanished and reappeared in front of my face, but he seemed to sense that he had crossed a line and didn't, and for that I was grateful.

I was tired and I had had enough. I flopped down on my bed in a huff. Despite searching all five of the passageways in the west wing we hadn't found the wavy wall or the safe, I wasn't any closer to figuring out Poppy's killer, and it seemed like I had lost my chance with Charlie. I felt like a big fat failure.

I put my hands over my face and tried to block it all out but I couldn't. For some reason I could smell flowers. I sighed and slowly sat up. Checking to see if my windows were open, I noticed a movement out of the corner of my eye and jerked around, expecting to see another sinister shadow standing at the window. But there was no sinister shadow; it was Charlie, and he was standing in his bedroom window waving his hands to get my attention.

He gestured for me to lift my window, so I pulled myself off the bed and walked over. Having not opened that particular window before I was unsure if it even opened but I unlatched the lock and tugged and pulled until it lurched up in a swift movement that almost made me fall out over the ledge. I recovered quickly from my ungraceful maneuver and looked up to see Charlie trying to hold back his laughter.

'Yes, can I help you?' I asked in a terse voice, feeling tired, irritated and embarrassed all at the same time. He put on his best handsome dimpled face and held out a rose that looked like it had been plucked from his garden. I felt my face relax and I smiled despite myself.

'Have you been avoiding me Weston?' I felt my face go a deeper shade of red as I feigned ignorance.

'I am sure I don't know what you are talking about.'

He smiled and pointed towards my house. 'There should be a delivery in your bedroom from my garden.' I looked around and saw the most beautiful bouquet of white roses in a crystal vase that looked like a priceless family heirloom. My heart fluttered around in my chest like a tiny bird trying to free itself. This can't just be in my head – boys don't pick flowers for girls they're not interested in, do they? I turned back to look at Charlie, feeling my face flush, 'Wow they're beautiful, thank you!'

'I also wanted to see if you are free tomorrow afternoon?'

'I think you will find tomorrow is Monday, which is a school day.' I cringed at the thought. I had two assignments and a paper to write that I had been neglecting due to my ghostly mansion searching, which I had absolutely nothing to show for.

'Nope, we have a long weekend. Didn't you know? The teachers have some sort of curriculum day tomorrow.'

'*Brilliant!* OK, well I'd better do some schoolwork in the morning but I should be done around 11 am. What have you got planned? Any other friends of yours coming over?' I asked, trying not to sound desperate.

'You will have to wait and see. Sweet dreams, sunshine.'

I walked over to my desk and inhaled the sweet smell of the roses, remembering again his lips on mine at the beach all those years ago. How had he managed to get them into the house, I wondered, and frowned at the idea of him presenting them to cranky Clara, nosy Marcel, or even worse, either of my parents. I was sure that I would hear about it at dinner if it was my parents, but they said nothing.

I was so tired that night I went straight to sleep, but instead of sweet thoughts about Charlie and our mystery date my dreams were full of running down long passageways, and no matter what I did I couldn't get out. I woke up feeling parched, with a pounding headache. I still wanted to go out with Charlie so after a poor attempt at both assignments and my paper I took two aspirin and skulled three glasses of water then went back to my room to appraise my wardrobe.

I had no idea where we were going, what we were doing, or whether there would be other people involved so I decided on a pair of light-green cut-off shorts and a blue-and-white striped long-sleeved top with white Converse shoes. I spritzed a couple of sprays of perfume, applied some tinted moisturizer, mascara and a light coating of tinted lip gloss. It wasn't much but it was more effort than I usually went to and my parents picked up on it immediately.

As soon as I walked into the kitchen Mom whistled at me and Dad put down his piece of toast and cup of tea like he was preparing himself for a long discussion. I grabbed an apple from the fruit bowl and, waving away their protests, walked out the back door and down to the beach. Charlie was waiting for me on the beach and I immediately felt better. He wasn't wearing anything too dressy, just jeans and a T-shirt. He was also distinctly sans friends. My heart fluttered again and I wondered if this was a date or not. He stood up and I saw there were two life jackets in his hand.

'Wait, what are those for?' I immediately felt tense again and I was pretty sure I didn't want to know what was coming.

He could sense that I was baulking at the sight of the lifejackets and put both hands up in the air as a sign of retreat. 'We don't even have to leave the dock if you're not comfortable. The other day you were talking about not remembering that one day on the boat with Gus and I just thought you sounded like you were trying so hard to remember that maybe getting on the boat might trigger some memories, like that night on the pier.'

I shuddered at the thought of that night on the pier but he did have a point. I reluctantly took one of the life jackets and walked slowly towards their dock. I was a little confused again. Was this a date or an attempted psychology session? And then I remembered the gift he had left for me in my room.

'Thank you for the flowers, they're beautiful.'

'You're welcome.' He smiled sheepishly at me and then his face went serious. 'It's a sort of apology, you know, for the other night. I feel like maybe you were upset and I haven't seen you all week at school. It sort of felt like you were avoiding me.'

I avoided his eyes and his implied question. 'How did you manage to get them up into my bedroom?'

'I gave them to Thomas actually. You know, when Gus was alive I always felt like he never really liked me that much. But he was really nice about taking the flowers to you.'

I thought about my talk with Thomas in his garden that he had nurtured so carefully.

'I spoke to him about Gus and I think he has made peace with it.'

'Still, it feels strange for me not being able to see him again, it must be so hard on Thomas,' Charlie said, pulling open the small picket gate leading to his dock and holding it open for me to walk through.

'Yes, I imagine it would be.' I bit my lip and thought about why Gus had never shown his ghostly apparition to his father.

There was a picnic basket sitting on the wooden planks and Charlie grabbed it as we walked past, leading me to the smaller of the two boats docked. It was a small white speedboat with an outboard motor and a cut-out section at the front that had cream-colored padded seats, which Charlie climbed down onto. He raised the gate and walked through putting the basket down at the back and came back to help me down.

'Climb aboard sailor!'

My feet were frozen to the spot. I looked out at the weather, which was sunny and warm, not a cloud in the sky, and then back to Charlie reaching his hand out to me. I took a deep breath and took his hand and he slowly eased me onto the boat.

'You can let go now,' he smiled, and I realized I had been crushing his hand. I let go quickly feeling a little foolish. He laughed and taking my hand back he quickly clarified, 'I meant you could let go of your breath, you don't have to let go of my hand if you don't want to.'

'Oh,' I said, trying to smile and relax and focus on Charlie being so sweet, but I couldn't. I sat down on the cushioned seats and concentrated on breathing in and out for a few minutes and began to feel more comfortable. I closed my eyes and breathed in the salty air. The sun was warm on my legs and I felt safe on the boat with Charlie. He was still holding onto my hands and I couldn't tell whether the butterflies were from him holding my hands or from being on the boat. I opened my eyes and saw him staring intently at me, waiting for me to give him the go-ahead.

'OK, take me out.'

'You sure?' he asked, studying my face.

'Yes. No … not really, but OK.'

He laughed and I couldn't help but smile back at him.

'Yes, let's go before I change my mind. Where are we going to go?'

'There is a place along the water that does amazing fish and chips. I also packed some snacks in case you didn't want to get off the dock so help yourself,' he said as he let go of my hands, expertly pulled the ropes off the dock and started up the boat. He had obviously been doing this for years because it only took him a couple of minutes and we were heading out away from the dock. I closed my eyes and leant back on the seat enjoying the boat bouncing across the bay and the saltwater spray in my face.

We drove for about fifteen minutes and re-docked outside a place called Beacon. Charlie was right, the fish and chips were incredible. After lunch Charlie took me to his favorite place on the water. It was a little cove not far from our houses. He pulled the boat in to the beach and we jumped down into the sand with his picnic basket and spread it out on the beach. It felt like we were the last two people on earth. We stayed on the beach until the sun started to go down and we had to go back.

When it was time to leave we waded out into the water and threw our things into the boat. Charlie climbed in first, pulling himself over the edge with ease. I tried a couple of times but the tide had come in and we were deeper than when we had climbed out so I ended up falling back into the water.

'Here, I'll help you.' Charlie reached down and put his strong hands under my arms.

My body tingled with his touch and I looked up into his face as he pulled me into the boat as carefully as he could. I was so distracted by his face being only inches from mine I caught the edge of the boat on the way in and fell into him, knocking us both to the floor of the boat.

'Sorry,' I mumbled, trying to pull myself up. I was so embarrassed I couldn't even look at him. But the next thing I knew Charlie put his arms around my waist and pulled me to him.

His lips were so soft but his kiss felt urgent, like he had been wanting to do it the whole time we had been together, and his arms around me were so strong. He pulled me in closer and I felt myself losing control in his arms.

The lapping of the water against the boat, his warm lips on mine, and the salty sea air triggered the memory and I was suddenly on the little sailing boat with Gus.

# CHAPTER 22

*We couldn't have been more than 200 yards away from Poppy's mooring.*

*'I had no idea you could sail!' I said to him in surprise as I watched his hands expertly pulling up the sail and navigating the rudder to take us in the right direction for the wind to guide us further out.*

*'There is a lot you don't know about me,' said Gus making a silly face at me, and I ignored him, looking over his shoulder at the growing clouds.*

*'Are you sure that we should go out now? I heard Clara saying something about a storm and those clouds look ominous. Maybe we could go tomorrow instead and Charlie could come too.'*

*'No!' he said quickly and a little crossly, 'It has to be today.'*

*I sat back in the boat feeling a little uneasy. Gus was always so kind and protective of me, I wasn't sure why he was acting strangely. He saw my uncomfortable expression and his face softened.*

*'Can I ask you something?' he said gently, his eyes probing my face.*

*'Sure, anything.'*

*'What if it had been me that day? That had reached you first when you pretended to drown. Would you have kissed me?'*

*Now I could see why he was acting strangely and had wanted Charlie out of the picture. Why it had to be today that we went sailing.*

*I shook my head, not entirely sure of my answer. 'But it wasn't you.'*

*He immediately picked up on my uncertainty and securing the sail he moved over to be next to me. He reached out and took my hands in his. 'I have had feelings for you for so long Sophie,' he said looking into my eyes. His face was so close to mine I could feel his breath on my lips and I could see what was going to happen.*

*'Gus don't,' I stammered. 'You can't. I'm with Charlie.' I turned my face away from his and moved to the other side of the little boat, putting some distance between the two of us.*

*His mood changed as soon as I said his name. 'What is it about Charlie? Is it because he has more money than me?'*

*'No!' I protested, feeling insulted that he would think that I would see that as being important. 'I couldn't care less about that.' I pulled my hands out of his. 'I think you should take me back now.'*

*'No, we still have the whole day to spend together.'*

*'Why would you want to spend the day with a gold digger,' I said unnecessarily harshly, but I was stung by his comment.*

*'Well I'm not going to go back yet.' He started to unfasten the ropes of the sail. If he was going to be petty then I was going to be petty too I thought stubbornly. 'Fine,' I said, 'there is not enough room on this boat for me and your temper.' He stopped untying the ropes for a minute and as he looked up I pulled off my T-shirt and shorts and took the opportunity to dive into the water.*

*'What are you doing?' he shouted. I'd caught him off guard.*

*'If you're not going to take me back I'll swim back!' I shouted at him.*

*He rolled his eyes and called my bluff. 'Get in the boat Sophie.'*

*'No,' I said obstinately.*

*He looked toward the shore and rolled his eyes again, 'Fine! I'm going for a sail.'*

*I hadn't expected him to let me swim back and I looked nervously at the shoreline. We were still no more than 300 yards off the shore and even though I wasn't a very good swimmer I was confident I could reach the beach. He must have been too or he would never have left me. I thought about the clouds that had been rolling in thick and fast and decided I was more worried for Gus.*

*'Gus, you really shouldn't go out in this weather. Those clouds look bad.'*

*'Oh, I'm sorry, I thought you didn't really care about me.' It was his turn to exchange blows.*

*'Please Gus! I never said that. Just because I wouldn't kiss you doesn't mean I don't care about you. You're one of my best friends. Please don't go out – look at the clouds,' I begged him, but he was just as stubborn I had been. Without a glance at the looming dark sky behind him he loosened the last of the ropes. The sail billowed out with the wind and he took off through the water. I watched him for a couple of minutes and then turned around and started swimming into shore.*

# CHAPTER 23

I opened my eyes and gasped. Charlie had his arms around me and was looking at me, concerned.

'What? What happened? Are you OK?' He studied my face and a look of recognition came across his. 'Did you remember?'

I nodded. 'I'm OK. I remember.' My eyes glazed over as I went back to that day again in my mind. 'Gus organized for just the two of us to go out on the boat that day. You had to go to a family function.'

'Yes,' he nodded in agreement, 'my great-grandmother's ninetieth birthday in New York.'

'He told me that he wanted to have me to himself and he had planned the day so we could be alone. That should have set off warnings but I just thought he was being silly. He told me that he had feelings for me and then tried to kiss me and we fought. About you. About my relationship with you. He asked me if it had been him that rescued me from the water whether … He said some pretty ugly things so I asked him to take me back and when he didn't I jumped into the water and told him I was going to swim back. I think at the time I was just trying to prove a point but he left me there. I begged him not to go into the storm.' My voice faded and I and started crying. It dawned on me that Gus had not told me what had happened that day because it had been partly my fault and he didn't want me to feel bad. 'Oh god, it was my fault wasn't it? I could have stopped him.'

'No Sophie, you remember Gus. He was like a stubborn mule. As soon as he decided something it was done. You couldn't have done anything to save him.'

Charlie wrapped his arms around me while I sobbed. In a way it was good that I remembered but I almost wished I didn't. We sat there like that for what seemed like forever and when the air started to cool and I began to shiver Charlie wrapped a towel around me and maneuvered the boat back to his jetty. He looked like he was deep in thought as he tied the boat back up and walked me back up to the house, holding my cold hand in his strong, warm one.

At the door he wrapped his arms around me and held me tightly. After standing there for several minutes he looked down at me while still holding me close.

'I used to wonder the same thing sometimes,' he said, like we had been in the middle of a conversation.

'You would wonder about what?' I asked, looking up into his magnificent face and wondering how I could be so lucky.

He looked away for a minute appearing to deliberate whether he should reveal his secret and then looked back into my eyes, 'Whether you had known that it was me that pulled you out of the water or whether you thought it had been Gus.' He saw the defensive look on my face and pulled me in tighter when I tried to pull back. 'Don't get me wrong! I think I can speak honestly on both our behalves when I say we were swimming as hard as we could that day because we were both in love with you and scared that you might have drowned.'

'You were in love with me?' I asked, feeling like I could burst but at the same time trying so hard to remain cool and calm. He smiled at me and chuckled under his breath, 'Of course; you didn't know? Gus was too. He never told me but I'm sure of it.'

He looked up at the house and then continued with his train of thought. 'We were all so close. You know sometimes I would look out my window over at the house before you came back and I thought that … Well, I would sometimes think that … You're going to think I'm completely crazy, but I thought I saw him there sometimes. And I wondered whether it was my guilty conscience. If I had been there that day maybe he wouldn't have drowned.'

I couldn't believe what I was hearing, could it be that he had actually seen Gus's ghost? 'Really? No I don't think you are crazy at all. Actually I wanted to tell you …' I was just about to tell him about the ghosts in the house when the front door opened. Clara was standing at the door and for once I was glad to see her and not my parents. I was not ready to have that awkward teenage conversation with them yet; there had been no need in Brooklyn because I had never gone out with any boys as more than friends.

'Hello Clara, lovely to see you!' Charlie said politely. She simply nodded at him and stood in the doorway awkwardly lurking. Charlie lent down and whispered in my ear so Clara couldn't hear, 'Were you going to say something?'

I smiled at Charlie and gave him a light kiss on the mouth and whispered in his ear, 'That day at the beach – I knew it was you, even with my eyes closed. Thank you for today, I had a really good time.'

He smiled as he turned around and started walking back to his house. Clara grumbled and walked back into the house and I waved at Charlie before he disappeared.

When I got back upstairs the last person that I wanted to see was Gus, so of course he was waiting for me in my bedroom.

'I've been looking at the blueprints and I think I've figured it out,' he said confidently. He hesitated when he looked at my face and saw me looking at him strangely. I wasn't sure whether it was the right thing to do, to bring up what I had just remembered from the day that he died. What was my motivation in bringing it up now? Was I just trying to relieve my guilt that I was partly responsible for his death? What if I had stayed in the boat that day? Would he have taken us back to land to talk it through or would he have sailed us both into the storm and I would not be here either? I stood there in the doorway with my mouth hanging open like a fish until he interrupted my thoughts.

'What? Why do you look like you have seen a dead person?' he said trying at humor.

'I just … well that is I was …' I stammered. Finally, I decided against it. 'You know what, never mind. What were you saying?' I said, looking down at the blueprints. We could deal with that awkward moment later.

He hesitated and then took a deep breath and said softly, 'I'm sorry I upset you yesterday, I really didn't mean to.'

'Sure, no problems,' I muttered, not meeting his gaze.

He paused and then, seeming satisfied that he had said his bit, picked up where he left off. 'OK, these houses were built back in the antiquated days of slaves right?

'I think you will find they were called servants and not slaves,' I corrected him. 'Poppy's family were vocally against slavery.'

He looked at me for a minute, 'Right, the *servants'* quarters are up here in the attic so they would have had passages down to their master's rooms.' He indicated the passageways on either side of the house on the plans, 'The original plans show that the lady of the house used the room on the opposite side of the house to the head of the house, which was the husband. The master bedroom is Poppy's room so your room, being on the opposite side of the house would have been the lady of the house's room.'

'So?'

'So it's likely that the servants would have been taking the jewelry to the lady of the house. So maybe there was a safe installed to house the jewelry for the lady of the house in the passageway leading to her bedroom.'

'Sounds reasonable, and besides, we have tried everything else. The only problem is that I don't remember there ever being a passageway out of my bedroom.' I looked around the wall for signs of an entrance.

'According to the blueprints there should be one,' Gus said pointing down at the plans.

I walked around the wall where the fireplace stood pulling down books, lifting up the mirror that hung above the mantle and even sticking my head into the fireplace before we found a latch inside a book on the bookshelf that felt like it hadn't been pulled out for decades. The door didn't spring open either, I had to push on it with every ounce of my strength. Because Gus couldn't push he sat on the edge of the fireplace calling out words of encouragement and occasionally telling me I had skinny girls' arms to make me angry so I pushed harder. Eventually it worked and the door slowly eased open enough for me to squeeze through. As we walked through examining the walls I started sneezing from the dust that I had disturbed, it was clear that no one had been in this passageway in centuries. The walls were narrow and the floor was made of a blue-colored stone. Aside from the dust the air in the passage was cold and smelt a little musty. After turning on my torch I made sure that the entry to the passage from my bedroom was hidden and started scanning the walls. On one side there were small air holes that also let in thin shards of light and between these holes there were small candle holders where the maid would have lit her way back in the days when battery-operated torches didn't exist. As it was I thought that the candlelight would probably have lit the passage better than my torch that was quickly running out of power, and I mentally cursed myself for not bringing extra batteries or a candle. I scanned the side of the wall opposite in the dim light. It was smooth and blue like the ground but halfway along the passageway I spotted a patch that wasn't smooth. My heart racing, I walked quickly over to the wall and examined it. There were what looked like little waves carved into the stone. It was only the size of a postcard but as I ran my hand across the markings it definitely felt like ripples.

'Found it!' I said feeling more relief than satisfaction. Gus came quickly from the other end of the passage.

'Now what do I do?' I looked around at Gus who was studying the indents in the wall.

# CHAPTER 24

Gus looked closer at the wall and then stepped back. 'Poppy said you have to run your fingers down the ripples.'

'Run my hand down the ripples,' I repeated as I looked at the wall again in mild disbelief. 'OK, here goes.' I took a deep breath and pulled my fingers down along the ripples. As soon as they hit the bottom on the indentation I heard a latch click and a door popped inwards. We both looked at each other in excitement and trepidation and I took a deep breath and pushed against the heavy stone door. Inside there was a room the size of a large butler's pantry and on all three sides there were shelves that were weighed down with a literal pirate's treasure of gold bars, jewelry, hats, paintings, antique clocks and a rack of beautiful old ball dresses. Gus and I could only stand there and gape in amazement at the treasure trove we had discovered.

After a few minutes I regained my senses and started searching the shelves for the fob watch. I sifted through jewelry boxes, looked into lock boxes that had their keys sitting on top and put my hand into vases that were sitting along the wall. I was leaning deep into a big vase considering the likelihood of spiders being able to access a completely sealed off room when I noticed a collection of paintings sitting behind the rack holding the dresses.

Momentarily distracted I walked over and pulled out the paintings one by one. As they were facing the wall I couldn't see each one until I had turned it around. There were two paintings of ballerinas that looked like original Monet's, a Vermeer style painting of a woman playing the piano and one that looked remarkably like a cousin of the flowers painted by Vincent van Gogh. I shook my head in amazement, wondering at the possibility that these were originals.

I didn't recognize the artists of some of the other paintings, one of which looked like a rough sketch of two young girls. It didn't look nearly as well painted or valuable as the other paintings and I wondered why Poppy had kept it. I went to lean it back against the other paintings and noticed the canvas paper was coming away from the back of the frame to which it was stuck. Pulling it back a little I could see that there was an additional piece of folded paper hiding behind the picture. I pulled the canvas down a little further and gently tugged out the piece of paper.

It looked old and the color had yellowed but it appeared to be a report from a hospital. The hospital was in a nearby town, not the local hospital. The writing had faded slightly but I could still make out some of the detail when I held it up to my torchlight. The patient's name was listed as Clarabelle Westlake and the date of birth was 29 February 1932. That was strange: Poppy's maiden name was Westlake but the date meant that this person was younger than Poppy and as far as I knew she didn't have any siblings.

I looked further down the form and found the doctor's comments. *Patient needs to be on bed rest for 10 days as her body has suffered a terrible shock. As a result of the inexperienced medical treatment she has received from a disreputable establishment to terminate her unborn fetus it is unlikely that she will be able to carry any further pregnancies to term.*

I stared at the page and read the comments again and again. The patient was unlikely to be able to have any more children. Clarabelle – Clara – it had to be a medical report for Clara; a young woman, who had looked so happy in a photo that presumably had been taken before this medical report. Before she had visited a backyard abortion clinic.

But why did the report have her name listed as Westlake? Had Poppy taken her to a nearby town to cover it up? Was Poppy blackmailing her to stay? Was this why Clara was so bitter and withdrawn? Had Poppy threatened her with scandal and so she had stayed, working for Poppy, even though she hated her? Maybe enough to want her dead. I had just found Clara's motive and I now had two people in the house at the time of Poppy's death who appeared to have strong reasons for wanting her dead.

'What are you looking at Nancy Drew?' I jumped when I heard Gus's voice right beside me. After explaining what I had found to Gus he reminded me there was still a whole room of treasures and because he couldn't use his hands, I was the only one who could go fishing around. I noted a sense of frustration in his voice as he moved around the cavernous room of treasures so I quickly tucked the piece of paper in my pocket and continued the search.

'Do you think these are real?' I asked Gus pointing to the gold bars stacked one on top of the other. I counted and there were twelve in total.

'It is more than likely,' replied Gus. 'This house has been in the family for centuries, the older generations didn't always trust the banks after the economic ups and downs.'

Shaking my head in amazement again, I stepped towards another row of shelves, which had what looked like a series of six drawers. As I opened each one I gasped as I found more and more incredible pieces of jewelry. The second drawer from the bottom held a number of men's watches and cufflinks so I paused and carefully examined each watch.

Gus, who was looking over my shoulder, pointed to one at the back of the drawer, and as soon as I turned it over we knew it was the one we were looking for. It had the same unique carvings as the key I had lost. The beautiful ornate rope-style circles curled around the outside and wrapped around each other at the top of the watch.

I breathed a sigh of relief 'Found it!' I murmured and carefully slipped the watch back into a small velvet pouch that had been holding another bigger fob watch. 'Ready to go?' I asked Gus. My torch was starting to blink and I felt like I had had enough of the darkness in Aladdin's cave. He nodded his agreement and I took one last look around the cavern of treasure. Shaking my head I pulled the door closed.

Once we were safely back in my room I found a better hiding place for the watch and the medical report, in a book I had discovered on my bookshelf that wasn't a book at all but a jewelry box disguised as a book. I slotted it back into the top shelf and hopped quickly and quietly onto my bed. If I couldn't figure out who the killer was I would need that fob watch to avert disaster. I had no idea who had taken the key but I was determined that no one was going to take the watch.

# CHAPTER 25

At school the next day I found it almost impossible to concentrate. My mind kept lurching from Clara to Charlie. I wondered whether Poppy had blackmailed Clara to keep working for her in return for keeping her dirty secret and it had eventually driven Clara to murder. But then I argued with myself, why would Poppy have taken Marcel out of the will and left Clara $100,000? That seemed an unlikely thing to do unless you had some affection for the person. Unless of course it was guilt from keeping her hostage for so many years, which could be a possibility, since maybe she had included Thomas from a sense of guilt about his son's death. You would think only having two murder suspects would make it easy, but I was going around in circles and could argue either way.

And then there was Charlie. Every time our eyes met he would smile at me and his dimples would make me dissolve into a blubbering mess. He swapped seats with the person who I had been sitting next to in history and when the teacher passed out one textbook per table I felt my heart lurch when we both went to open the book and our hands touched.

I couldn't stop thinking of his lips on mine in the boat and I hoped that I wasn't building it into something that wasn't there. But then my conscience would argue back that he had told me at the front door when he dropped me off that he had been in love with me. He didn't say he's in love with you though, he said he and Gus *were* in love with you, back then, years ago, when we were just children and before you killed his best friend and then left and forgot all about him.

At lunch I went over and sat with my friends and Charlie sat with his, although he did spend a lot of time looking over at the table that I was sitting at. So much so that Alice caught me looking over at him and the smile that passed between us. 'Well Miss Sophie, there are some serious eyes being thrown across the room today!'

Emma's ears must have pricked up and she turned around to where Alice was looking and caught sight of Charlie, who was now in conversation with another boy sitting opposite him. Looking back she rolled her eyes and snorted at my likely lovesick expression. 'Don't waste your time Sophie. I don't mean to be rude but there is no way that is ever going to happen.'

'No, you're probably right,' I said focusing on eating my lunch. I didn't have to lower myself to her level – I would prove her wrong at the dance in a couple of weeks and then I would sit back while she ate her words. I just needed to muster the courage to ask Charlie again. I wasn't sure why I was hesitating. He said that he never went to the dance but maybe he would reconsider. He obviously still liked me but I was nervous that he would say no; and then my mind would spiral back into doubt again. Maybe he was spending time with me for old times' sake and he would realize that he was happy I had left three years ago and never made contact. I was sure that we were both different people than who we had been back then, before Gus had died.

My stomach churned and I took one last glance up at his table as everyone started packing up their lunch. He was looking at me with a look of concern; I must have looked as miserable as my thoughts. 'OK?' he mouthed at me, and I snuck a look Emma's way. She was too busy packing up her bag to pay any attention to me. I smiled back at Charlie and nodded my head feeling much better than I had a minute ago. I shouldn't let a miserable person make me miserable too, I told myself.

The next period I had English with Alice and we had been working on *Macbeth*. With Halloween approaching Mr Clarkson had decided to discuss the ghostly apparitions that had haunted Lady Macbeth and Macbeth. 'Do you believe in ghosts?' was written on the board in scribbled chalk. I glanced at Alice out of the corner of my eye as she read the board. Her brow furrowed and she looked around the room at the others in the class, obviously concerned that someone might mention her grandmother, but for the next fifty minutes the discussion stayed firmly on *Macbeth* and not on local folklore and I could see the tension release from her body the minute the bell rang. Again, I thought about raising the topic with her, but she hurried off straight after class claiming to have a paper she had forgotten to hand in.

After school I walked over to the bikes and pulled my bike off the rack. I was pushing it back when a flower appeared in front of my face from behind and startled me so much I almost dropped the bike. 'Oh!' I said, looking around to find Charlie sheepishly holding the flower.

'Sorry, I didn't mean to scare you. I thought you would have heard me.'

'No, that's OK.' I shook my head quickly and took the flower from him. It was a white daisy that had a couple of petals missing and the petals left were drooping. He looked at the daisy and then back up at my face 'Yeah, I actually picked it after I saw you looking like someone had run over your puppy at lunch. Sorry, I think it has seen better days.'

'That's OK,' I said smiling back. 'I think it's perfect.'

'Have you got much homework on tonight?'

'No just a couple of sketches for Art tomorrow. We're supposed to draw something that has been weathered. I was thinking I might draw some of the boats or our rusty old dock but maybe I could sketch Clara,' I said jokingly.

'Yeah, even though we live next door I haven't seen her much in the last couple of years – she is looking really old! Would you mind having company while you sketch?' he asked seriously.

'That would be great. You can do some sketching with me.'

'I can't even draw stick figures! But if you must use me as entertainment I will be at your service,' he said and took an elaborate bow. 'I need to meet with the coach for twenty minutes. Meet you down at the beach in forty-five?'

I nodded my head and tucked the flower gently into the side pocket of my bag. As I slung it over my back I watched him jog off to the football ground in awe. He made it look so easy to cover so much ground. Shaking my head, I climbed onto my bike and tried to replicate his athletic prowess by riding faster than I ever had before so I could get ready before he got back.

Arriving at the house puffing, with a light sheen of sweat, I flew into the house and up the stairs to throw on some makeup. I could feel butterflies in my stomach as I assessed myself in the mirror. My long honey-colored hair looked like it could use a bit of a trim and my cheeks were flushed red from the mad dash home on my bike but altogether I thought I looked alright. I threw my hair into a topknot and changed into a ripped pair of jeans and a T-shirt with flip-flops and a cardigan because the air had started to cool down a little. I assessed myself in the mirror again quickly to make sure I didn't look like I had dressed up for the occasion – I didn't want to seem like I was trying too hard.

On my way out the door I heard my mom swear under her voice and something heavy clattered to the floor. I rounded a corner in the hallway and stared in surprise at the sight of my mother, heavily perspiring, kicking one of the doors leading off the hallway. 'Mom, are you alright?'

'Yes, this damn door will not open no matter what I throw at it!' She looked up at me and was instantly distracted from her assault on the door and the crowbar that was lying dejectedly at her feet. 'Well you look nice. Where are you off to?'

'Nowhere special,' I lied. 'Just going down to the beach to do some sketching for my art assignment.' I held up my sketchpad and charcoal pencils as evidence. She raised her eyes, obviously knowing how often I wore makeup but deciding not to pry.

'OK, well don't be too late.'

'Thanks Mom, good luck with the door! Try not to hurt yourself.' I took one last look at the crowbar and headed out the front door.

Half an hour later Charlie and I were comfortably sitting on the sand at the side of the weather-beaten pylons of my run-down jetty. We both had sketchpads and pencils but instead of sketching in his book Charlie was drawing lines in the sand with a stick and watching me drawing with a pensive look on his face.

'Have you always known that you wanted to be an artist?' he asked looking at my drawing.

'Actually, I had never drawn before until Gus died. My parents started taking me to art galleries and live art shows where artists would be doing demonstrations. I could stand there for hours just watching an artist perfecting their masterpiece. There are so many artists in the city – they're like bees to a honeypot! Like Steven Paul – he was only a high school senior at my school in Brooklyn when he won a gold medal prize for his photograph of a girl and I got to watch while artists recreated this amazing photograph on this huge wall in Williamsburg – it was so inspiring to watch. After that I just knew that was what I wanted to do. I wanted to be able to create that feeling of magic for other people. There is incredible street art all over the city. Just around the corner from the giant mural of the girl there is a life-size painting by these Iranian brothers and stencil artists, Icy and Sot – they're amazing! Their use of color is perfection and the way they just share their art, they inspire me.' I realized that I had been excitedly babbling and I turned to see him studying my face and instantly blushed.

'I wish I had that kind of light-bulb moment,' he said looking towards the ocean.

'You've never felt passionate about anything?'

'Sure,' he turned and smiled at me, lifted me up off the sand and pulled me into a bear hug. 'I fancied myself a pretty good lifesaver once upon a time.' I laughed along with him. 'Truth be told I think I would be happy staying here and joining the family business – get into property development with my dad. I always loved going out to the sites with him when I was younger and the past couple of summers, with you and Gus gone, I had nothing to do so I've been working on the sites, learning what the laborers get up to. It was also a part of my probation, which is why I dropped out of school for a while. Dad thought it would do me good to spend some time with the guys, people he looks up to, so I could have some role models and people I trusted that weren't just my parents. It was the best thing he could have done. They helped to get me on the right path again. It would be amazing if Dad could do more behind the desk, designing, doing the architecture side of things, and I could be out on site.' He got lost then, wrapped up in telling me about their current project and all of the ins and outs and I realized that both Charlie and Gus would stay here forever, while my dream had always been to leave.

I wondered whether it was because they would both stay, or whether I was starting to like living here, that my resolve to move back to the city was starting to crumble ever so slightly.

# CHAPTER 26

I had taken to spending time in Poppy's lounge room. No one else seemed to be interested in coming in so it was a nice refuge from having to speak to anyone or try to figure out whether there was an axe murderer cleaning the house or cooking my dinner. I snuggled down into Poppy's old leather chair and closed my eyes to rest for a couple of minutes.

'That was my husband's favorite chair in the house.'

I recognized Poppy's voice immediately but when my eyes flew open it was still a shock to see her sitting in the leather chair next to me. I realized that I had only really seen her a handful of times away from her usual place – sitting at her dressing table looking miserable – since we had moved into the house. She smiled her warm smile and I relaxed immediately.

I thought again about all of the times that I had seen her staring out at the water and I realized that I had never seen other ghosts in the house apart from her and Gus. Gus had told me that the spirits that were not tied to the house – either from living there or dying there – would only come in or out when the clock was turned on a full moon, but surely Poppy's husband was connected to the house, so why hadn't I seen him?

'Where is he?' I asked her, hoping that I was not being too nosy.

She shook her head sadly, 'I don't know. I believe that he died in the Battle of Normandy in France, he was part of naval bombardments. Overall the battle was a success but they still lost thousands of men to the German forces. They never found his body and by the time the rest of his crew came back there were only a handful and none could remember seeing him after the landing. I have always imagined seeing his spirit coming across the water and returning to me. It's possible his spirit is dwelling in a house where he died, or he may have even crossed over. When the spirit has resolved any unfinished business it is no longer tethered to this plane. He is part of my unfinished business – just to know what happened I feel would give me some peace. You can't even imagine the suffering when you lose someone but it is never confirmed that they are gone.' She closed her eyes and in the lines on her face and the shaking in her voice I could feel some of the anguish and despair and I hoped that I would never experience that feeling. I wondered whether asking Poppy about her husband would make her sad or cheer her up. I suspected a little of both.

'What was he like?'

'He was tall and strong and handsome but so gentle and kind and loving. He always knew how to make me feel like I was the only person that ever mattered. I lived in a different time to you my dear. A lot of my friends were being paired up with people that they had never met, by their parents of course. But not me. Before we were married we were friends. I think that is important in a relationship.' I picked at a loose thread on my sweater, thinking about Charlie and Gus, and when I looked up she was smiling in a kind, knowing sort of way.

'That must have been difficult for your friends getting married to total strangers. I can't imagine that.'

'Yes, fortunately times have changed. Some of those women never got to know the men they married as they were sent overseas with the war and never came back.'

I thought about the stories Poppy used to tell Gus and me, about the soldiers coming in and out of the house, and wondered how it worked. 'Isn't there some way that you could contact him? Some of the other spirits that might have seen him?'

She shook her head and looked around the room as if seeing it all for the first time. 'I've tried. The ghosts that have come in and out of here have helped me look but so far we have not been able to find him.'

'My experience in the ghost world is limited but maybe I can help you try to find him from the non-spirit side. It's amazing the information you can get these days from the internet.'

Her face cleared a little and for once she looked even hopeful, 'That would be wonderful, you are very thoughtful Sophie.'

'Not at all, I'm happy to help. Even though it sounds

like there isn't much information available I think I'll have an easier time finding the last resting place of your husband than I will trying to uncover the truth behind your death, and trying to find the key and stop the ghosts from being unleashed on Halloween!'

It was meant to be a bit of a joke but I saw Poppy's face fall and she studied my face before voicing her concerns. 'I know that we have put a terrible burden on your shoulders Sophie and I am sorry for that. Please make sure you are careful and remember that you are dealing with someone who is mentally unstable.'

'Of course,' I said, and when she looked a little unconvinced I followed up, 'I promise I'll be careful.' She looked a fraction more placated.

'Do you have any of your husband's military records? Anything that I can use to identify him? It might be helpful when I contact the people responsible for veterans' affairs.'

She thought for a moment before her eyes widened and a stricken expression came across her face. 'All of that information would be in my husband's study.'

'OK,' I said slowly, not understanding the cause for her alarm. 'Was your husband's study cleaned out after he died?'

'No, it is exactly as he left it.'

Again I felt like I was missing something. 'Well I'll go and have a look through now then.'

She shook her head, 'You can't. It's in one of the sealed rooms.'

'Ohhh, OK, I see now. Well then how do I get the

doors open? And now that you mention those rooms, I've been wondering why they are sealed. That must be some serious superglue! They don't even budge a little. How do I get into them?'

'No one can get into those rooms. But more importantly, no one can get out. Do you still have the notebook that was with the key?'

I nodded my head, 'Yes.'

'That notebook has the details of the spirits that I have met in the rooms and when. The names with a star next to them are the occasions when I was scared. Scared for my life. There are evil spirits in those rooms Sophie, spirits of people who had no redeeming qualities when they were living. On the whole most of the spirits who enter the house are harmless but there are some that mean ill will. I worked with a local woman who understood the spirits – to draw these bad spirits into a handful of the rooms, which she then sealed with magic. You will find their names and their locations in the book. You must keep the doors sealed and never let those spirits out. You can't just go up to the doors and open them with your hands.' I thought of my mom trying to pry the doors open on my way out to meet Charlie.

'What about a crowbar?' I asked anxiously.

'Why would you do that?' she looked at me incredulous.

'Not me – my mom. She was at one of the doors a couple of days ago with a crowbar.'

She shook her head, 'That won't work. You'll need a

witch to reverse the spell and even then you need to find a way to get rid of the evil spirit inside before you even think about opening the door. You'll need to find my witch; her name is Isadora.' Remembering something she pointed to the shelving with the photo albums, 'Get me the album with the dark blue spine.'

I walked over to the bookshelf and pulled down the photo album she had been pointing to. Holding it up she nodded her head and I carried it over to the table next to where she was standing and started flicking through the photos. She glanced at each page and when she shook her head I would continue to turn. The photos must have been more recent than some of the ones I had looked at because they were in color and Poppy looked a lot older. The color from the photos had started to fade a little though and the quality didn't look very good. From the clothing I would have guessed they were from the 1980s.

'Wait, go back to the last page,' Poppy said excitedly.

I turned back and held the page open and she pointed to a woman standing with Poppy in a beautiful garden.

'That's Isadora.' As soon as I saw the lady she was pointing to I knew who she was. She was a lot younger than Poppy, maybe in her late thirties in the photo, and she was the spitting image of her granddaughter; one of my closest friends at school, who had told me about her grandmother that everyone thought was crazy, who had been institutionalized multiple times for thinking that she was talking to the spirits. It was Alice's grandmother, who Alice had told me had passed away.

'I won't be able to get help from your witch Poppy,' I said looking dismayed.

She looked at me with concern. 'Why not?'

'She has passed away. I'm friends with her granddaughter.'

'Is her grandmother her father's mother or her mother's mother?' she asked urgently.

'Her mother's.'

'Why, but that is perfect,' she said sounding excited.

'I'm confused again … what part of that is perfect?' I looked at her, incredulous.

'It is likely that she has the same gifts as her grandmother. The gift is passed on through the mother.'

I knew that Alice was aware of her grandmother's gifts and believed in her ability rather than thinking she was crazy like the rest of the townspeople that knew her, but I was sure she wasn't going be all that excited with me turning up on her doorstep and asking her if she might be a hocus pocus witch herself.

Poppy was nodding enthusiastically and I sighed; another day another challenge. 'OK, I'll ask her but I'm not sure she's going to like it.'

# CHAPTER 27

I decided the best approach would be to take up Alice's offer for dinner at her mom's restaurant and I subtly invited myself over the next time I saw her at school. She was more than happy to oblige, inviting me around that day. When I arrived I nervously checked Poppy's photo that I had taken from the album. I was unsure how Alice's mom would take my questioning in relation to her mother when it sounded like she didn't even talk about her to Alice, and they obviously had a strained relationship.

My nerves were immediately eased. Her family couldn't have been more wonderful and welcoming. Her mother opened the door to the restaurant, which was closed because it was still early, and wrapped her arm around my shoulder. 'Hello Sophie! Come in, we've heard so much about you from Alice. I'm Alice's mother, Sally.'

'Oh dear – all good things I hope!'

'Of course!' Her brother and sisters immediately pulled me into the kitchen where they were making some pasta.

'There is no such thing as a free meal here Sophie,' Sally laughed and handed me an apron.

I spent the next hour being instructed on how to

make homemade pasta, mixing a ricotta filling and then how to press the little parcels into neat little pillows. My pasta looked a bit like a three-year-old had made it but I was proud of my first attempt. Next we all whipped up a salad and a fruit punch and set the table together. Coming from a single child family I spent most of the time wishing I was one of five. I mentioned this to Alice when we were setting the table and she snorted.

'Sure, you've had ten minutes of this crazy house – come and live with us for a week and I guarantee that you would be running back to the peace and quiet of being by yourself!' Her mom shot her a look and she immediately recanted, 'Calm down Mom, of course I'm kidding … sort of. Most of the time we get along but if someone loses an item of clothing wait for the yelling to begin!'

'Do you miss being in the city Sophie?' her sister Annabelle asked. 'I wish I could go and live in the city, living in a small town is so boring.'

'Yes, I plan to move back the minute I finish school,' I nodded in agreement. 'I mean, there's nothing wrong with here …' now it was my turn to backtrack and qualify my comment because I felt everyone's eyes on me, and my conviction had certainly been waning in the past couple of days. 'But I really loved living in the city and I'd like to be an artist. To be totally honest I don't really feel like I belong in the big house that my parents are doing up.'

'How are your parents going doing up the old Westlake mansion? I don't envy them; they have a big job ahead of them.' Alice's mom said.

'Have you been to Storybook House?'

'Yes, when I was very young, my mother used to take me up there sometimes to play.'

I knew this was my opportunity and I reached down to my bag and pulled out the photo.

'Actually, I found a photo and I thought it might have been Alice's grandmother. The woman in the photo looks a lot like Alice.' I handed the photo to Alice's mother and glanced at Alice. Her face looked a little pinched and she was looking down at her food, pushing it around the plate. An uncomfortable silence fell over the table like a heavy blanket.

'Yes, that's her,' her mom nodded with a very straight poker face. 'How fantastic, where did you find it?'

'There is a wall of albums in a lounge room on the ground floor. We have a history project coming up and I thought I might write my report on the house. Everyone seems to think the place is haunted.' Sally knocked over the water glass she was reaching for and I watched her face going from showing nothing to being visibly annoyed.

'Yes, my mother would tell me those ridiculous stories too but you don't need to worry yourself Sophie, it's total rubbish!'

I could see I wasn't going to get any help on the sealed rooms front from Alice's mom so I backed down and laughing said, 'You'd better not tell the social committee at school that or they will put a gag on you. They are banking on the reputation of the house being haunted to add some atmosphere for the dance!'

She immediately thawed and laughed along with me. With a final glance at the photo of her mother she handed it back to me and lifted one of the bowls, 'More salad Sophie?'

The topic was officially closed and we started talking about when she had opened the restaurant and how she would like to open a second restaurant in the city in the next couple of years. After dinner we all pitched in to help clean up before the dinner staff arrived. Everyone gave me a hug goodbye and as Alice walked me to the gate I called out to Sally that I could be her first waitress when she opened her restaurant in the city. I had given up on the idea of raising the ghosts again for that day but when we reached the front gate Alice surprised me by turning to me and saying, 'I believe there are ghosts in your house Sophie.'

I tried to contain my excitement and remain impassive. 'Why do you say that?' I asked carefully.

'Because I've seen one there. The day of the bonfire. I'm sure of it now – I saw my grandmother, Isadora.'

'You did? Really?' My mind was doing somersaults at the idea that there was another ghost in the house. Why hadn't I seen her? What room was she in? Why hadn't she made herself known? Did Poppy know about her? I looked back up at Alice and realized that she was observing me going through the catalogue of questions in my mind.

She looked at me curiously, 'You don't seem that

surprised. You've seen her ghost haven't you? That's why you came to dinner, isn't it? You wanted to ask my mom about her?' she looked at me with excitement dancing across her eyes.

I shook my head, 'I'm sorry Alice, I haven't seen Isadora at the house.'

She picked up on my choice of words and started nodding, 'But you have seen others, haven't you?'

I nodded my head, 'Yes. There are two. One of them is Poppy, the other one is my friend Gus.'

She stared off into the distance, her own thoughts running around in her mind. 'I've been thinking about it ever since that day. I'm positive I saw her in the window – she was looking straight at me.'

I thought of the sealed rooms and an idea occurred to me. 'Why don't we ask Poppy and Gus – would you like to meet them?'

She looked nervous but excited at the same time and she only hesitated briefly before answering, 'OK, when can I come over?'

'Come tomorrow. Actually, there was something I was hoping that you could help me with.'

'Alright,' she said slowly, looking unsure now.

'Some of the rooms are sealed closed. I have been speaking to Poppy and she said your grandmother helped her to do this. Have you read anything in her books about the house?'

She looked pensive and thought. 'She does mention some things in her books about your house, I'll have to take another look. I better go in and help my mom set up for the dinner rush. I'll have to help Saturday morning too – can I come around in the afternoon?'

'Yes, that would be perfect. There is something that I will need to look into before we try to get into the room.'

I saw the glint return to Alice's eyes as I jumped on my bike and headed back to my haunted house.

# CHAPTER 28

The trip to Alice's house had gone better than I had expected but I still had work to do if we were going to solve some of these mysteries. I knew that I would have to find out more about the spirit that was trapped in Poppy's husband's study before we even thought about unsealing the room. From what Poppy said it seemed the rooms had been sealed for very serious reasons so unsealing the door was not to be taken lightly. I wondered what my mom would think if I told her why she couldn't get the door open with a simple crowbar and I wondered whether Dad had also attempted to open the doors. I knew that Poppy was convinced that the doors were impenetrable but surely with enough firepower the doors could be unsealed. Fortunately, my parents had plenty of other things going on in the house that were distracting them from focusing solely on those rooms.

I was also thinking about what Alice had said about seeing her grandma in the house that day on the beach. I would be extremely surprised if Isadora was in the house – I hadn't seen her and neither Poppy nor Gus had mentioned that she was there; in fact, I was sure that they had told me that only the spirits that were connected to the house in some way would be able to be seen in the house. But Alice was absolutely certain that the person that she had seen was her grandmother and given she bore absolutely no resemblance to Poppy I had to wonder if it was possible that Isadora was stuck in one of the sealed rooms. From Alice's description of where she had seen the apparition, it sounded like Isadora could be in the upstairs room next to Poppy's.

As soon as I got home I headed upstairs and tried the handle of the door next to Poppy's room and it was exactly like the others. If you didn't know better you would think that it had just been glued shut. I walked further down the hall and popped my head into Poppy's room. She was sitting, like she always was, at her dresser table, looking out the window.

I knocked quietly on the door and she turned around. Her face looked so sad I wanted to put my arms around her and give her a big hug but I knew that I couldn't. 'Oh, hello Sophie darling.' She straightened up and pulled her face into a smile. 'To what do I owe the pleasure of your visit?'

'I've spoken to Alice and she's going to help me.'

'That's fantastic news. If she is anything like her grandmother she'll be a valuable asset and a wonderful friend.'

'Yes, about her grandma, I was wondering whether her spirit could have ended up in this house?'

She looked at me, confused. 'I don't think so. Why would her spirit have returned to this house?'

'I don't know, but Alice thinks she may have seen her in the window of the room next door and it is one of the rooms that's sealed.'

She looked more confused. 'We never sealed the room next door. It was a nursery I think, for when my parents had more children, but my mother couldn't have any more after me so it was never used.' Standing up, she walked through the door and came back moments later. 'It is definitely sealed, I can't get in there either. Maybe we did seal it, but I can't see why we would have. I'm sorry Sophie, it's my memory – I just can't trust it during those last couple of years!' She looked dismayed again and I tried to reassure her.

'Don't worry. I'll look into it and see what I can find in your book.'

I walked down the hall to my bedroom and, making sure that no one was around, I closed the door behind me, climbed back up to the bookshelf and took down Poppy's notebook from its hiding place.

I slowly looked through each page for any references to the study and also any information regarding the room next door to Poppy's that would confirm her suspicion that it had been a nursery.

At the beginning of the notebook there were a couple of notes that mentioned the study but it must have been before the room was sealed with the bad spirit inside because there was no sign of a star next to any of the rooms earlier on in the book.

As I flicked through I wondered what Poppy meant

when she said that they drew the spirit into the room. How did they do that? Did that mean that if you had something powerful enough you could draw the spirit into something else? Something like a box or a suitcase, and trap them in that instead?

Unlike Poppy, who had lived in the house her entire life and probably had understood that the spirits lived there for almost as long, my understanding of the spirit world was a matter of months. Alice was arguably better equipped than I was, having had the benefit of speaking to her grandma about the spirits before she died. I had no idea how I was going to try to unseal the room and get the spirit out before my mom gave up on the crowbar and tried something with a bit more firepower.

I had just conjured up the vision of my mom with a chainsaw when I spotted the star on a page that mentioned the study. The name next to it was Diana Faraday. I got on my computer and tried to search the internet for references to the name but nothing came up. I glanced again through the book looking for a mention of the nursery but there was nothing in there.

Armed with only a name I headed off to the library to do some research. A kindly looking librarian offered to help me look through the records, which was fortunate given there were rows and rows of them. I looked around the library and realized there were no other people in there so she was probably grateful for the distraction.

There had been dozens of Faradays that had lived in the area but only one Diana. She was born in 1890 and died in 1918 so she had only been twenty-eight years old when she died.

'What terrible thing happened to you?' I said quietly, under my breath.

The librarian, who had been checking another section, wandered past and overheard me. With her head still buried in the folder she was holding she said, 'From the looks of it she was hanged,' and held up the death records from 1918.

'What for?' I asked, completely horrified.

'These records say that she murdered a baby by the name of …' her voice trailed off as she looked through the report. 'Oh, here it is, yes, Edward Westlake. He was eighteen months old. There are old news articles on the computer in the back. I can set it up for you if you like. There might be something in there.'

'Thank you, that would be great.' I thought of little baby Edward with the same last name as Poppy. As far as I knew there were no other relatives that had lived in the house with small children. Could it be that Poppy had been wrong? Had the nursery next door to her bedroom been used by a baby brother that she appeared to know nothing about, her baby brother who had been murdered?

After forty-five minutes of scrolling through the articles from 1918 I found what I was looking for. From the records it looked like Diana had been a nanny to little Edward. She had come with good references and she gave no explanation why she had killed the infant. The reporter had interviewed her family who said she had been made to give up her own baby boy a year before going to work with the Westlakes, and they believed she may have suffered a mental breakdown from the pain of looking after another child so soon after giving up her own.

I wondered if it was possible that Poppy had known she had an older brother who had been murdered but had perhaps forgotten. On the other hand, Edward had been born years before Poppy. It was possible that she was never even told what had happened. It was also possible that her parents never mentioned the baby but were so haunted by his death that they kept his room just the way it had been before he died.

Maybe the key to getting rid of Diana's ghost haunting the study was not to trap it in something at all but to find her son and help her cross over. Perhaps her unfinished business was to know what happened to her son after he was taken from her.

I spent the next four hours poring through old records and researching until I had to leave to meet Alice at the house. I was armed and ready with the information that I thought might help us in our attempts to calm the ghost of Diana Faraday.

# CHAPTER 29

Alice was waiting for me at her gate. Her face looked excited but nervous and she had a backpack that looked like it was overflowing with information. As soon as we got back to the house I took her into the secret garden, because I knew no one would bother us in there and we would not be overheard. After she had finished marveling at the beauty of the garden we spread our information out on a picnic rug I had taken from the house and she looked at me expectantly.

'OK, tell me everything from the beginning,' she said.

I told her about what had happened with Gus, meeting Poppy and finding and losing the necklace, about the book that reported each of the ghost sightings and about the spirit visits in each of the rooms. Her eyes widened when I explained my dilemma with the Halloween ball being in the house on the same night that the spirits might come out and trying to find out who in the house was a killer. I also told her what I had found out at the library about Diana Faraday and the baby that she had murdered.

'OK your turn, what have you found?' I asked

looking at all of the material that she had brought with her and hoping that the answers we needed were in it.

'Wow, that's a tough act to follow! So I went through all of my grandma's stuff that I managed to salvage from her house before Mom could just throw petrol on the house and burn it down!' I raised my eyebrows, questioning whether she actually did this, and Alice laughed and shook her head.

'There were a couple of mentions in some earlier books but nothing that would help us, and then I found this diary.' She pulled out a notebook and it had a photo of the house on the front of it. The photo was obviously taken long ago as the house still looked grand and well maintained, not the dilapidated mess that stood next to us.

I opened the book and started flicking through the pages. At the top of each entry was a date and the name of a room, followed by a detailed description of the spirits that Poppy and Isadora had encountered. I had brought Poppy's book down from its hiding spot in my bedroom and started comparing the dates and entries. 'This is amazing Alice! Poppy left me this notebook that has the dates and names but not a lot of other information. Not like Isadora's journal – this is a goldmine!' I flicked through the book looking for the study and found it towards the back. It described Isadora's experience with Diana Faraday. She sounded like a very angry spirit. Isadora's notes indicated that she was able to move things around the room, smashing vases and throwing books. From Isadora's description it seemed she had decided to try to seal her in the room as a result of her attempting to stab Isadora with a letter opener that was sitting on George's desk.

At the very back of the journal there were notes on how she drew the ghosts into the room with crystals and spells that were used to seal the rooms so that the ghosts could not come out and people could not come in. There didn't seem to be any notes on how to reverse the spell but Alice had gone through some of Isadora's other journals and found a list of spells and reversing spells.

Alice pulled a glass jar out of her bag that was the size of her hand and looked like it had previously held jam but now it had some long, narrow, glass-looking clear crystals at the bottom of it. 'They are Lemurian seeded crystals,' she explained. 'I think they are the stones that my grandma used to draw the spirits into the room that they are in. I figured we could try to draw them into an object, then they won't take up a room.'

'Do you think that will work?' I eyed the jar dubiously.

'It is a glass jar with crystals in it, I really doubt it,' she said dryly, and we both started to laugh.

I looked back down at the book and kept flicking through the pages looking for some more ideas but like Alice had said, I couldn't find anything else that might be useful. A few months ago I would have laughed hysterically at the thought of ghosts and witches and even though the rooms had clearly been sealed shut by something a little stronger than superglue, I still had some doubt as to the power of magic to seal a room closed.

'God I hope that this works,' I said.

'Me too,' Alice agreed, looking as nervous as I felt.

A thought occurred to me and I looked back through Poppy's journal and then Isadora's. 'I haven't been able to find anything in these books about an evil spirit in the room where you saw your grandmother. Perhaps it would be best to try to open that room first. If she is in there she might be able to help us.'

'Absolutely,' she agreed, nodding her head vigorously. I don't think either of us was ready to try to deal with the ghostly spirit of a book-throwing baby murderer.

'But first I think you should meet Gus and Poppy. Are you ready?'

'Ready as I will ever be to meet two ghosts!' she answered nervously, pushing all of her stuff back into the bag.

We walked upstairs to Poppy's bedroom, where I had told Poppy and Gus to wait so I could introduce them to Alice. I wasn't sure who was more nervous: Alice, whose hands had started to shake at the thought of coming face to face with ghosts, or me. I hadn't completely decided whether I believed what I was seeing was actually there and not just a figment of an overactive imagination. I knew that if I had mentioned the ghosts to my parents they would have laughed at me initially and then sent me to a psychiatrist. What if Alice couldn't see them and she went to the school, my parents, or a medical professional and told everyone how crazy I was. I had to believe that the Alice I knew would never do that, and the fact that she was convinced she had seen Isadora in the house made me believe that she would see Gus and Poppy too.

We reached the top of the stairs and walked towards Poppy's room. Putting my hand on the doorknob I turned to Alice, 'You don't have to be scared, they were both really lovely people and they are wonderfully nice ghosts. I actually can't believe I said that sentence, did it sound as crazy to you as it sounded in my head,' Alice nodded and smiled, 'It's OK,' she encouraged, 'I'm ready.'

With that bit of encouragement I took a deep breath and opened the door. Poppy was sitting at her dressing table and Gus was standing by the window looking nervous too. They both turned to look when we walked through the door and I quickly closed it behind me and looked at Alice's face. Her head was tilted to the side and she was looking in the direction of where Gus was standing. I looked at her face and then at Gus and then back at Alice.

'Can … can you see him?' I asked her nervously.

She turned to look at me, 'Well … you never said how good looking your ghost friend was.' We all laughed and immediately the tension was broken.

'Hi, I'm Alice,' she stepped forward with her hand out as if to shake Gus's hand and then looking down at Gus's hand and then her own, she shrugged her shoulders and did a small wave instead.

'Hi Alice, I'm Gus,' Gus said, waving back.

'And I'm Poppy,' Poppy said, standing up and walking towards Alice. 'I must say you bear a striking resemblance to your grandmother.'

'Yes, a lot of people have said that. I think my mother

finds that particularly annoying. They didn't get along very well when she was alive. Speaking of my grandmother, do you remember if she ever told you of a spell to seal the spirits into something other than a room; maybe an object like a jar or box? We found lots of notes on how the spirits were drawn into the rooms and how the rooms were sealed but never anything on sealing them into an object.'

Poppy shook her head, 'No, sorry. I do think she looked into drawing the spirits into an object but I think she decided it would be too difficult.'

Alice turned to look at me, 'Well we'll just have to go off what we have in the other books and give it a go.'

Turning to me Poppy asked, 'Did you find what you were looking for at the library about the ghost in my husband's study?'

'Yes actually, I did. It was a woman by the name of Diana Faraday. She was hanged for murder.' I hesitated but decided to continue. 'She killed someone in this house. A baby.' As I said the words I watched Poppy's face to see whether any recollection came across but she just looked shocked.

'Oh! How terrible! How could a woman do such a thing?'

'I have no idea,' I said sadly, wondering how I was going to break it to her that she was never an only child, that the child the woman had murdered was her own flesh and blood.

'Ready Sophie?' Alice pulled me out of my thoughts and I turned around to look at her. Her voice was shaky

and she looked even less enthusiastic than she sounded.

'Ready as I will ever be! Let's go.'

We walked back down the hallway leaving Poppy and Gus in Poppy's room. Alice opened the notebook and lay it open at her feet, lifted her hands to the door and checking the words again mumbled quietly '*Aperio.*' We both looked at the door expectantly.

'Did it work?' I asked her looking at the door, unsure what to expect – whether it would pop open like the safe in the secret passageway. 'I don't know,' Alice sounded unconvinced. I reached out and tried to turn the handle. The door didn't budge. I tuned to look at Alice and shook my head. She let out a deep breath, relaxed her shoulders, rubbed her hands together and, closing her eyes, she held her hands out again and this time said the words with strength in her voice. We heard a noise like the sound of a key turning in a lock and we both looked at each other with shock on our faces.

'I think it worked that time!' I said excitedly.

She reached her hand out to the doorknob and this time it turned like a well-oiled handle. We pushed the door inwards and it creaked as it opened. We both stood there on the threshold to the door peering in, not yet ready to step into the room. The floor was covered with a thick layer of dust that looked as though it hadn't been disturbed in a hundred years. The wall to the right was covered with soft baby-blue wallpaper that had little hand-drawn white feathers floating down the walls and into the crib that was pushed against the wall. There was a circle-shaped royal blue rug in the middle of the room and a small rocking horse over left next to a chest of drawers. Beside the window there was a small table and an armchair and in the armchair was a woman who looked just like Alice.

# CHAPTER 30

'What took you so long?' said the woman with a deep husky voice, and I spun around to look at Alice who had tears streaming down her face. She ran into the room and tried to wrap her arms around her grandmother but she couldn't, and as soon as she realized this she stepped back and put her hands over her face and cried harder. I rubbed her back gently as she sobbed.

'There, there, my darling child, there's no need to cry!' Isadora said softly, her face next to Alice's as she knelt down. She looked up at me and I smiled and stepped forward, putting a reassuring hand around Alice's shoulder and pulling her to me. 'You must be Isadora?'

'Yes and I think you might be Sophie.' I nodded but was a little confused as to how she knew my name. She smiled at me, her beautiful big chestnut eyes glistening with tears from seeing her granddaughter.

'You might not remember me but I came over sometimes when you stayed with Poppy when you were little.' As soon as she said it I could vaguely see in my mind a big group of women walking through the house when I was younger. They would sit in the big living room, set up at little card tables, and drink port, giggling away like schoolgirls and playing their hands with the confidence of seasoned professionals.

'The bridge club?' I asked looking up at her face.

She nodded her head, 'Yes, that's right. But of course I would do other things when I came over,' she smiled, gesturing toward the door.

'How did you get stuck in this room? Why is the door sealed?' Alice asked, although having stopped crying, the remaining tears were still making pathways down her face.

'Well that is a long story, where shall I begin? I guess by telling you that there is another spirit in this room. He is sleeping at the moment.' Isadora gestured to the cot and Alice and I looked at each other alarmed. Walking over to the cot I looked down at the sleeping baby and then looked back at Isadora. I thought back to what I had been reading at the library, 'Edward Westlake?'

She looked confused and she shook her head, 'I never found out who he was. Poppy said she heard noises in the room next door to her sometimes – like the sound of a baby crying. I became obsessed before I died with trying to release his spirit and when I died I found myself in this room and the door was sealed. I don't know what happened. I must have said the wrong spell.' A look of recognition came across her face. 'So this little boy is …'

'Poppy's brother? Yes,' I nodded, 'but I'm fairly certain that she knew nothing about him.'

'Grandma, how do you release a spirit?' Alice asked, obviously thinking about the ghost that we were going to face downstairs next.

'You have to show it the light. The good that has come in life after they have gone, and help them finish anything left unfinished. Anything that is holding them here. Bad memories, wrongs that need to be righted – there is something that is holding them here and that needs to be resolved before they can be released. In saying that, I think that some spirits just want to stay here and never cross over.'

'What if we introduce baby Edward to his sister?' I asked, glancing at the door and thinking of what Poppy would think if she knew she had an older brother.

Isadora nodded, 'Yes that could work. I have never encountered the spirit of a baby before.'

Excusing myself I left Isadora and Alice to catch up on lost time. I walked back down the hall to Poppy's room and knocked on the door. Turning the handle I peered around the door expecting to see her sitting at the dressing table but she wasn't there. I was relieved to see that Gus had gone too because I thought it was a personal conversation that I wanted to have with Poppy alone. I stepped into the room as she was walking out of her wardrobe.

'Oh! Hello Sophie, did you manage to unseal the door? Was Isadora there?'

'Yes, we did,' I nodded. 'And yes she was there, but actually she wasn't alone. There is a baby in the room also.'

I looked to her face for any kind of recollection but she just looked confused.

'A baby?'

'Yes, a little boy. Your brother, actually, as it turns out.'

She shook her head, 'But I didn't have any brothers or sisters. My mother told me she couldn't have any more children after I was born.'

I studied her face and considered whether or not it was a good idea to tell her. I decided that the shock and possible grief of finding out about having a sibling would have been worth it to me; and in the end I decided the shock wasn't going to kill her when she was already dead! 'Well, I'm not really sure about after you were born but this little boy died before you were born – he is your older brother. Do you remember me speaking about the woman in the study, Diana Faraday?'

I watched her face as the realization sunk in of what I was telling her. 'She was hanged for murder? Yes, you said she murdered a baby. A baby.'

I went to sit beside her as she processed the information. Even if I could not comfort her by holding her hand I could make sure she knew I was there for her.

'She murdered my brother?' she said slowly. She held her hand to her mouth and it looked like there were tears forming in her eyes, and then she started to smile and let out a short laugh. 'Now that you say that there were a lot of things that happened when I was young that I really didn't understand. I think I understand now. Why my parents were so protective.' She was nodding to herself, seemingly recalling memories from a time decades before I was born. 'I once took a pillow and blanket from the house and slept in the sunken garden because my mother and I had a terrible fight. I was only ten and by the time I went back to the house in the morning they had the National Guard searching the entire east coast of America for me. My mother hugged me so tightly and for so long I thought she would never let go.'

I sat quietly and waited for her to fully absorb the information. She appeared to be vacillating between extreme grief, happiness and confusion and when she finally looked back up at me she had questioning eyes.

'Is he … can I see him?'

'Of course. He's having a nap in his crib. Isadora said she was trying to release his spirit before she died because you could hear a baby crying.'

'Yes, I remember now,' Poppy nodded in agreement, in a rare moment of clarity about the not-so-distant past. 'We thought that maybe if he sees you then he'll be able to find his peace and move on, to be with your parents.'

We walked slowly down the hallway and I moved quietly into the bedroom and looked down into the cot to find Edward still peacefully sleeping.

'Poppy!' Isadora walked the five steps to the door and pulled Poppy into a tight embrace.

'Isadora, I'm so sorry! I had no idea that you were trapped in here! I guess I have been so deep in my own thoughts these days.'

'Not a problem – I have had wonderful company!' Isadora chortled, moving happily back into the room and gesturing towards the cot.

I looked down again to see if all the noise of their happy reunion had woken baby Edward, but his eyes were still firmly shut, his soft pink lips puckered. I turned and saw Poppy, still standing at the doorway, looking unsure, and I nodded to her in encouragement. She looked into my face for a long moment, and then at Alice and Isadora, whom she smiled at, and nodded solemnly. Taking a deep breath, she steeled herself and stepped into the room, looking around her as if taking in her surroundings for the first time, and then walked slowly over to the cot.

Taking another deep breath she looked at my face again and her lips curled into a half smile like she was nervous but excited and then she slowly looked down and as she did her face melted.

'Isn't he beautiful!' she said, her voice almost a gasp, 'sleeping so peacefully!'

As if he had heard the sound of her voice Edward's mouth twitched at the edges before he opened his eyes and looked up at Poppy's face. His face broke into a broad smile and he wriggled around in his cot and stretched his arms above his head before reaching his arms up to her. She stood back as if checking that he wasn't reaching up to someone else. Realizing it was her, she put her hands down carefully into his crib and lifted his little body into her arms, gently, holding him close to her with tears running down her face.

'I don't even know his name. What is his name?' she asked me, wiping away her tears.

'Edward Theodore Westlake.'

She held him slightly back from her with trepidation, as if she never wanted to end their snuggle, looked into his eyes and whispered quietly to him, 'Your name is the same as our daddy's. I bet that he loved you!' It was like they were the only people in the room. Their eyes locked together, Poppy gently cooing to Edward and him gurgling back.

Alice, Isadora and I quietly moved out into the hallway and left Poppy to have some time alone with baby Edward. I led the way into my room so that Alice and Isadora could have some time with each other.

With Poppy snuggling baby Edward and Alice giving Isadora a detailed run down of everything that was happening with her family I decided we could postpone the confrontation with the ghost of Diana Faraday to another day.

# CHAPTER 31

All of the amazing family reunions had me wandering around the house in search of my own family but instead I found a note on the kitchen table from Mom saying that they had gone into town to meet with a plumber. I walked down to the beach and breathed in the fresh air.

As I stood, looking out at the water I thought about mortality and what happens when you die. It seemed to me that all the ghosts I had met were in limbo: not with the living and not quite with the dead. So much for eternal rest; it seemed to have totally bypassed Gus, Poppy, Diana, Isadora and even baby Edward, who couldn't have done a thing wrong being only a baby, I thought sadly, shaking my head. How were we supposed to help him get his happily ever after? And what was the unfinished business of the others? Obviously Diana's would be to know what happened to her son, Poppy's must be that she could not let go until she found out what happened to her husband, Isadora must have been trapped in that room. I couldn't imagine why Gus was still here.

'Penny for your thoughts?' a deep voice said from behind me and I felt Charlie's warm arms wrap around me from behind. I could feel his breath on the back of my neck which sent shivers of pleasure down my spine and when he nuzzled his face into the side of my face I could feel him smiling. I could stand here with him forever I decided and my face blushed scarlet at how deeply I was falling in love with him, for I felt certain he would never feel as strongly for me.

'Just pondering life and what happens to us when we die.'

'Well that is timely,' he said, which caused me to panic mildly; had he known what I was doing inside with the ghosts? Even worse, had he seen Gus?

'Would you consider going on a trip with me that may result in your premature death?' he continued with a quiet chuckle next to my ear.

Still mildly confused and thrown off guard I turned around and asked, 'And where might this trip be to?'

'Nowhere terrible my beautiful neighbor, my brother has asked me to bring his motorbike into the city. I thought you might like to come for a ride with me. No need to worry either,' he said trying to smooth out my frown lines with one of his fingers but failing, 'I was only slightly joking about the premature death part – I'm actually a very good driver. Do you trust me?' He raised his eyebrows at me and I reached out and pretended to smack him in the arm. With his quick reflexes he took my arm, kissed the back of my hand and then pulled me closed to him, leaning his forehead against mine, so close that I could smell his breath and all I wanted to do was kiss him, but I hesitated. I had never been on the back of a motorbike before and was embarrassed to admit that the thought was actually quite exciting. Thinking about my parents, I knew they wouldn't approve but Charlie had just offered me a trip back to my sanctuary and the chance to spend time with him and I couldn't say no.

'I trust you,' I said pulling back and smiling. 'Give me ten minutes OK? I'll grab a couple of things and meet you out the front of your place.' I moved to start walking up to my house but Charlie, still holding my arm, pulled me back into a tight embrace and then, leaning back, kissed me gently on the lips. My heart fluttered and I felt myself go weak at the knees.

'Just wanted to do that so you don't change your mind,' he winked at me. 'See you soon,' he said, turning and running back up to his house. As I watched him I realized that he was wearing his gray hooded jumper that I had worn the night he had rescued me from the water. The jumper had been swimming on me but on him it stretched slightly, emphasizing his muscles.

As if I would change my mind, I thought, smiling to myself. I would use any excuse to spend more time with Charlie. I started walking up to the house in case he turned around and caught me in the act, watching him. Thankfully I had because when he had almost reached his back door he turned around and yelled back, 'Sophie? Don't worry about a jacket, I have one for you to wear.'

Inside, I popped my head in on Alice and told her she could stay as long as she liked, my parents wouldn't be back for a while, and grabbed a couple of things from my room.

'OK' she said, and barely glancing around she continued telling her grandma a story about what sounded like something her mother had done with a hose and Isadora's old house. They both let out cackles of laughter as I closed the door. I grabbed my keys and phone and pulled on a thin sweater to wear under the jacket that Charlie said he had for me. I touched my lips again, feeling his kiss still lingering.

When I walked around the corner of the house he was standing next to a shiny black motorbike holding a black leather jacket and a helmet. He already had a similar black leather jacket pulled on over the top of his gray sweatshirt and if possible, he looked even better in leather. I felt my pulse quicken as I looked at the motorbike. It looked like it had never been ridden before. The body was a shiny black with the exhaust pipes curving up the back of the seat, the wheels were black with red lines curving around the inner circle of the wheel and the seat did not have a scratch on the perfect black leather. In a word it looked fast. 'Wow!' was all I could manage as I stood there with my mouth hanging open.

He handed me a black helmet and leather jacket, which I pulled on.

'Ready?' he asked

I looked at the bike and then looked down at the helmet that I was holding starting to feel anxious. Sensing my hesitation he ducked down so that he could look me in the eye. 'Have you ever been on one of these before?

My face went crimson. 'Sure I went on one when … And also there was … no, actually, never.'

'I will drive safely, Scout's honor,' he said, holding his hand up in mock salute. His face looked so sweet and sincere and I really didn't want to miss out on a chance to spend time with him so I took a deep breath, gave myself a mental shake and slid the helmet firmly down on my head. Charlie gently helped me fasten it so that it gripped lightly beneath my chin. He gave me a squeeze around my hips, whispered into the side of my helmet 'Hold on tight' and then turned back to the bike and threw his leg over. Zipping up the jacket I took another deep breath and climbed onto the back, sliding into place behind Charlie I actually felt snug and secure. He pulled my arms around his back and after turning the key he revved the engine and took off down the driveway.

At least if I did die I knew a handful of ghosts that I could have fun with in the afterlife, I thought to myself dryly, as the sound of the motorbike roared in my ears, and I realized that I was closing my eyes, holding my breath and squeezing Charlie so hard I was probably cutting off his circulation. I loosened my grip, let go of my breath and slowly opened my eyes. As I saw the road rushing past us I tightened my grip again slightly but I heard a peel of laughter and realized it was my own.

I spent most of the drive laughing and by the time we reached the city my face was sore from smiling. We pulled up outside a beautiful red-brick building in the heart of

Tribeca that had an art gallery on the ground floor. Of course his brother would live in the most expensive and trendy part of New York City I thought to myself with a cringe. I wasn't sure I wanted to meet someone who was likely to be just as attractive as Charlie but even more intimidating being older.

'Sounded like someone enjoyed themselves,' Charlie said with smirk.

'Are you kidding? That was incredible! I'm actually disappointed we're not going back on it! Speaking of which, I only just realized we have to get back; how are we getting back?'

'Don't you worry about that, I have it all sorted,' he said mysteriously as he walked towards the sidewalk. I could see the entry of the apartments above but instead he moved towards the entry for the art gallery below and pulling my hand, he walked through the entrance with me trailing behind him.

The artwork was magnificent. As we walked through the gallery I was drawn to the incredible works of Dustin Yellin and Mickalene Thomas. Looking closely, I realized with shock that they all looked like originals. With my head spinning at the thought of the cost of all the pieces in the gallery we reached the counter at the back where the owner was sitting.

'Bonjour Monsieur Charles!' The owner kissed the air around Charlie's face in a dramatic display of a greeting. He was dressed in a tailored black suit which would have made him look like a banker or a lawyer had it not been for the frilly white shirt that was popping out over the top, and his black hair styled into a gravity-defying wave on top of his head. It almost looked like a theatrical wig. 'And you must be Miss Sophie,' he said turning his attention to me. He subtly gave my outfit a quick once over and I had the feeling he was distinctly underwhelmed by the lack of style he found in his examination.

'Hello,' I said sounding unsure. How did this unusual character know my name? Luckily it seemed that he was anticipating my confusion and he guided me towards a door at the back of the store.

'We have a wonderful surprise in store for you!' he said enthusiastically. Charlie, who seemed to be well aware of this surprise nudged me to follow the peculiar man and followed behind me, chuckling quietly to himself at the look of concern mixed with confusion on my face.

When we got to the back of the store the gallery owner stood back and ushered me towards a passageway. I turned around to look at Charlie and he smiled encouragingly. I walked into the narrow corridor that was made almost impossible to squeeze through due to all of the paintings leaning up against the wall with bubble wrap on them. I thought of the masterpieces in Poppy's hidden safe and wondered what the odd gallery owner would do to get a hold of those sales commissions. When we squeezed out at the end there was a slim, chic-looking woman in her early twenties sitting at a desk, wearing designer glasses and tapping away at a keyboard. She looked up when we popped out of the hall of paintings and looked approvingly towards Charlie, suspiciously at me, and then behind us at the gallery owner who barked out an order to her: 'Sara go out the front. I'll be back down in ten minutes.'

As he ushered us up a staircase I could hear her grumbling behind me and when I turned around to glance at Charlie I noticed her appraising his backside. This day could not get stranger if I found a ghost in the gallery, I thought to myself. We moved up three more flights of stairs and just when I felt my thighs beginning to burn in protest we reached the top of the building and Pierre (not his name but the name I had decided to give him because it sounded like something a French art dealer might be called and I hadn't been introduced to him), pushed open the heavy metal door to go outside. The sky was a perfect clear blue and after the darkness of the staircase I had to shield my eyes for several seconds from the bright sunlight that reflected off the rooftop. Once my eyes adjusted to the glare I stood looking around me in complete shock.

The 360-degree views of the city from the rooftop were breathtaking but the rooftop where I stood was even more so. There had to be a hundred different flowers and plants laid out before me. It was like a secret garden oasis in the middle of the city. I carefully stepped down the decked steps to the courtyard below that had low-lying hydrangeas and camellias on either side. Down the end of the path I could see two bench seats facing each other, surrounded on either side by bright red rose bushes and a water feature that created a peaceful tinkling sound.

There were two people sitting on one of the seats

talking to each other but before I could make out their faces I breathed in and a beautiful smell caught my nose. Turning around to the doorway that we had walked through I could see that even that was covered in jasmine vines that were producing the most amazing perfume.

I reached out and pulled a sprig of it to my nose, closing my eyes and the smell instantly took me to the secret garden at Poppy's house. A memory of pulling the tiny flowers off the branches and sucking out the nectar with Gus came to the surface and I fought back the sadness that I could feel pulling me down. No, I thought, I can't be sad in this most beautiful place, in the city that I love, next to a guy that I could feel myself falling in love with.

I opened my eyes and was surprised to see that Charlie was no longer beside me but had walked down the other end of the garden with Pierre and they were speaking to the mystery guests, who were sitting at the table. They stood up and pulled up a big blank canvas, and now that my eyes had adjusted fully I noticed that around them they had set up paint pots, spray cans and other blank canvases leaning up against the walls.

My curiosity was piqued and I held on to my sprig of jasmine and my memories while I walked down the pathway to see who it was they were speaking to. My surprises had not yet finished it seemed, and as I reached the tables I came face to face with Icy and Sot – the Iranian street artists that I had mentioned to Charlie as being some of my artistic idols.

I was so starstruck I could barely stammer out a hello

when Pierre slapped Charlie on the back and, telling him to make sure he sent his mother over to spend more money at his gallery, took his leave. As he left he did a short bow in front of me and said with a wink, 'I look forward to seeing what you produce Miss Sophie. Perhaps one day I could have the honor of representing your artwork.' I managed to stammer out a thank you and turned to look at Charlie, gaping.

'Great to meet you Sophie,' Sot said and shook my hand warmly. 'We heard that you liked some of our pieces and wondered if you'd like to help us with our next piece.'

'Are you kidding? I'd love to!'

The next forty-five minutes I was completely engrossed watching Icy and Sot demonstrate and explain their techniques to me, and I was able to help them apply some of the paints and stencil work. I was so engrossed that I completely forgot where I was and by the time that we had finished the sun was starting to go down. Even though I was desperate to stay and absorb more of their knowledge I realized I would have to get home. I reluctantly turned to Charlie who had popped out during the session to return the motorbike to his brother.

I walked out of our art lesson on a cloud of happiness. 'That was incredible! Thank you so much Charlie! You are full of surprises!'

'One more to go!' he said as he held the door open to a car that had pulled up out the front.

Charlie watched my face as the car weaved through streets and I tried to get a bearing on where we were heading. As soon as we got closer to the river I began to suspect I knew the destination and if I was right, I was not going to be happy.

# CHAPTER 32

'How are we getting home?' I asked Charlie nervously and he began to chuckle again.

'I feel like you're getting a real thrill from torturing me but I have to tell you now if you're planning on taking me in a helicopter you need to know that I am *really* afraid of heights! Also, I think you should know that I have never been in a helicopter before.' I squeaked out the last part of my sentence as we got closer to the helipads sitting next to the river.

'You had never been on a motorbike before and you *loved* that,' he reminded me.

It was getting late and my parents would start to get worried if I wasn't home soon. I knew that a helicopter would be an extremely quick way to get back to the Hamptons but my hands broke out in a nervous sweat and I felt a lump rising in my throat.

'Don't worry,' Charlie said, trying to calm me, 'you can close your eyes and just hold my hand.'

The car pulled up next to a huge-looking helicopter. As I gingerly climbed out of the car I could see the pilot sitting in the cockpit, looking down at the instrument panel in front of him. The rotor blades had already started their slow looping around and the engine was so loud I could barely hear my own thoughts. I knew that I should be walking towards the helicopter but my feet felt like they were stuck in wet cement. I eyed off the helicopter suspiciously. From where I stood it looked like a big black coffin with razors rotating around the roof, and Charlie's dad's company logo on the doors.

While I stood there and debated the two-hour drive versus the twenty-minute flight and certain death, Charlie had a quick word with the pilot and then came back to where I was standing like a mannequin. He took my face in his hands and looked into my eyes, blocking my view of the helicopter momentarily. 'There is nothing to worry about. I'll be with you the whole time, OK?'

He registered a slight weakening of my resolve so he took my hand and led me over to the door. As he helped me into the helicopter I looked up and could see the blades moving faster and wondered macabrely how many people had their heads chopped off by helicopter blades. I climbed over into the soft leather seat and grabbed for the seat belt, fumbling clumsily with the clasp. Charlie climbed in after me and gently took it from my hands, easily clipping it into place, pulling the straps tighter and securing me in my seat. After Charlie strapped himself in he reached over and took my hand in his. I smiled nervously and looked out the window over the river. 'Please God, let us not crash!' I thought and as the door slammed shut I closed my eyes tightly. I felt the helicopter lurch off the ground and closed my eyes tighter still.

I felt Charlie's hand gently touch my face and his lips press softly against mine. As soon as he pulled back from our kiss I opened my eyes to see his face right next to mine. He pointed at his eyes and then pointed outside encouraging me to look outside. He squeezed my hand reassuringly and even though I couldn't hear him over the roar of the helicopter motor and blades I could see his lips mouthing the word 'amazing.' 'Look!' he mouthed and pointed outside again. I reluctantly took my eyes away from his face and glanced quickly outside.

He was right – it was incredible. All the lights sparkled like a blanket of diamonds and I could see the city rising up into the night sky.

We moved low over the Chrysler building and Central Park, watching the wind from the helicopter blow through the trees. We flew so close to office buildings I could see people sitting at their desks finishing up their work for the day. I moved closer to the window trying to see the river below. The Brooklyn Bridge appeared and I motioned to Charlie, who was looking over my shoulder, where my neighborhood was. I traced the outline of the bigger buildings to where I knew my house was and felt myself getting a little emotional at the thought of strangers walking through the house, cooking on our stove and filling the house up with their furniture, their family and their smells. I wondered whether they had found the indents in the wall next to my bedroom door where my parents had tracked my growth over the years or whether they had repaired the crack in the terracotta tiles of the kitchen where I had dropped my mom's mortar and pestle.

Charlie must have asked the pilot to take a scenic trip past my neighborhood because I knew it would not have been on the flight path. We veered back around and headed towards the coast. I kept my head pressed against the glass trying to track the landmarks all the way back to Poppy's.

The pilot touched down and, as had been the case in the morning my face was sore from smiling. Charlie had organized a car to pick us up and he dropped me home at least thirty minutes before my parents pulled up in the Volvo. Alice had left a note on my desk thanking me for helping reunite her with her grandma.

'How was your day?' Mom asked as she walked into the kitchen where I was devouring Marcel's latest creation, slow-cooked lamb shanks with mash potatoes and green beans.

'Great! How was your day?' I asked quickly, trying to avoid any awkward follow-up questions that would require me to lie. It worked. She started ranting about how expensive plumbers were and how Dad should maybe retrain so that they could afford the renovations required to get the building up to code. I thought guiltily about the money I knew was hidden in the safe, not to mention the priceless gems, paintings and antiques hidden in the passage safe. I still hadn't thought about how I could slip that into conversation but I knew I needed to do it soon.

After her rant Mom headed off for bed claiming fatigue, but I suspected that she was going to have a walk through the house to perform another review of the bathroom situation, so I used the opportunity to climb the stairs to my bedroom and retreat into my cocoon of blankets, smiling at the memory of my amazing afternoon with Charlie.

'You look very happy about something.' I opened one eye and saw Gus's face looking suspiciously at me from the other side of the covers.

'Hey Gus.' I immediately felt guilty like I had been caught doing something I shouldn't.

'So, you guys are hanging out again are you?' He gestured to the window in the direction of Charlie's house. He must have been watching me out the window.

'Yes we are.' I closed my eyes and pretended to go to sleep. Neither Gus nor Charlie were my boyfriend and yet I felt that when I was with one I was cheating on the other.

'Was it a date?' his eyes narrowed as he waited for my response.

'I don't know. He didn't call it a date.' He seemed to be mildly satisfied with that response until his next question occurred to him.

'Did you two kiss?'

'Yes we did. Not that it is any of your business,' I said and immediately regretted how defensive I sounded. Gus wasn't my boyfriend and he wasn't my dad. I didn't understand why he was being so jealous.

'Well if that's the way you feel perhaps I should pop over there and let him know that you've been sleeping with me the past couple of weeks.' My eyes flew open.

'Don't you dare!' I squealed, sitting upright in bed. Gus immediately disappeared and I lay back down, wide awake, wondering if he could really go over to Charlie's house and if he did whether Charlie would see him. I stayed awake for another two hours waiting to hear screaming coming from Charlie's house or for Gus to come back, but he didn't.

# CHAPTER 33

He didn't come back for the next two nights either and I hated to admit it – especially to Gus – but I didn't sleep nearly as well without him there. I kept quiet and hoped that he would retake his place in my bed at night.

The lack of sleep wasn't helping me solve the problem that we had with the sealed rooms either. After having a serious conversation with her grandma, Alice and I had spent every opportunity over the past two days with our heads buried in a variety of books and school computers hoping to find more about how to trap or at least calm bad-tempered spirits but we weren't having much luck. Isadora was concerned that Diana Faraday was a very dangerous spirit and if we unleashed her it could have dire consequences.

Later that week we found ourselves spending lunchtime yet again on the school library computers reading through another account of a woman claiming to be haunted by a Patrick Swayze–looking ghost. I finally decided to just give up and take our chances.

'Ahhhh!!' I cried in exasperation and received a scolding look from the frumpy middle-aged librarian. I lowered my voice to a whisper and turned to Alice who was on the computer next to me, 'What are we doing?!' I hissed. 'This is ridiculous! We are never going to find anything that remotely resembles real life on these sites.'

Alice turned to look at me glumly and sighed heavily. 'I don't think I'm getting anywhere either.' She turned her computer screen to face me and I could see Casper's friendly smile grinning at me madly from the screen. 'Maybe we should just give it a go.'

'Really?' I knew that she felt, as the more skilled of the two of us, that it was her responsibility to take care of us both and her grandma had emphasized that she believed if we were unprepared it could go very badly.

'Well I figure it was easy enough to open the door, so surely it will be just as easy to seal. So I reckon we should unseal the door and have a quick look. If the crazy lady starts breathing fire we retreat and seal the door immediately. Grandma had more years than me to find the answers and the best she could do was to seal them in a room.'

I nodded my head solemnly, 'Yes and she said that the only way that we can get rid of them for good is by showing them the light. I think I have enough material to do this for Diana. God knows she doesn't deserve it after smothering a defenseless baby with a pillow, but if it means she is gone from the house it will be worth it.'

'Let's do it,' Alice said firmly, both of us convinced that was the right course of action.

That afternoon Alice and I rode back to my house in silence. The bravado we had at lunchtime had worn off and we were both nervously thinking about the chances a murderous ghost would be hesitant about murdering the two of us. By the time we reached the house and ditched our bikes in the shed I could swear that my knees were shaking.

I looked up at the house, which was looking a fraction more welcoming. My parents had replaced all of the shutters with new ones and they had been painted a glossy white. I really should be helping them more, I thought guiltily; but then realized that unsealing the rooms and getting rid of the evil spirits inside them was probably more beneficial than painting the staircase banisters with double coats of lacquer or sanding the floorboards to be polished. I looked over at Charlie's house and wished more than anything I was sitting inside with him planning another trip into the city. Alice was standing next to me looking at the house with trepidation too but she looked more determined than I did. I think if she had chickened out I would have been right behind her running for the hills.

'We can do this!' she said firmly. 'Ready?'

'No,' I said meekly then quickly recanted, 'Yes, yes I am. Let's do it. We can do this!' I repeated what she had said, trying to convince myself.

Unlike me, Alice seemed to grow in confidence the closer we got to the room and by the time we got to the door she confidently held her hands over the handle and said with a clear voice, '*Aperio!*' I heard a click on the other side and held my breath waiting for something to happen.

The door remained motionless just as any normal door would. I heard a whooshing noise and took a step back until I realized it had been the sound of me releasing my breath. Alice looked at me as I giggled nervously. I stepped forward, took the handle, and it turned as easily as if it had been used every day. I pushed the door open and we peered nervously into the room.

# CHAPTER 34

Everything was still and quiet. I'm not sure what I had been expecting – maybe for a giant fire-breathing female apparition to appear with flames licking out of her head – but the dust lay thick on every surface of the room, as it should. The room was laid out as a study and lounge room. The heavy oak desk and chair was positioned to look out onto the stone driveway and behind that a small couch and two chairs with a coffee table in the middle and a large ornate fireplace with bookshelves either side full of books. I put one foot inside the door, intending to head towards the books, but something behind the sofa on the right caught my eye and I walked over to see what it was. Alice was following closely behind me, looking over her shoulder, but as we got to the couch she saw what I had been looking at. It looked as though someone had picked up a giant glass vase and thrown it against the wall. The shards of glass lay strewn across the Oriental rug.

We were standing together looking down at the glass on the floor when the jar that Alice was holding with the crystals inside was flung out of her hand and into the wall behind us.

'Why did you do that?' I asked her, looking at her like she was mad.

She had gone white and was shaking her head, 'I didn't!'

We both turned to look at the other end of the room where the ghostly apparition of a woman stood. She wasn't breathing fire but she may as well have been. She looked furious. The door to the hallway slammed shut and another projectile came hurtling across the room and slammed into the wall. Fortunately our first impulse was to duck as several more objects followed in quick succession behind it. I wondered if the smashing would alert anyone else who might be in the house but we had made sure that everyone was out.

Thomas was helping my parents fix the wooden struts of the dock, Clara was in town doing a mail run and Marcel had gone with her to buy some food for dinner. The smashing against the wall stopped and I went to peer over the couch but before I could the books started to fly out of the shelves and against the walls. At least she had run out of breakable glass and porcelain objects, although I was quite certain she could do just as much damage with a book and there looked like there was ample supply for her to continue for a while. I had to do something.

'I found out what happened to your baby boy!' I yelled, hoping that she could hear me over the sound of books thudding against the walls, furniture and windows. The books stopped in mid-air. I took that as a sign to continue speaking. Looking over at Alice, she nodded and slowly moved closer to the crystals that had fallen out of the glass jar when it smashed.

I spoke quickly trying to keep her listening to my voice. 'He was adopted by a really lovely couple that lived in New York City! They could never have children and they dedicated their lives to him. He studied medicine at university and became a doctor, he married a woman who was also from New York and they had five children.'

I peered over the edge of the couch I was hiding behind. She was standing next to the fireplace, and while she still looked like she was mad, some of the anger in her eyes seemed to have dissipated so I took a deep breath and stood up. 'He only died a few years ago at the ripe old age of ninety-five! He has twelve grandchildren and they have all gone on to achieve great things. It sounds like he was a wonderful father.'

Diana's anger seemed to be evaporating but she looked like she was debating whether I was telling the truth so I pulled out some of the pictures that I had printed off at the library and held them up. Her breathing seemed to slow and she lowered her hands and squinted like she was trying to see what was in the pictures. To show her the pictures I would have to leave my safe haven behind the back of the couch so I took a deep breath and slowly moved towards her, watching for signs that her anger might again flare. I could hear my heart pounding and my legs felt like they could give way at any moment but I tried to keep a calm expression on my face to not betray the fear that I was feeling to Diana.

I needn't have bothered; she wasn't looking at my face at all. Her eyes were transfixed on the pictures that I was holding and she was searching them desperately for signs of her son.

I reached the other side of the room where she was standing and held the pictures out for her to see, forgetting that she couldn't take them. 'Oh sorry,' I mumbled, kicking myself for the oversight. Quickly looking around the room, I spotted the coffee table a couple of feet from where she was standing and motioned for her to follow me over to the table, where I put the pictures down and spread them out.

'This one is a picture from when your son was a baby. I got it from the adoption agency,' I said quietly and when she didn't say anything I turned slightly to look at her. She had tears streaming down her face and she nodded her head sadly, obviously recognizing his dimpled little cheeks, full head of curls and mischievous eyes.

I picked out another page that had two photos on it; both were of a couple proudly holding the same baby boy from the first photo. In the first the couple were smiling happily for the camera. The next was a more candid shot that seemed to be taken by accident as the couple were not looking at the camera. They were both staring at the child with a look of total wonder and profound happiness.

'This is him with the parents who adopted him,' I said, holding it up for her to see. She still had tears rolling down her face as a result of the first photo but the second seemed to give her a sense of release and she let out a sigh.

I made the most of the moment of calm to look more closely at Diana. She seemed to have shrunk in size from when she was projecting objects at us. She was dressed in a maid's outfit of black with a white apron over the top. Her hair was a deep russet color that she had tied in a bun at the back of her head and her nose was sprinkled with freckles that made her look younger than she really was. I picked up another photo and put it on top of the pile.

The photo was again from the adoption agency and had been taken as a file update and welfare check when the boy was fifteen. It looked like he was looking not at the camera but into the distance at someone who was standing next to the photographer, perhaps his adopted mother. His face was dusted with freckles and his mouth, which also looked to have been inherited from his birth mother standing beside me, wore a broad smile like he was trying to stop himself from laughing and his eyes seemed to twinkle with mischief. His curly hair had grown longer and seemed to be darker than in the earlier photo.

I looked at Diana's face and she was completely immersed in studying his features so I risked a glance around my shoulder at Alice who was standing still behind the couch. 'OK?' she mouthed at me. I shrugged my shoulders and the movement seemed to spark Diana from her trance. She also looked around and saw Alice standing behind the other couch holding the retrieved crystals in her hand. 'That won't work,' she said calmly, glancing at the crystals and at the smashed glass on the floor. 'You need a lot more crystals and you can't trap an adult spirit in a glass jar,' she said shaking her head.

'You knew what we were doing?' Alice asked in bewilderment. Given we hardly knew what we were doing it occurred to me that maybe we could ask her for help.

'Yes, I was a witch too. It is the reason why my boyfriend, the father of my child, would not marry me. So my parents made me give him away,' she ran her fingers down the little boy's features in the picture. 'I have half a dozen books on the topic in my trunk. Or I did before I died. I'm not sure what they would have done with my books after I died.'

'How is it that you can control objects?' I asked her, feeling my confidence had increased incrementally as her anger disappeared.

'I think if you feel enough emotion then you can channel it into an object. Enough hate, anger, love …'

The thought occurred to me that if Diana had figured out a way to control objects maybe she had also discovered a way to touch a person.

'But you can't touch people?'

She held her hand up and gestured for me to do the same. When our hands touched the same chill ran through me as when I had walked through Gus. I was surprised to find myself disappointed. She noticed my disappointment and considered what I was asking again. 'I think that it would be possible, if enough emotion was involved.'

Thinking again of what she had said about the crystals and being involved in witchcraft I made a mental note that we needed to find out what had happened to Diana's belongings after she had been executed. Would they have given them back to Diana's parents? Would they have left everything that she had with Poppy's parents and if they did would Poppy's parents have destroyed all trace of her because it was too difficult to look at. That seemed unlikely, given they had effectively left baby Edward's room exactly as it had been when he died, even after they had a new baby in Poppy. I decided I would go back to the safe hidden in the secret passageway, where it seemed every other secret that needed to be buried had been kept.

She turned her attention back to the table. 'Can I see more of the photos?' she asked beseechingly.

It didn't seem like she was particularly concerned about or hostile towards Alice's presence in the room so she came out from behind the couch and joined us at the table. I wondered if her heart was beating as fast as mine. I looked down at my folder where the photos sat and collected my thoughts.

'I couldn't find any others from when he was a young boy. The next one I could find of him was at university,' I said, pulling out another image. He stood next to a tall tree in a garden wearing a university cap and gown and smiling proudly at the camera. He still looked like the young boy that had been in the earlier photo from the adoption agency but his face had thinned out a little and his hair was almost entirely brown with faint red highlights that you could only see because this photo was in color and had been taken outside in the sun. 'He studied medicine and went on to become an obstetrician.'

She looked up at me in surprise. 'He delivered babies?' she said in awe tinged with a little bit of sadness, and then a look of horror came over her face. 'Oh god! I wonder what he thought of his own mother as he handed over each one of those tiny miracles to their adoring mothers. He must have thought me to be the worst person in all of the world,' she said sadly, putting her hand to the photo even though she couldn't touch it.

'Well, the records that I could find documented that the grandparents of the child had given him up due to the mother being unmarried. I think from that he would have known that you didn't give him up by choice,' I said, trying my best to ease her concern.

She looked through the rest of the photos in silence, simply nodding her head when she wanted me to go to the next picture. There was a photo of him receiving a prize for his study in genetics of birth defects and a photo in the paper of him with his children talking about the importance of healthy lifestyles for children. When I reached the end of the pile I glanced at her face and she turned to me and smiled.

'Thank you, both of you, for helping me when I didn't deserve it. I think I am ready to leave now.'

Just then the sound of a baby giggling echoed from the other side of the room and we all spun around to face the source of the noise. Poppy stood in the doorway holding on to little baby Edward who was reaching his hands out for Diana. I turned to look at Diana in surprise, unsure what her reaction would be to the loving gesture from the infant that she had murdered. Diana looked at him lovingly with tears cascading down her face and then up at Poppy in horror.

'You? You are not his mother, but you look so much like her. Are you … Did she … did she have more children?'

'Just one more,' Poppy said nodding her head. 'Unfortunately she couldn't have any more after me.'

'I am so deeply sorry for the pain and suffering that I caused your family. I know that it is no excuse but when my parents took my child away and thrust me into work so quickly after I fell into such a deep depression. And then when I saw your parents with Edward … they were so happy and I was so, so unhappy. I think I blamed them. I wanted to take away their happiness and show them what it was like to suffer. There is not a day that goes past that I do not think about what I did and wish to God that I could go back and reverse it. I wish there was something that I could do to undo some of the pain.'

Poppy looked down at baby Edward who was still reaching out to Diana and then looked back at Diana. 'Actually, there is something that you can do.' Diana looked up at Poppy hopefully and Poppy indicated toward the photos of Diana's son that I had just shown to her. 'Now that Sophie has helped you make peace with your unfinished business, you will be able to find peace and cross over to the other side. I'm not sure why my lovely brother has not been able to cross over but you can take him with you when you go. Take him to my parents and help them be reunited.' Diana was already nodding and before Poppy had finished talking she was reaching her hands for Edward's little chubby ones that were still reaching out for her. Poppy gave him one last cuddle and whispered something quietly in his ear.

Diana and Edward's hands connected and when she drew him in to her he touched her face softly and they looked into each other's eyes. There was a bright white light, the sound of a baby's giggles echoed through the room again and they both were gone.

I looked again at Poppy who appeared to have her heart broken into a thousand pieces. With one last tear-stained look at where her brother had just been she nodded her head, turned on her heel and walked back towards the staircase that led to her room.

'That would have taken a lot of courage,' Alice said to me, looking at the doorway where Poppy had just been. I just nodded my head. I would go and speak to her later but for now I thought it was best to give her time to heal. The whole experience had been exhausting. And to think that there were five more rooms like this one in which Poppy and Isadora had deemed the spirits too dangerous and sealed them shut. I went over to the couch and slumped into it, a cloud of dust rose up into the air as I sat, which made me start coughing loudly. As I swatted the air in front of my face, Alice sat down gently next to me, avoiding disturbing the dust down her end of the sofa.

'We were lucky today that she wasn't actually that dangerous or scary … in the end. If we are going to try to unseal the other rooms I think we should try to find Diana's trunk with the information she knows about how to trap the spirits. Hopefully it has been kept somewhere,' I said to Alice. No sooner had I spoken than the door handle began to slowly turn. Alice and I looked in horror as the door opened, but no one appeared. I counted off twenty seconds in my head before slowly standing up and tiptoeing towards the door.

# CHAPTER 35

As I was reaching for the door it swung open and I saw Mom on the other side of the threshold looking down at her phone.

'Oh Sophie, it was you in there.'

Mom spotted Alice sitting ramrod straight on the couch and cheerfully called out, 'Hi Alice! Wow you managed to get the door open! I was working on that for hours the other day. What's your secret?'

'Magic,' Alice said and laughed, and my mother laughed along with her because there was no such thing as magic.

'Well we have another four or five doors that I might need your magic touch on. This room is a right mess isn't it! I wonder what happened in here,' she said, looking around at all of the smashed pottery and books lying scattered around the floor.

I looked longingly at my comfortable position on the dust-covered couch and started gathering books. 'Why don't you leave this room to me Mom, you have enough to do.'

'Great, thank you Sophie. Nice to see you again Alice.' She looked back down at her phone and walked back out of the room. I suspected Mom was happier to see I had made a friend than she was that we had opened the door.

As soon as she left I flopped back down on the couch and coughed as another plume of dust went into the air. We had just sent an angry spirit into another realm with a little spirit baby, I felt like I had earned a little bit of relaxation. My heart was slowly coming back to its normal rhythm and the enormity of what we had done was slowly sinking in.

Alice looked around the room again and then back at me. 'Exactly how many other rooms did you say were like this one? As in, locked up, sealed, throw away the key, too scary to enter the door of this ghost train?'

I put my head in my hands and mumbled out the word that I myself didn't want to hear, 'Five.'

'*Five*?' I peeked through my fingers at her horrified expression. 'We have to figure out the key to getting rid of *five* more crazy, serial killing psychos?!'

'I will understand if you're not with me on this. I can try to find another witch maybe,' I said with absolutely no enthusiasm.

'Please! As if they can hold a candle to me – I'm practically an expert now! And I'm in this with you, all the way. It would help if we could find Diana the crazy witch's box of goodies though, since she wasn't all that forthcoming with information before she poofed off into the unknown.'

I nodded my head, 'I was thinking the exact same

th …' I stopped short and we both looked at each other in alarm as we heard a rustling noise from outside the room. Who could that be? Had someone been listening to our conversation, or could there be another ghost in the room?

The noise stopped and we both leapt up and looked around for weapons as the doorway remained empty before we saw a mop of hair come around the door looking down into a plastic bag where a very live human hand was fishing around.

'*Mom!*' I stammered, my heart racing again. I was unsure how many times my heart could go from zero to one hundred beats per minute before I suffered a heart attack and joined the other ghosts in the house.

'Oh yes, me again,' she said absentmindedly as she looked around the bag for her keys or phone or whatever it was that she had lost in there and caused us to suffer our momentary panic. 'I forgot to mention before that I was looking around in Poppy's room the other day and I found something that I thought you would find interesting.'

My heart quickly went back to racing as I pictured Mom walking around Poppy's room and coming across her spirit sitting at her dressing table, staring out into the ocean for her long-lost love. But she looked far too calm and collected to be recalling a ghostly encounter so I tried to hide the look of shock on my face and probed, 'Really?' I had meant for the word to come out naturally but unfortunately it came out as more of a timid squeak, which Mom instantly picked up on and she looked up from her fishing expedition to look at my face. She studied my features as I tried to make myself look as relaxed and natural as possible, but I was a terrible liar and she called me on it. 'Is … anything the matter?' she asked lightly, trying and failing to sound carefree because she was obviously aware that we had company in the room and clearly didn't want to embarrass me in front of Alice.

I remembered the article that I had found about Gus's drowning in Poppy's safe and decided that it was as good a reason as any to tell my mom. 'I was in Poppy's room the other day and I found something too …' Making a show of expelling air like a big sigh, I pulled the article out of my jeans pocket and handed it to her. She only had to read the headline and her face instantly clouded over and she looked back at me with wide eyes, searching my face for signs of distress.

'It's OK Mom,' I reassured her. 'I remember everything now and it's OK. Really.' I gave her a reassuring smile and she looked from me to Alice and obviously decided to let it slide until later when she could speak to me alone. If only she knew that Alice had met Gus – and not when he was a living person.

'So what did *you* find?' I probed, trying to contain my curiosity. After looking down at the article once more, she recollected her thoughts and put on a smile that I could tell was a little forced because it was not touching her eyes. When my mother was genuinely happy the corners of her eyes would crinkle and her brown eyes would sparkle.

'Well, I found the most amazing collection of gowns and I think they are about your size.' She looked over at

Alice and quickly sized her up. 'You too Alice, you look around the same size as Sophie.'

I laughed, relieved that it wasn't something sinister that she had come across. 'And what pray tell will we be wearing these lovely gowns to? Do we have an engagement at the White House?'

I couldn't contain my sarcasm and Mom looked at me like I was a little dim-witted- 'Well the Halloween ball of course – it is this Saturday night, silly.' I could feel my expression change from amusement to one of horror.

'*This Saturday night?* As in five days from now?'

'Yes you duffer, when did you think it was. I've been receiving a lot of emails from your friends, those red-haired twins, and they are very enthusiastic.' She paused and looked mildly frazzled and confused for a minute and then walked out the door mumbling to herself, 'In fact a little too enthusiastic since they will be coming over here every day for the next five days by the sounds of it …' Her voice trailed off as she walked off down the hall.

As soon as I was sure she was out of earshot I spun on my heel and started pacing, 'Argh! What am I going to do Alice!' I hissed out in a whisper in case we had any other unexpected visitors eavesdropping in the hallway. 'I have no idea who murdered Poppy – what if they turn back the clock and unleash the ghosts and, and, and …'

'Calm down Sophie, just breathe.' Alice stopped me in the middle of the room and put a reassuring hand on my shoulder. She looked into my eyes and waited while I took some deep breaths.

'You have the fob watch so we will put that in the ball room to protect the visitors and keep them in there while we go around to the other rooms and speak to the ghosts that are free to roam around. The scary ones who might hurt people are all sealed in the five rooms that we haven't opened so they can't get out. At the end of the night we simply get the ghosts to stay in their rooms in the mansion while we escort the guests out. They will be none the wiser.'

I had finished my deep breathing exercise and was surprised that Alice's plan made complete sense, 'We may actually be able to pull this off,' I nodded my head, feeling a lot better that I was in this with someone else who was also living and breathing and could calm me with a stern touch.

'Now to more important matters,' said Alice. I looked back up at her face concerned about what she was going to say; I didn't think I could handle any more stressful situations today. 'I really think we should go up and take a look at these dresses your mom was talking about because I don't have anything to wear to this party!' I laughed and felt my whole body relax, the tension slowly eased as I realized Alice was right – we would try our best to keep our classmates safe but I wondered again whether Marcel or Clara had other ideas for Saturday night.

Poppy was delighted that Alice and I wanted to wear her dresses and told us to help ourselves to anything that we liked. It really was an impressive sight: she had four walls covered with shoe racks, ball gowns and a collection of twinsets in every different shade of pastel, which I had fond memories of. I smiled as I imagined her wearing them with her string of pearls, a dash of lipstick and mascara. She had dressed very casually but always looked stylish. I had often wondered how on the outside she had looked so put together and normal and yet she also had this element of eccentricity to her. For starters her house looked like it was about to fall down and she told these outrageous ghost stories like they were true. On reflection they obviously sounded so convincing because they were in fact based on reality.

I picked out a dusty pink gown that went to the floor. It had little pink and white roses stitched into the length of the gown with embroidered leaves and cap sleeves that I loved. I couldn't believe how lucky I was finding one that fit so well and was amazingly stylish vintage rather than being a moth-eaten relic.

I was so happy with my find I thought I might burrow deeper into her wardrobe to see if she had any shoes to match. Even though Poppy had said we were welcome to anything, I popped my head back out of the cupboard to check if it was OK, but she was gone. I turned to look at Alice who was holding up a dazzling floor-length bronze dress.

'Wow! You should definitely try that on! Did you see where Poppy went? I wanted to check if I could have a look through her shoes.' I looked around the room again but she had definitely gone. She must have thought we needed privacy, or maybe she didn't want the memories of the nights she had spent in the dresses decades earlier.

Alice turned around to look at me and shrugged her shoulders, 'She said we were welcome to anything. I think her exact words were, 'I don't have any use for them anymore.'

I giggled as Alice did a graceful twirl with the dress still held up against her body and walked back into the wardrobe. I followed her in and walked over to the shoe racks. I was looking down the bottom at a pair of nude-colored pumps when I spotted a pair of bronze-colored strappy heels that would match perfectly with the dress that Alice had been holding up in the mirror. 'Alice,' I called out to her, but I heard only a muffled response about pulling on the dress.

I reached out to take the shoes out of the bottom of the cupboard, 'Well if Mohammed won't come to the mountain, then the mountain must come to …' I trailed off as I saw the corner of a picture frame poking out from the bottom shelf. I pulled out the shoebox that was sitting on top of it and wiped away the thick layer of dust that coated the glass. I put down the shoes and went to sit with the photo on the soft velvet seat that sat in the middle of the wardrobe.

I ran my hand over the picture of Gus's face smiling like he was posing for a Ralph Lauren catalogue. He wasn't looking at whoever was taking the photo but at the girl standing next to him with her arm slung casually around his shoulder, a look of absolute adoration on his face. It was me. I didn't remember the photo being taken but we were standing down at the beach, our sun kissed faces and radiant smiles spoke of days spent running along the sand and climbing up trees – not a care in the world. Looking at the picture made me yearn for him to resume his nightly vigil in my room. I missed him more than I thought I could.

I didn't realize that I was crying until I heard Alice in the doorway. 'Are you OK?' she asked quietly. I quickly wiped away the tears that were making silent rivers down my face and nodded.

'He was really special to you, wasn't he?'

'He was, I mean he is. At least I still get to see him right? Even if my suspicions are correct and he has simply stuck around to spend eternity teasing me. I found you a pair of shoes,' I said, trying to sound light and move the attention back to the matters at hand, 'That dress looks incredible on you. Percy is going to just die when he sees you in it,' I quickly realized my slip of the tongue and we looked at each other and burst out laughing.

That night when I went up to my bedroom I hoped that Gus would be in there but he wasn't.

'Gus,' I called out softly. Nothing happened so I called out again and he appeared sitting on the seat next to my window. He sat there silently staring out the window towards Charlie's house.

'Please Gus, you can't stay mad at me forever,' I pleaded.

'Can't I?' I sat down next to him on the window seat. 'I remember what happened the day that you died. Are you angry with me because it's my fault that you died?'

His anger disintegrated immediately and he turned to look at me and moved closer to me on the seat so that we were only a foot apart. 'Of course not. It was never your fault Sophie. Not one bit of it.'

I could tell that he believed that but I was not sure that I did. I looked down into my hands and tried to stem the tears that threatened to spill.

'If I had just stayed in the boat …'

'Then you would be dead too. I'm glad that you jumped off.' I looked back up at his face and a couple of tears ran down my face. Gus reached out to touch my face but couldn't and let his hand drop to his lap.

'Please don't be sad Sophie. I never want to make you cry. I could never stay mad with you – even though you haven't been able to see me I have been in here the past couple of nights.'

The thought made me feel better and I managed a smile. 'Really?'

'Yes really. Now go to sleep. Poppy told me that you had a battle with a scary ghost today and you should probably rest before your body goes into shock!'

I lay down on the bed. With Gus back in his spot beside me I went to sleep quickly and woke the next day feeling a thousand times better than I had in a while.

# CHAPTER 36

The rest of that week I spent half-heartedly trying to figure out whether Clara or Marcel could have been responsible for Poppy's death, but really my mind was on Gus and Charlie and the dance. I was still yet to ask Charlie if he was going to come because he had seemed completely disinterested the one time that I had brought it up with him. I had also decided to tell Charlie about the ghosts. I wasn't sure how it was going to go and I was petrified that he would run for the hills. I knew my heart would struggle to recover if he did.

My mom had also been giving me nervous glances, obviously thinking about my revelation that I remembered everything about Gus. She clearly wanted to talk to me about it but struggled to find time for us to speak given the twins and their ball committee were spending every waking moment at our house. I was unsure of what I was going to say to her. I couldn't tell her that I was dealing with his death quite fine thank you given I was currently spending even more time with him now than before he died. Most nights I fell asleep with him sitting on the window seat in my bedroom looking out at the water, or lying next to me telling me stories about some of the ghosts that he had met. It was strangely comforting.

The night before the ball Mom and I had dinner together alone and she finally had her opportunity. 'Sophie, honey, I don't want you to feel angry or disappointed that we didn't bring you back here after Gus died and I don't want you to feel responsible for his death either.'

'It's OK Mom. I think if you hadn't been distracting me in the city with all of the galleries and exhibitions I might never have discovered my love of art. I do feel guilty about that day. Sometimes I think maybe I could have stopped it happening, but I know I can't blame myself forever. I'm OK, really.'

I pulled out the photo of Gus and me that I had found in Poppy's closet and passed it to her to see. She smiled and touched the photo with her hand.

'He was a very good-looking boy, wasn't he? I always thought that you might have ended up together.'

'*Mom!*'

'Well I know you were very close with Charlie next door too. I spoke to his mother last week. Have you seen him at school?"

'Yes' I took a deep breath; it was now or never and she was bound to find out at the ball tomorrow night anyway. 'Actually, we've sort of been seeing each other again.'

'Really? Well that is a surprise. I mean I know you and Charlie might have had a little summer romance one year but I always thought that you were more interested in Gus. Of course the three of you were thick as thieves back then but I would see the way that you and Gus looked at each other. I knew that he loved you but I always suspected that you could have been in love with him too.'

'Don't be ridiculous Mom,' I said with a laugh, but even I didn't believe what I had said and her words brought up memories that I had buried.

When I went up to my room that night Gus wasn't there. Given his ability to be in a room without being seen, even by me, I wondered if he could have overheard what Mom had said. I went to the window seat and looked over to Charlie's house. He was sitting on his bed with the blinds open and saw me standing in the window when he looked up. He smiled at me and waved his hand in hello. I waved back and thought about what my mom had said. I could see how she thought I had feelings for Gus; we were really close, but it didn't compare to the way my heart would flutter when I saw Charlie.

Sliding my window open, I waited until he did the same and summoned up the courage that I hadn't found in the weeks before.

'I'm not sure if you're aware but there is going to be a party over here tomorrow night. I think there are a lot of people coming.'

'Really? I didn't know that. All good friends of yours?' he asked with a smile on his face so I could see his dimples.

'Um, no; actually, I think a lot of them may be good friends of yours though, so if you're not too busy tomorrow night it would be great if you would consider getting dressed up and coming over to hang out.'

'Sounds interesting. I might see you there!' That wasn't a yes and it wasn't a no but I got the sense that it was the best I was going to get so I smiled and said goodnight.

'Goodnight Sophie. Sweet dreams.'

As I pulled my window down I had the sensation of not being alone in the room and I turned around quickly. Gus was standing next to my desk with his back to me looking at the photo of the two of us that I had found in Poppy's closet.

'Gus! You startled me,' I said, feeling like I had been caught doing something I shouldn't be. I didn't want to have another argument with Gus over Charlie. I quickly drew the blinds and went to stand next to him.

'If I was still alive would you go to the ball with me?' he asked, still looking at the photo of us. I thought about that for a moment.

'Yes.' Technically I wasn't going with anyone so I told him what he wanted to hear, which also conveniently happened to be the truth. That seemed to make him happy and he went and lay down on my bed and closed his eyes with a big smile on his face. I lay down on the bed next to him and thought again about what Diana had said at the start of the week.

'Did Poppy tell you that the ghost we cleared out of the study was a witch and, as a ghost, she could move objects?'

'No' he said, sounding disinterested, without opening his eyes.

'She said that the way she did it was by focusing all

of her emotions and energy into an object. She said that it might be possible for a ghost to focus all their energy and maybe touch a live person.'

He opened his eyes and looked into mine, just inches away. I felt my heart flutter from the way that he looked at me with such intensity. He looked down at his hand, then at mine, then held his up. I reached my hand out and put it alongside his.

He seemed to focus everything he had and then put his hand to mine. It didn't feel quite the same as before but his hand still went through mine. I realized that I had been holding my breath and released it with a sigh. He looked extremely disappointed but not like he had given up. I got the feeling that this was not the last time he would try.

# CHAPTER 37

The next night Gus sat in my room looking gloomy while I got ready to go. He was pretending that he was irritated by the fact that I had yet to discover the killer or recover the key. But I was too excited to be dragged down by his mood. I hid behind the cupboard door so Gus didn't see me getting changed and pulled Poppy's beautiful gown over my head. Once I knew that it was on properly I stepped out from behind the cupboard into the center of the room and did a little twirl for him. 'What do you think?' I asked spinning around the room and laughing.

I could see in his eyes that I looked good. 'I'm not really into dresses. I suppose you look alright.'

I stuck my tongue out at him and sat down at my desk. 'You're just sulking because you can't come,' I said as I put on lip gloss in the mirror.

'Just make sure that you are back by midnight Cinderella! Or all your friends down there might turn into pumpkins.'

But Gus's sour mood could not put a dampener on mine. I pulled on a pair of strappy shoes I had found in Poppy's cupboard and ran lightly down the stairs to help with the rest of the set up. My mom whistled her approval and even the twins who barely paid me any attention now that they had Mom's cell phone number on speed dial heaped praise on the dress. There was only one thing that would make me feel more excited than how I was feeling now. I kept popping my head out the front to see if Charlie had decided to come; I thought my heart might burst if he didn't.

While I was waiting at the top of the steps glancing at Charlie's house the first guests started to arrive and I saw a familiar face coming up the drive. Uh oh, I thought to myself and turned quickly to try to disappear inside the house, but I wasn't quick enough. I heard someone call out 'Sophie? Wow that is you, hi, you look amazing.' I turned around and Alex was standing at the foot of the staircase with Emma lagging behind him, stumbling up the driveway and looking inconvenienced as Alex had let go of her hand and she had to make her way across the stones in her six-inch stilettos. I was happy that he had a date even if it was Miss Sourpuss. Emma had caught up with Alex and I could tell that she didn't appreciate the way he was taking in my dress.

'Were you looking for your date? Who is your date by the way?' Alex asked, trying to look back down the driveway.

Having realized that she was the second choice and clearly not the object of his affections, Emma turned her nose up, sneered and said in a pitying voice, 'Sophie doesn't have a date.'

He looked at me with his sad puppy dog expression

and I willed myself to come up with a good lie. 'Well actually … I … it's a really funny story. My date is …'

'That would be me. Sorry I'm late!' I heard coming from my left. As I turned I saw Alex and Emma's mouths drop. Charlie jogged across the stones of the driveway from his house. He held out his arm for me and I grabbed onto it.

'Hi,' I stammered feeling as shocked as Emma and Alex obviously did. Charlie kissed me softly on the lips, his face staying close to mine after he pulled back from the kiss.

'Ready?' he asked. I was still speechless and merely nodded. We moved towards the house before I recovered my voice. I turned back to Alex and Emma, still standing at the bottom of the steps.

'See you inside,' I said. Alex simply nodded at me.

'Oh my god! Thank you! I have never been so happy to see someone in my whole life,' I whispered to him as we walked through the front door, leaving Emma and Alex behind us.

'You look so beautiful,' he said giving me a twirl then pulling me back to him and kissing me lightly on the lips again. We walked into the ballroom together and Charlie went to get us a drink while I sat down in one of the large leather lounge suites my parents and Thomas had moved into the ballroom and placed around the sides of the room.

They had really outdone themselves. Apart from the lounges there were bales of hay to sit on that they had collected from a nearby farm. Lifelike cobwebs hung from various points around the room and came together on the ornate chandelier in the middle of the room. Someone from the drama department had borrowed giant spiders from the school and their black bodies were dotted across the white cobwebs. The lights of the chandelier had been dimmed and the only other light came from the candles placed strategically around the room and inside more than a dozen pumpkins carved with ghoulish faces that cast eerie shadows on the walls. There were more pumpkins lining the driveway leading up to our house. I marveled at the efforts of the social committee who had spent a whole day working on the pumpkins alone.

I watched as more and more people began to filter through the double doors that led into the room, all of them excitedly marveling at the decorations and the lighting. The DJ had been set up on the wall opposite the entrance, with a table laden with food on one side and a table with drinks on the other. As I ran my eyes along the drinks table I spotted Charlie talking to our science teacher Mr Keller. Further along the table stood Emma and Alex. It looked as though Emma was talking in an extremely animated way but Alex didn't seem to be listening and was sipping his drink and glancing around the room as though he was looking for someone.

I spotted Percy and Alice come in and started to get up and head over to them but was stopped in my tracks by the voices of two girls discussing my date.

'Did you see Charlie is here?!' I glanced to look at where the voices were coming from. A tall dark-haired girl I had never seen before was speaking to one of the social committee, a brunette with tight curly hair. She had spent several days helping the twins prepare the house for tonight but I had never caught her name.

'I know! He never comes to these school dances. He is so good-looking! But who is that girl that he's here with?' the dark-haired girl asked.

'She's a nobody. She lives in this creepy house and he lives next door so her parents probably asked him to come with her.' The dark-haired girl sniggered and they moved off towards the DJ booth.

The rational part of me knew that it wasn't true but their words tapped into my deeply held insecurity about why Charlie was spending time with me. I tried to shake off their rude conversation and walked over to Alice and Percy. On the way I was intercepted by Charlie, who was now talking to Ben and Pat.

'Sophie,' Ben and Pat said in unison, and I laughed nervously, looking at Charlie. I wasn't sure what he had said to them about whether we were dating or not and it occurred to me that the two girls that I had just overheard were probably in the same circle of friends. Based on their conversation I guessed he hadn't mentioned to any of his friends that we might be seeing each other. I felt my heart sink a little at the thought but tried not to let it show.

Charlie laughed at something Pat said, which I couldn't hear, and Ben turned to me and spoke quietly under his breath. 'I don't know how you did it Sophie but thank you for getting Charlie here tonight.'

'Because he never comes to the dances?' I asked.

'Oh he always used to come but a couple of years ago he just stopped coming and nothing we said could convince him. Just quietly he got into a bit of trouble with the law,' I let his comment slide, pretending not to know what he was talking about.

'Yeah,' he continued, 'he got drunk and stole a car.' I had known about the car but I didn't know about the drink-driving. I glanced over to where Charlie was talking to Pat.

'I think it may have been over a girl. When he got back to school the following year he said something about being completely over her. Not over it but over her.' As I studied Charlie's face he seemed to be involved in a serious debate about how the football training sessions should be run. I didn't want to hear any more of what Ben had to say. I already blamed myself for Gus drowning I didn't need Ben telling me I could have been responsible for Charlie getting drunk and stealing a car. I spotted Alice and Percy and made a quick escape.

'Excuse me for a minute, I see some of my friends,' I mumbled, quickly walking away from the group.

'How does it feel to be with the best looking date?' I asked Percy as he gave me a hug hello. Percy turned to look at Alice with a mischievous smile.

'I think she's speaking to you Alice!' She swatted him on the backside and gave me a hug.

'You look amazing Alice!'

'Thanks to our spiritual stylist,' she whispered in my ear as she gave me a hug. I stood back and took in the gown of Poppy's that she had chosen. She really did look incredible, like the gown had been made for her.

Percy's eyes went from my face to the dance floor behind me. Someone cleared their throat behind me and then I heard Charlie say 'Hi' from the direction Percy was looking. When I turned around he was standing awkwardly behind me, just outside our circle. He looked shy so I pulled him into the group and Alice and Percy both said their hellos.

'Mustered up the courage to ask someone to the dance eh?!' Percy whispered, raising his eyebrows. I looked around to make sure that Charlie hadn't seen his little display of humor and hit him on the arm when I was sure that he hadn't.

'Ouch!' he said still chuckling and Charlie turned back to see what had caused Percy to let out his little yelp. I smiled at him and glared at Percy. A song came on that had half the room up and on the dance floor and Percy dragged Alice into the throng of people moving around the floor. I felt Charlie's hand move into mine and I forced myself to look at him, hoping he couldn't read my thoughts as he looked into my eyes with a concerned look on his face.

He lent in and asked, 'Everything alright?'

'Sure. Everything's great,' I said smiling, and shrugged my shoulders, pretending to be interested in the people dancing, but he wasn't fooled.

'What's going on?'

'I just wasn't sure that … whether you really wanted to … you didn't have to come if you really didn't want to,' I stammered.

'What happened? Did Ben say something to you?'

'Well … yes and these other girls. I heard them saying that I was just a bit of a pity date and I thought they might have been friends of yours and then I just felt … I just felt a little stupid to be honest.'

'You can't be serious! Look at you! You are no one's pity date. You are the best-looking girl here tonight. Haven't you seen all the guys and most of the girls looking at you? The only reason I'm here tonight is to spend time with you. Come on. If we're at a dance we may as well dance!' He put his arm around me and dragged me onto the dance floor next to Percy and Alice. Percy made a loud wolf whistle, which made Charlie laugh and me shake my head at him.

Charlie pulled me to him and started to lead me around the dance floor. I felt like I was floating on air, like a ghost. Ghosts, I thought, pulling my mind back to reality. I decided it was now or never – I needed to tell Charlie the truth.

'There's something I have to tell you,' I blurted out, trying to swallow my nerves, but it felt like my heart was beating in my mouth. This was going to be harder than I thought. I started to doubt myself again and thought about how I would have reacted if someone had told me six months ago that they could see ghosts. I took three deep breaths and looked up at his face.

'What a coincidence, there is something that I have to tell you too,' he said looking directly into my eyes.

'OK.' My heart was still in my throat. Is this the point where he tells me that he is not really interested and this whole thing was in my head?

He lent in and whispered into my ear, 'I love you.'

My heart swelled and I couldn't take the smile off my face. 'Well that's convenient,' I tried to play it cool but couldn't, 'because I love you too,' I whispered back. All thoughts of ghosts disappeared in that instant and I felt again like I was floating. There could have been no one else around us as we danced around the room, it was like a fairytale. But as in most fairytales there was something sinister overshadowing my happiness and sure enough it soon bubbled to the surface. While we were taking a break sitting on the seats at the side of the room and joking about my dancing technique, or lack thereof, Charlie joked that I may have broken some of his toes.

'Ha ha, very funny.'

'No, I'm serious,' he laughed. 'I need some urgent medical attention!'

'Do you see a nurse's badge on this outfit?' As soon as the words came out of my mouth I knew who had murdered Poppy. Charlie saw my expression change and grabbed my hand.

'What is it? Are you alright?'

'Yes … I mean I think so … Yes. Can you just wait here a minute?' I said to Charlie, dodging people milling around as I ran over to the door that led to the kitchen.

Without even checking if Marcel was in there I grabbed the photo of him with his mother and ran out to find Thomas.

# CHAPTER 38

Thomas was on his way back to his cottage from visiting his garden and I thrust the picture in front of his face. 'Is this the badge that Poppy had in her hands?' I asked him urgently.

He took a step back, 'What?'

'When she died you said that she had a red badge in her hand. It looked like it had been ripped off something.'

He still looked confused but he glanced down at the picture and nodded. 'Yes that's it.' He saw that the other person in the photo was Marcel and looked up at me with alarm. 'But wait, are you implying that …?'

'I'll explain it all later,' I said running back up into the house and almost colliding with Charlie.

'What is going on? You just took off like there was a fire.'

'I need you to do something for me and I don't have time to tell you why, I just need you to trust me OK? I promise I'll explain everything.'

'OK' he said slowly, although his face was not at all convinced.

'I need you to make sure that no one from the dance leaves the room for the next thirty minutes.' I looked at my watch, it was 11.50 pm. 'Get Alice – she'll be able to help.

Just tell her … tell her I know who it was. And I'm going to stop them but I need her to help you keep everyone safe.'

He looked completely confused but he agreed. I walked back into the ballroom, pulled the fob watch out from my bag, wound the handle and hid it under the photos sitting on the mantelpiece.

'I love you,' I said again, kissing him passionately, and then ran up the stairs where I knew Gus would be waiting. I started talking as soon as I opened the door and, sure enough, he was sitting next to the window staring out into the water like I had seen Poppy doing so many times.

'It's Marcel, I'm sure of it now. And I'm pretty sure I know where he would have hidden the key – there's a secret passageway out of the kitchen.' I walked over to the desk and pulled out the blueprint pointing out the path.

'How can you be so sure?' he asked, wondering where my newfound confidence in Marcel's guilt had come from.

'The badge that your dad found on Poppy after she died was Marcel's mother's nurse's badge,' I explained it to him, and he agreed that my argument was sound.

'Well it's almost midnight, let's go down and find him,' I said walking towards the door.

'Wait,' Gus said sounding unsure of himself for a minute.

'Wait why? We have to go now,' I urged him, a note of panic creeping into my voice.

'It could be dangerous down there, something bad could happen and I … I … I just want to tell you … I *need* to tell you something first.'

OK, this couldn't be happening. 'Gus, we have to go now,' I urged again and moved closer toward the door.

'Please,' he said so quietly that I bit my lip and turned around.

'I just want you to know … I have for a while been thinking … and I know that there is nothing I can do to … well it's just that I want you to know … I love you.' He looked up into my eyes. 'I love you Sophie. Always have and always will.' he shrugged his shoulders like there was nothing he could do about it even though he had tried.

'You love me?' I said incredulous. 'You can't be serious – you tried to kill me that night when I first saw you. I almost drowned!' I reminded him.

'*Kill you*? No way. I was trying to get you to remember. You slipped and fell all by yourself. I have been watching you for the past few months and you are very accident prone – did you realize that?'

'Argh! You are impossible! And you are see-through like a jellyfish.'

'Jellyfish? What does a sea creature have to do with this?'

I was flustered but it dawned on me that he wasn't the first person who had declared his love to me that night. 'And anyway, I'm dating Charlie.'

'Do you love him?' Gus asked with a pout.

'None of your business,' I said turning around because I couldn't look him in the face.

'You have dreams about me you know. I've heard

you saying my name when I watch you sleep,' he said with a mischievous smile.

'You *what*?' I shrieked and, forgetting I couldn't touch him, I turned around and smacked him in the arm. As soon as my hand made contact with his arm we both looked up at each other. The incandescent appearance of a jellyfish was gone and he stood solidly in front of me as if he had never died. Slowly it sunk in. I looked at my watch – it was one minute past midnight.

'Marcel has turned the key!' we both said in unison.

Before I could think about what this meant and how we were going to fix it, Gus reached over and pulled me into his chest and hugged me to him. It felt so good to have his arms around me, hugging me tightly to him. We stood there for what seemed like hours before he relaxed his grip and lightly kissed the top of my forehead, sending tingles down my spine.

'I've been wanting to do that since the night that you decided you were responsible for my death!' he said, and before I could respond he started moving towards the door. 'OK, let's go and get that key!'

We ran down the stairs and almost crashed into a group of adults standing at the bottom. At first I thought that Charlie must not have taken my request seriously and had allowed some of the staff members and chaperoning parents to leave the ballroom, but as I looked closer I realized that they were not members of the school staff. They were ghosts. There were half a dozen of them, all dressed in military clothing. The oldest one, who looked like he had walked out of the pages of my history book with his blue uniform covered in brass and a strapping salt-and-pepper beard looked over at me when we reached the bottom of the stairs. He gave my clothing a once over and then, seemingly unconcerned introduced himself.

'Good evening, we have been invited to a bridge party. Can you please kindly show us to the parlor?'

I looked around at Gus and he muttered under his breath, 'Don't let them leave. If they leave the house while the clock is turned back and we turn the clock back again they could be stuck in limbo.'

I cleared my throat, 'Right this way gentlemen,' I said and led them over to one of the living rooms that had a large table and chairs. 'Help yourself to a drink,' I said pointing to the collection of old crystal scotch decanters and some glasses. 'And if you please, don't leave this room. Thanks!'

I quickly backed out of the room and closed the double doors.

'Quick, let's go!' I said to Gus running along the hallway. We could see groups of people in the rooms that we passed along the way and with a rising surge of panic got to the ballroom and were relieved to notice that the door was still closed.

We rushed into the kitchen, pulling a latch in the pantry. The wall on the left-hand side sprang open to reveal a staircase. Taking them two at a time we made it to the bottom in seconds. 'Be careful, stay behind me,' Gus said pulling me back behind him. It felt strange to have his hands touching me when they had until a few minutes ago been going straight through me. There was a room at the end of a passageway that looked as though someone had been living in it. A bed was set up against the wall with a side table and a desk off to the left. As my eyes slowly adjusted to the dark I could see a set of shelves pushed to the side that revealed a second passageway going up to another room. Gus started walking over to the second passageway and I saw a jet of light before the back of my head exploded in pain. The room went black again as though someone had turned out the lights.

# CHAPTER 39

I blinked open my eyes and felt the back of my head throbbing. I tried to put my hands to the back of my head but I couldn't. It took me a minute to realize that I was tied to a chair in the room below the kitchen and another minute to remember why I was there. My eyes blurred and came into focus on Marcel, standing next to his little desk pulling liquid from a small bottle into a syringe. I scanned the room looking for Gus. He was tied up on the other side of the room with his mouth taped. His head was tilted to the side and his eyes closed like he had fallen asleep watching a movie.

'Hello sunshine,' Marcel said with a high-pitched creepy voice that sounded nothing like the Marcel that I had gotten used to seeing around the house. I stared at him in hatred and said nothing.

'Now now, no need to be grumpy. You were so happy when you came running into the kitchen before and pinched my mother's photo. You think that you have it all worked out don't you? But you really know nothing.'

'You will never get away with this!' I spat at him with all the venom I could muster.

'Oh Sophie, I already have. No one even knows that

you are here. I will just write your parents a sad little note about how you couldn't take it anymore and then, once I have injected you with this nerve immobilizer, I will take you out on that precious little boat that you used to kill your boyfriend over there and in true Romeo and Juliet style you will perish the same way. I thought you would like it – it seems quite poetic to me.'

'*No!*' I could feel the tears welling up at the thought of my parents finding my body. 'They will never believe that I killed myself!'

'I am afraid they already do. While you have been spending your nights trying to figure out who killed your precious Poppy I have spent every dinner telling them that I have seen you crying by the dock and sobbing into your breakfast cereal.' I couldn't believe it but he was right. I had spent hardly any time with my parents and they had obviously been trying to give me the space that I needed. Given my history of mental breakdowns around this house Marcel's story wouldn't be a stretch.

'Look on the bright side,' he said flicking the needle to get rid of any bubbles, 'at least you will be with Gus forever now.'

I looked over at Gus who had come to and had heard what Marcel was planning. He was shaking his head with tears in his eyes. I had an overwhelming feeling of sadness and regret.

'Oh Gus, I'm sorry I didn't figure it out sooner!' I sobbed. 'I do love Charlie but I love you too.'

Gus tried to talk but the tape stopped his words.

'Oh! That's touching,' Marcel said sarcastically as he walked towards me, focused on the needle in his hand.

'Why are you doing this? Why did you kill Poppy?'

He paused for a moment considering his response. 'Poppy was standing in my way. She showed me her ghosts one day you know. I walked into one of the rooms when she was turning the key. She was surprised that I was there at first but she let me stay.' His eyes were off into the distance as he remembered that day and I took the opportunity to try to get out of the binds that were around my wrists. It was useless, he had left nothing to chance and secured them tightly using cable ties and they were digging into my wrists.

'It was amazing,' he said with his eyes glazed over. 'The room that had been empty was suddenly full of people having a party. I had always thought that she was completely off her rocker but this was just incredible. We should have haunted house parties, I told her, bring in some money for the property, which was starting to look a little shabby. But she said no, she was trying to help all of the lost spirits that landed on her property, who were looking for some peace and quiet. And besides, she told me, if she wanted to put money into the house she could, there was plenty of money and treasure and jewels in the safe in one of the secret passageways.' Gus and I exchanged a glance, thinking about the room where we had found the fob watch.

'Can you believe that?!' he said, looking at me now. 'She had millions of dollars stashed away and she just didn't care. She just wanted to be some ghost whisperer. I vowed then and there that I was going to find this hidden safe of treasures and rob her blind. Unfortunately for her, she cottoned on to my plans because the rooms started getting sealed up and no matter what I did I couldn't find that safe. I decided I could get on with it with her out of the way and she made it so easy for me, sitting there in her greenhouse having a little nap. She barely felt the needle, at least that is one thing Mommy dearest taught me – how to do an injection properly.' He looked back at me again. 'I'm really very good; I promise you will hardly feel a thing …' He started to move closer to me, the needle held high.

'I know where the safe is,' I said, seeing my opportunity. He looked over at me and then at Gus, trying to gauge whether I was lying. 'Poppy told me where to find the blueprints to the house so we could find the safe and try to protect my school friends tonight from you releasing all of the ghosts.'

'Where is it?' he demanded, lowering the needle.

'I can't describe where it is, we'll have to show you where it is,' I said gesturing to Gus and hoping that my face wasn't transparent. 'It took us days to find it and that was with a map and Poppy's help. I don't think I could have found it otherwise.'

Marcel considered for a few minutes but obviously realized it would be quicker and easier to get me to lead him there. 'Fine; just you though – your boyfriend has to stay here.'

I looked over at Gus who was shaking his head like a mad person. 'Fine,' I said.

He led me over to the other side of the room. I turned

around and took one last look at Gus who was fighting madly with his restraints and trying to yell but was being muffled by the tape on his mouth. Marcel pushed me hard into the second secret passage that led to the lounge room and I stumbled and almost fell. I looked down at his hands, in one he had a knife and in the other was his needle.

The exit to the second passage came out of a hutch outside, next to the greenhouse. Marcel pushed past me and pried open the wooden beams then pushed me in front of him into the cool night air. He walked me around the house and through the greenhouse. I wondered if this is how he had escaped detection when he killed Poppy. Before we walked into the house I thought of all the ghosts roaming around the rooms inside. I eyed off Marcel's knife.

'Won't it look strange if my hands are tied?'

He glanced at the door trying to decide how likely it was that we would see any of my classmates. 'Where is the passageway that has the safe?'

'You can only get to the passage through my room,' I said lying, knowing that we could probably access it through at least three different rooms, all of which would have avoided walking out in places where we might be seen.

'OK, but if you make any attempts to flee I will make sure I find your other boyfriend, the one that is still living next door, and stick a needle in him while he is sleeping.' He used the knife and cut the ties around my wrists and pointed to the needle in his hand. I nodded my head and walked slowly through the door.

Unfortunately, it seemed that Charlie had followed

my directions and we didn't come across any of my friends or schoolmates from the Halloween ball that I could have subtly alerted to my predicament.

As we walked from the living room, we passed ladies in full ball gowns like they had walked from the pages of a Jane Austen novel, a group of handmaids waited on them pouring glasses of sherry and passed around coffees and tea. In another room the group looked like they had appeared from the great Gatsby with their flapper dresses and overdone makeup telling of that era. But they were all focused on their groups and none of them paid us any attention. I was surrounded by people and yet I had never felt more alone. Finally we got to the bottom of the staircase and went upstairs, down the hall and into my bedroom.

All the while I had been looking feverishly for something that I could grab and use as a weapon against Marcel but he was walking so close with the tip of the knife pressing firmly into my back that I didn't dare make any sudden moves for fear that he would drive it through my shoulder blades. I heard a creak of the floorboards outside my bedroom while I was pulling the leaver of the secret passageway. Glancing at Marcel, it didn't look like he had registered the noise and he started talking again in his odd singsong voice.

'It was that stupid badge that gave me away wasn't it? I don't know why I kept it – I didn't even really like my mother that much. She was always nagging me about being a chef for Poppy and where was that going to get me but she is the one who is stupid now. When I am richer than all of the arrogant morons who live here put together – then who will be laughing!'

'Can you put down that knife? What do you think you are going to find in the safe once you find it Marcel and how do you propose to get all of the stuff out?' I asked a little bit too loudly, hoping that the creak in the passageway was someone who could help me, or at least someone who could go and get someone to help.

He looked at me with a blank expression. 'That is not for you to worry your pretty little head about,' he snarled and then gestured with the knife for me to continue into the passage.

I also wanted to ask exactly how much money he thought was sitting in the little treasure chest he had envisaged in his mind but I decided that it was probably not a good idea to continue questioning the clearly unstable homicidal maniac when he was holding a sharp kitchen knife in my back.

I walked through the passageway, still looking for any possible weapon and racking my brains as to what I could do when we got to the safe. Was there anything in there I could use as a weapon? I struggled to remember what had been in there when we retrieved the fob watch. There had been some old-looking clocks and some big boxes; I could try and throw one of those at him. But if they were too heavy or I was too slow it would only take him seconds to spin around with that knife and it would be all over for me – and for Charlie, not to mention what he would probably do to my parents if he went on a murderous rampage.

We got to the point in the wall where I could see vague outlines of the wavy lines and I stopped. I felt along the wall until my hand touched the ripples then I slid my fingers down the lines until it I heard a click and the door sprang open into the wall. Marcel pushed me over to a seat near the entrance and pulled out ropes, which he used to rebind my hands and tie me to the old metal candlestick holder coming out of the wall. I would not be getting the chance to try to find a weapon in the safe then. He went back to the entrance of the safe with the torch and I heard him whistle in delight at what he saw.

While he was distracted in the safe I looked up to the ropes and candlestick that were holding me prisoner. I tried pulling the candlestick out of the wall, hoping that like most things in this house it had aged badly and would just pull out of the stone but it was firmly jammed into the wall and wouldn't budge. The ropes had more give than the cable ties but he had tied them really tightly.

I could see the moon coming through a small window in the wall and it hit me, I wasn't going to get out of this alive. I only hoped that I had given Gus the opportunity to escape. Maybe he could tell my parents what really happened. Thinking of my parents made my resolve crumble and I started to sob quietly. In my blurred vision I saw something glint on the wall just under the candlestick. It was a nail! Brilliant! I thought and started to try to rub the rope up against it to get it to fray.

I had been working on the rope for ten minutes when I heard Marcel coming back out again. He was muttering about how he was going to get all of the loot out of the house and he seemed distracted with his excitement. As soon as he saw me standing there though he remembered that he had things to deal with before he enjoyed the spoils of his discovery and he turned back into the safe and retrieved his knife and needle. I cursed under my breath and looked at the rope. There wasn't enough time to free myself. I was not going to stand here while he injected me. Marcel started to walk towards me, a glint in his eye. 'Like I said before, you won't even feel a thing. I promise.'

# CHAPTER 40

I closed my eyes, pretending to go quietly but actually waiting for him to get closer so I could kick him. Instead there was an almighty crash and the thud of a body hitting the ground. I gingerly opened my eyes and was immediately confronted by the sight of Marcel on the ground, his eyes closed, and the needle sitting next to my foot. I looked up to see my rescuer pulling the ropes off my wrists.

'Are you alright?' the voice said above me.

'Clara!!!'

'Yes, who were you expecting? Superman?'

'How did you know that I was here? How did you find us?'

'I heard you say in your room that you were coming to the safe.'

'That was you I heard in the hallway?' my body flooded with relief and I couldn't stop myself from reaching out and hugging her. I had never been so happy to see someone in all my life. I turned back to look at Marcel's motionless form on the floor of the passageway.

'What are we going to do with him? Is he dead?' I poked my foot into the side of his body and he rolled over.

'No, but he probably won't be using this frying pan

again any time soon. I hope they like omelets in jail! Since he was so hell-bent on getting all of Poppy's treasure why don't we lock him in there until we can call the police? We need to find the clock that he used the key to turn back.'

'You know about all of that?'

'Oh yes. Who do you think it was that left you the clue on your desk so you could find the key?' She smiled at me. 'Poppy gave me an envelope before she died. She made me promise that you would be the only person that would see the contents of the envelope.'

It was the only time I had seen Clara smile. It was a pity really; she looked a lot younger when she smiled and so much less scary. We grabbed Marcel at each end and lifted him into the safe where we used the ropes he had used on me to secure him so that he wouldn't be able to move. As we pulled the door back into place Clara turned to me, 'Sophie,' she hesitated for a minute, 'Before you turn back the clock I have someone that I would like you to meet.'

I followed her back down the passageway, and upstairs into the servants' area where Clara and Marcel's rooms were. She opened the door to her bedroom and stood back for me to enter. After suspecting she was Poppy's killer for weeks I still wasn't sure if I should trust her, but she had just saved my life, and was absolutely not Poppy's murderer, so I decided it was probably best to give her the benefit of the doubt.

Clara's room was not at all what I had been expecting. She walked around the house with her severe and sinister dark clothing and I'd just assumed that her room would be sparse and dark, but it was homely and inviting. She had a beautiful floral-printed bed cover and a light gray and white flower-patterned rug with an oversized armchair sitting next to her fireplace. The small picture windows were framed by white lace curtains and I realized that hers was the window I saw a figure standing in on the day that we arrived. 'It was you standing in the window that day,' I said without thinking and then immediately I retracted it. 'No, it couldn't have been, you were downstairs at the front when we arrived. Then who was it standing in the window?' I turned around to look at her and realized that we were not alone in the room.

There was a man standing at the fireplace looking back at me. He was taller than Clara, maybe six feet tall, and he looked young in the face, but he had a full beard and mustache of dark black hair. He was wearing a suit like the uniform of a butler and while his face looked kind, I had just been attacked by someone who had been cooking me dinner for the past couple of months so I wasn't feeling all that relaxed. I reached for the fire poker but the man got there first and lifted it away from its rest.

'Stop, please, I am not here to hurt you,' he said in a rushed voice.

I assessed my surroundings: by now both the man and Clara were between me and the door and the only way out were the windows behind me. I looked from him to Clara and back, all the while backing towards the little windows. We were only three stories up I reasoned – I'd probably end up with broken bones but I'd still be alive.

Who knew whether the windows still opened though? Would I be able to open them before one of them grabbed me? I peered down at the windowsill assessing if they had been opened recently.

'Sophie,' Clara's voice, strong but gentle, made me turn back to look at her. Her face didn't look angry or bitter like it usually did and she crossed the room to the man and put her arms around him. I was so confused and I searched her face for answers. 'This is my husband, Roland.' He smiled at her and tenderly kissed her on the forehead.

'Husband? You never told us you had a husband.' I stopped backing towards the window and waited for her to respond. I studied his face and realized that he looked a lot younger than she did. Hats off to you Clara I thought, surprised, and then it occurred to me I had never seen him before. How odd. Did he just stay up here in the servants' quarters and never come out or did he live in the village? I recalled the day that I had overheard Clara arguing with someone and realized it must have been him that she had been speaking to.

Clara looked at him again and smiled, but at the same time tears welled at the corner of her eyes and when they dropped he wiped them away gently with the back of his hand. His face was sad too and I wondered what was behind the sadness they both felt.

'No, I didn't. I guess that it just wasn't something that I wanted to speak of. Roland died such a long time ago, long before you were born Sophie.'

'Wait, what? So you're a ghost?'

'He is the only reason that I have stayed here all this time.' She took a deep breath. 'Let me try to explain to you so that you understand. Where do I begin? We started working here around the same time, when we were just teenagers. Roland was the assistant butler and I was just a chambermaid. We fell in love, got married and planned our future together.' Her face clouded over as she continued her story. 'But it was not to be.' She attempted to wipe away the tears that were working their way down her face. 'After we had lost seven children from miscarriages and in childbirth, Roland was so depressed that he jumped from the roof of the house. He died in my arms.'

'Miscarriages? You wanted children?' My thoughts went immediately to the medical report that I had found in the safe. 'But I found a medical report for Clara Westlake. It said that you had an abortion,' I said gently.

She turned back to look at me, a little surprised. 'Yes, the doctor at the clinic warned me that he thought the likelihood of being able to bear children was low but I didn't want to believe him.'

'That bastard robbed us of our chances,' Roland spat with an angry look on his face.

I looked back at Clara still confused. 'I'm sorry, I don't understand,' I said.

'Not long after Roland and I began seeing each other I was attacked by a man. I got pregnant. I couldn't have the baby. I was an unmarried maid for a wealthy house and the man he was … he was … I would have been thrown out if the boss even heard a rumor that I was pregnant. I spoke to a maid at one of the other houses that I trusted who told me her sister had been in the same situation as me. A real doctor's clinic, she told me.' Clara shook her head. 'But it wasn't a clinic at all. I doubt that the doctor was even a doctor. If Poppy's father had found out he would have …' She stumbled over her words. 'Well he would have had to fire me.'

'Fire *you*? Why would he have fired you?'

'It was Poppy's uncle who raped me,' she explained. 'But Poppy and I had become friends and so she took me to a proper clinic in a nearby town to recover and she didn't mention it to anyone. Not even when people would wonder aloud at why I wasn't able to carry a child to term. She even paid for everything for me and told her father that she needed the money for a trip.'

'When I found that medical report I thought maybe you had stayed because Poppy had blackmailed you to stay,' I confessed.

'Oh no, Poppy would never have done that. She saved me. I owe her a great deal and I would do anything for her. When Roland passed away she also told me of the ghosts in the house and she helped me find him.' She looked lovingly into his face. 'I have stayed here ever since so that I could be near to him.' Looking back to me she whispered, 'He has helped me watch over you and keep you alive when Marcel was trying to kill you. I did overhear you in your bedroom but the only reason that I was up there was because Roland had seen you when you left the passage in the living room.'

I looked over at Roland who was restoring the fire poker I had minutes ago planned to hit him with to its rightful home. 'Thank you for helping me,' I said, sheepishly, feeling a little foolish. He simply nodded his head and looked back at Clara with a sad expression on his face again. She smiled sadly, nodding back at him. They seemed to be having a conversation without having to say a word. She reached into her pocket and pulled out the key on the chain that I had found in my flowerpot and handed it back to me. 'I found this on our slippery chef. You will need to turn back the clock that he turned thirteen times.'

Clara then walked back to Roland and wrapped her arms around him, burying her face into his chest. Her back began to rock with sobs.

'I guess this is goodbye again my love,' he said pulling her close. He started to rub in circles over her back. 'Don't cry my darling, I will be here with you always, until it is time for you to join me again.'

I felt like I was eavesdropping on a very private moment and so I moved over to the door, squeezed through the opening and closed it quietly. I stood there for a moment thinking about Clara and Roland's situation. Was it better to be with the one you loved for a lifetime as a ghost or be able to think of them in another place, in peace, with the ability for you to move on. I guess it was hard to ever truly 'move on.'

Unless, I thought, flinching, you had amnesia about the person like I had with Gus. *Gus!* Oh my goodness, I had completely forgotten that he was possibly still tied up downstairs. I stuck my head back through Clara's door and they both looked up with surprise, not realizing that I had left the room. 'It was lovely to meet you Roland but I have to go and find Gus. Marcel tied him up in the passageway beneath the kitchen.' They both simply nodded, like it was the most normal thing that could have come out of my mouth, and continued to hold each other.

# CHAPTER 41

I took the stairs two at a time down to the bottom floor, dodged the uninvited house guests, went through the living room, into the kitchen and down the staircase that led to the underground room.

'Gus?' I hissed, trying to will my eyes to adjust to the light. As soon as I said it I realized he would still have his mouth taped so he probably couldn't answer back.

I didn't have a torch and my eyes hadn't had time to adjust to the darkness so when I flew across the room to where I thought he would be sitting I ended up knocking over the seat he was sitting on and falling on top of him. Pulling myself up slightly I reached out and touched his face and ripped the tape off his mouth.

'Gus! Gus – are you OK?' I asked urgently, feeling his face to make sure he wasn't bleeding.

'Next time you want to get into some role playing can I tie you up?'

I was so relieved to hear him speak I let his rude joke slide. I traced my hands again over his face and down to his lips and lent down to touch my lips gently on his. I felt his body tense in surprise before he eagerly kissed me back.

When we parted I sat on top of him hugging him until I heard him clear his throat next to my ear.

'As much as I am enjoying this do you think it would be possible for me to lose the cable ties?'

'Oh, god, I totally forgot,' I said, wiping the tears of relief from my eyes. I pulled the chair into an upright position and hunted around the bunker for something to clip the cable ties. Finally I found a pair of scissors in one of the desk drawers.

My eyes still hadn't completely adjusted and it was still pitch black so it took a while for me to make sure that I wasn't going to accidentally cut his wrist. After fighting with my eyesight for a few minutes Gus cleared his throat again and muttered, 'Um Sophie, technically I'm actually already dead so you probably don't have to be too concerned about killing me with a blunt pair of scissors.'

'Right, I'd forgotten,' I giggled nervously, and carefully cut them enough for Gus to wriggle out. As soon as Gus was out of the chair he turned around and hugged me so tightly I was sure he was going to smother me. Finally his grip eased. 'Don't ever do something like that again – I was so worried about you. What happened? Where's Marcel?'

'Oh he got exactly what he was looking for,' I said smiling mysteriously, and before I could expand on my explanation I heard footsteps coming down into the room. Gus and I scrambled around for somewhere to hide but before we could find somewhere we heard Clara's voice call out my name and I relaxed again. Soon after Clara and Roland appeared in the doorway.

'Not interrupting anything are we?' Clara asked, looking sheepish.

'Well actually …' Gus put his arm around my back.

'Not at all,' I said batting away his arm. He pretended to wince. 'I was just about to tell Gus how you clocked Marcel over the back of the head with one of his favorite frying pans. Gus turned to look at Clara in disbelief, 'Really?'

'I used to be quite a good tennis player back in the day,' she said smiling at Roland. Then she turned slowly back to me. 'I'm sorry to upset the jovial mood but I think it's time we turned back the clock Miss Sophie.'

I nodded my head but had a sudden thought. 'Do you think we can hold off for another ten minutes?' Clara looked confused but nodded her head, 'I can't see why not. I think your friends Charles and Alice have everyone happily caged in the ballroom; I'm not sure that anyone has really noticed. Your mother and father were going to go looking for you a while ago but then they started speaking with Charles and he has had them in raptures ever since.'

Gus rolled his eyes. 'Everyone's ideal son-in-law,' he said a little maliciously, and I elbowed him in the ribs. 'We'll meet you at the back door to the kitchen in ten minutes.'

Turning to Gus, I grabbed his hand and ran up the steps and back into the house. Graceful ladies and gentlemen let me step through their groups until I got outside and ran down to the garden towards Thomas's cottage. Gus figured out where we were going halfway down the hill and started to pull back on my hand and slow down.

'Wait, Sophie, do you think this is a good idea?'

'Why? You don't want to see him?'

'Of course I want to see him but I don't know if he wants to see me. He's moved on with his life; shouldn't I respect that?' he looked sadly down at his shoes.

'I spoke with him about you and I feel like he would be so disappointed if I didn't give him this chance. It can be his chance to say goodbye.'

'OK.' He took a deep breath and started walking down the hill again.

When I knocked on the door I couldn't hear any noises inside so I thought he might not be there or could even be asleep. I knocked again and heard him move towards the door. Gus quickly ducked out of sight. When he opened the door he was very surprised to see me and his brow furrowed, looking behind me for my parents.

'Sophie, what's wrong? Has something happened?'

'If I could tell you that you could see Gus again, one more time, even if it was only for a couple of minutes, would you want to or do you feel as though that would just upset you?'

The furrow in his brow deepened. 'What are you talking about?'

'Please just tell me – if there was an opportunity would you take it, no matter what?' I knew that I sounded anxious and out of breath but we only had a short amount of time and I couldn't waste it being sensitive and dragging out the question.

He looked at his hand resting on the doorknob and

his face twisted like he might cry. 'Absolutely. I would do anything to see him again, to speak to him again.'

I stepped back from the door and Gus stepped slowly into the light. Thomas gasped and stepped backwards, reeling from the sight of Gus. Gus turned to me looking unsure, just as Thomas lunged forward and wrapped him in a big bear hug. Tears cascaded down his face.

Slowly Thomas eased his grip on Gus and looked him in the face with astonishment, grief, happiness and love all mixed in to one. He looked as though he had a thousand questions running through his mind but all he could stammer was, 'How?'

'Remember what Poppy said about the house being inhabited by spirits? I'm one of them now, I guess. I know how that sounds and I didn't know whether to see you tonight because I didn't want you to feel like you need to hang onto my memory … and I wasn't sure whether you would even believe that it was me but I just … I just … I'm rambling and we don't have much longer but I just wanted to tell you that I love you and you don't have to stay here if it makes you unhappy.'

'So you're a ghost. But why can I see you and touch you?' Thomas looked unsure of himself again and looked to me for some reassurance.

'It is a really, really long story which I can tell you later,' I said. 'But let's just say you can see Gus any time you like now that you know he is here and you believe in ghosts. You won't be able to touch him for much longer though so probably best if you use this time to hug it out!'

Thomas and Gus embraced again and I used the moment to politely start wandering up to the house and leave them to have a private moment to themselves. When I reached the house Clara and Roland were waiting for me at the steps. I had been unsure whether I had made the right decision in telling Thomas about Gus and the only people who could tell me whether it was right or wrong were standing in front of me, but I couldn't do it. How could I ask Clara in front of Roland whether she would have lived a happier life had she just moved on after his death. So I just stood there with Clara and Roland, quietly watching Gus and Thomas until the two figures started heading towards the house.

Turning to Clara I pulled out the key on the chain. 'Right, so how do I do this?'

'You just need to put it back into the clock that Marcel used and turn it backwards by one turn.'

'How will I know which is the right clock?' I asked uncertainly, looking at the key.

Clara put her hand on my hand and I looked up at her weathered face that was no longer the least bit scary and she squeezed my hand. 'You will know.'

I looked down at the key again and then up at Gus and Thomas as they reached the bottom step. 'Ready?' I said to the group, although I think that I was asking myself as much as I was asking them. Everyone nodded and began moving towards the door to the house. We walked into the kitchen and past a harried looking butler who looked like he had stumbled out of the 1980s. 'Hello Bertie,' Clara said kindly. He turned around looking for the source of the interruption of his thoughts and spotted Clara. 'My dear, can you just see what these lunatics have done to the place!'

'Don't fret Bertie, they will be gone soon and I'll clean up the mess. Why don't you go and have a tonic and a lie down,' Clara said, and he nodded his head and wandered off looking mildly confused.

# CHAPTER 42

I tried the clock above the fireplace in the kitchen first but that seemed a little obvious and nothing happened. So we moved from one room to another, dodging temporary houseguests dressed in various costumes from a wide range of different centuries, inserting the key into each of the clocks.

Finally we arrived in the parlor where I had sent the first group in their military attire to play bridge and drink scotch. The dust under the clock on the mantle above the fireplace looked recently disturbed and my heartbeat started to quicken. Gently I pulled the clock around so that I could see the keyhole. I held up the key on the necklace that was hanging around my neck and slowly pushed it into the keyhole at the back. The back of the clock began to glow. Clara nodded at me and then turned to Roland. He gave her a light kiss on her forehead and wiped away a stray tear that was making its way down her cheek.

Thomas also seemed to know what this meant and he reached over to Gus and pulled him in close for one last hug. Once the last farewells had taken place I turned back to the clock and turned the key counterclockwise. When I looked around again to see if it had worked Gus had regained his translucent glow and Clara's hand was going through Roland's. As the clock struck one am the members of the military who were gathered in the room slowly disappeared and the room went back to looking empty, dusty and old.

'Well, I'd better go and tell Charlie that he can release the prisoners!' I said, walking over to the door. I looked into the rooms as I walked back to the ballroom and they too had become quiet. The ghost party had definitely come to an end for this full moon but I felt a thrill of excitement to know that they could all come back again next month with a few twists of the key in one of the clocks. All of the stories that Poppy had told me must have been true and although I couldn't remember a lot of them I recalled being spellbound listening to them as a child.

I slowly opened the ballroom door expecting there to be an angry mob of people on the other side of the door demanding to be released; or potentially a frightened group of students who had encountered the hoard of ghosts that had until minutes ago occupied most of the house, but it looked as though no one was any the wiser. More than that really, it looked like no one wanted to leave.

My parents were standing at the dessert bar that had been set up next to the entry talking to Charlie and I casually walked over and put my hand in his. He looked down at me and trying his best to sound casual asked, 'All OK?'

'Yes, more than OK. Everything is perfect.' I squeezed his hand tightly.

Unlike Charlie, Mom looked mildly irritated. 'Where have you been hiding young lady?' she asked.

'You're lucky that we have had your friend Charlie to talk to. He's offered to take me out fishing,' Dad said enthusiastically, even though I knew he had never been fishing and never had any interest in fishing.

'I just had to pop upstairs for a little while, something that I ate didn't agree with me. Must be Marcel's cooking.' An idea came into my head. 'Actually, I don't think he's going to be working here anymore. When I was upstairs I walked past Poppy's room and saw Marcel trying to steal money out of a safe there. Clara was with me and she called the police.'

'What?' my parents both said together, looking shocked. 'A safe?' Mom said.

'Yeah, there must be hundreds of thousands of dollars in there.'

They both looked at each other, shocked, then excused themselves, presumably to find Clara and head off the police lest the school party be concerned about why they had been called.

'So, is this where you tell me why I had to create a diversion every time someone wanted to leave the room?'

I turned to look at Charlie with a guilty look on my face. It wasn't just the fact that I had yet to process what had happened in the basement when I had kissed Gus and told him that I was in love with him. It was also because, even though I had revealed the ghostly secrets of the house to Alice and that had not yet blown up in my face,

I was doubting my conviction of telling Charlie in case he thought I was completely insane. 'I'm not sure you'll believe what I say.'

'Try me.'

'Well, you remember those times that you said you looked over at the house and thought you saw Gus? There's a good chance that you did.'

He looked confused. 'Gus didn't drown?'

This was going to be harder than I thought. 'Well, yes he did but …'

I watched Charlie's face turn from confusion to a look of concern: I wasn't sure whether it was concern because he had figured out that there were ghosts or because he was genuinely concerned for my mental health, but before I could ask we were interrupted by Mrs Hodges, the school principal.

'Sophie this is a beautiful house. It's so wonderful of your parents to allow us to use it for the Halloween ball. Hello Charles.'

'Thank you Mrs Hodges,' I said politely, glancing back over at Charlie and wondering what he was thinking.

'I think it might be time for us to finish up for the night. Can you both help me round up the troops and get everyone to say their farewells?' Mrs Hodges said politely, stifling a yawn.

I didn't see Charlie for the next fifteen minutes as we moved through the room, telling everyone that it was time to wrap up for the night. There were more than a few groans of disappointment and, even though it was due to the organization of my parents and the social committee rather than me, I felt great that everyone was having such a good time that they didn't want to leave. I didn't have much part in the decorations, entertainment or refreshments but I felt I had played a vital role in avoiding any disasters caused by Marcel or the ghosts in the house. Charlie's friends Ben and Pat even came up to me to say goodnight, which I took as a good sign.

I looked over at Charlie a couple of times as we finished clearing the room but his face wore a relaxed, social mask as he high fived and hugged his friends and I couldn't tell whether he was still considering our discussion from before. As we rounded up the last stragglers and walked outside he reached out and held my hand, squeezing it briefly which made me relax a little. At least he hadn't gone running back home!

I stood at the top step with my parents, Clara and Charlie watching as cars arrived and picked up laughing, happy students who were finishing up a wonderful Halloween night out, none the wiser that this year's Halloween party had been a lot more of a ghostly encounter than they realized.

Sharing a farewell hug with Alice on her way out she had whispered in my ear and reminded me that we still had several other rooms to try to unseal and I had promised Poppy that I would try to find where her husband's spirit was. On top of that, I would also need to do my fair share of work around the house helping my parents to get it ready for guests.

For a place that I had thought would be incredibly boring, the next year was looking like it was going to be action-packed. As the last of the partygoers waved their farewells, Clara looked up to the top of the house in the direction of her room. I followed her glance and saw a shadow move. Clara glanced back at me and smiled momentarily before bidding us goodnight and heading inside to clean up. Mom followed behind her.

'Well that was a success, I thought,' Dad said looking proud but exhausted. 'It's a bit late to clean up this mess now – let's work on that tomorrow. How about a hot chocolate before bed?'

'Sounds great Dad, I'll come in a minute.' I didn't really feel up to going through the whole story tonight but I could feel Charlie's glances in my direction becoming more urgent and I knew that he needed an explanation.

'Sure kiddo, I'll leave it on the stove for you. Goodnight Charlie, I look forward to coming out on the boat with you.'

'Sounds great Mr Weston. Goodnight.'

'Please call me Ted.' He smiled as he walked back into the house.

As soon as my dad was out of earshot Charlie turned back to me. 'I knew that I wasn't crazy when I saw Gus. OK, let's have it – from start to finish.'

I sighed. I suspected that my hot chocolate would be cold by the time I had finished my explanation but at least it seemed for now that Charlie didn't think I was imagining things.

# Acknowledgments

I read a book years ago that used astrology to provide the personality traits for people born on each day of the calendar year. Initially I thought it was ridiculous to blanket every person born on that day with the same personality but the characteristics they listed for my birthday were bang on. The first line listed me as a dreamer.

I am a dreamer and I want to thank everyone who supported my dream for this book.

Thank you to the whole team at New Holland especially Francesca and Liz for believing in Sophie's story.

To my amazing Skye I am so grateful for your encouragement and enthusiasm and volunteering to proof read no matter how rough the draft.

To my beautiful Nanny who told me that if I loved writing I need to just get on and write.

To my wonderful parents who have encouraged me in everything that I do.

Lastly to the three loves of my life, Sophie, William and Sam. I started writing this book when we embarked on an adventure together to live in Shanghai. It was crazy and it was overwhelming but I loved it because I had you with me. We are a team and you are the best team I could ever hope for. I look forward to many more adventures with you three by my side.

First published in 2021 by New Holland Publishers

Sydney • Auckland
Level 1, 178 Fox Valley Road, Wahroonga, NSW 2076, Australia
5/39 Woodside Ave, Northcote, Auckland 0627, New Zealand

newhollandpublishers.com



A record of this book is available from the National Library of Australia.

ISBN 9781760791452

Group Managing Director: Fiona Schultz
Publisher: Francesca Roberts-Thomson
Project Editor: Liz Hardy
Designer: Yolanda La Gorcé
Production Director: Arlene Gippert

Printed and bound by The SOS Print and Media

10 9 8 7 6 5 4 3 2 1

Keep up with New Holland Publishers:

 NewHollandPublishers

 @newhollandpublishers

US $14.99